Thought Bubble

Volume II

Ethan Thomas

Brennaman Publishing

Thought Bubble: Stories From My Mind
Copyright © Ethan Thomas
All rights reserved.

This is a work of fiction.
Any names, characters, places, and events are products of the author's imagination
and are used fictitiously. Any resemblance to persons living or dead is coincidental.
Any opinions expressed are those of the characters and should not be confused with
the author's. No part of this book may be reproduced in any form or by and means,
electronic or mechanical. This includes storage and retrieval systems without written
permission from the author, with the exception of brief quotations in reviews.

Published 2026
ISBN: 979-8-234-05295-7 (Paperback)
ASIN: (eBook)

CONTENTS

DEDICATION

Thanks for picking up Volume Two! This book includes a few of my shorter stories, but is mainly Novelettes/Novellas. I hope you like them!

> FLASH FICTION

THE TRACKER

They snuck off the path through the woods. He pushed her up against a tree and kissed her, touching her breasts as she put her hand down his pants. This was it.

Then she pushed him away. "We have to go to the tracker first," she said.

"Why? What are the odds we are related?"

"There are only six hundred people on this planet. It's a good chance."

"Come on, I thought the reason we were sneaking around like this was because we didn't want it to be public." He ran his thumb, still in her dress, over her nipple.

"We're sneaking around because my mother hates you. Now come on. Accidentally fooling around is one thing, but I'm not going to have sex without knowing if you're my cousin."

They walked back to the trail, out of the woods, and towards town. They passed the sheep that provided their clothing and food, all lounging in the sun. With no predators, their sheep had evolved to have no sense of caution. They passed the early habitat that now served as the government buildings since the terraforming was completed. Both had vague memories of attending daycare there before the schoolhouse was built.

Walking down the thoroughfare, they got to the office of the tracker. They didn't have paint, but it was hard to miss. It was one of the oldest buildings on the street, having been up since the first generations started breeding. The inside was now shelves of books and papers that were bursting with the births, deaths, and genealogies of six hundred people. The man, whose name was Greg, was a portly man in a rough shirt and vest, suited for his bookish work that left little time to exercise.

"Name?" he asked, though she was fairly sure he knew it. "Georgiana Raymond," she told him. He walked over to a shelf on the right side of the wall.

He took out a scroll with a leather cover and moved over to a long table. "Any homosexuals that you know of in the family line?"

Georgiana shook her head. "No sir, not directly. My mother's cousin is a lesbian, but her wife and she have only just gotten their assigned breeding partners."

Greg nodded. "I see here you are descended from Martha Gramfin, correct? That's your first generation colonist?"

Georgiana nodded. "Yes sir, that's my grandmother."

He scanned the scroll again. "She had kids with..." His voice trailed off.

"How long will we have to trace our families back just to have sex?" John asked.

Greg looked up. "That depends. Do you want kids who are born dead, with six toes, or who die early?"

John looked at his shoes. "No sir."

The bare minimum is about two hundred more years. That's when enough people will have been born and separated from Generation One far enough that you'll only have to worry about direct relations, say third cousin and closer.

"Damn," John said. He looked out at the sun setting over the horizon. "Can you get those alone? I've gotta get back."

Georgiana nodded. "I'll tell you what he finds." John left, putting his hat back on as he exited the building.

Georgiana turned back to Greg and his tracking. He had retrieved a book from the shelf that looked like a personal journal. No one really felt weird about keeping them, considering they didn't end up here until after you were dead. "So, it looks like your grandmother did a few things with both of his grandparents at an orgy. But she says she didn't get pregnant until well after that.

"Oh, wait, did you just say orgy?"

Greg nodded. "It was a long trip. They'd been locked in the generation ship for a long time, and they were all in their twenties. Gen one was weird, man. But I don't think you and he are related. I could check the generation ship records, but I don't think that's necessary.

"Do you mind if I ask why?" she asked, genuinely curious.

"Sexual activity was very closely monitored on the ship. Women were given enough birth control to kill a horse, and their school curriculum taught them to, shall we say...it taught them other activities. You're good to go with the boy. Let me know if you get pregnant."

"I will... wait, did you factor in—"

Greg held up a hand. "I know all about your momma's youth. You're your daddy's, or at the very least you aren't his daddy's... wait, you were born in twenty-five eighty-five, right?"

"Yes sir, that's me."

"Perfect. This chart has birthdays and doctor records. Good to go."

"Thank you, Tracker."

Greg smiled. "See you in a couple of months." He winked.

FOR HER

"Welcome to Jose's, what can I get for you?" Good god, I hated this job. I hated his voice even more. I walked behind Dennis as he took an order and tied my hair back.

"Why must you get ready here?" Dennis asked as I tied my apron. Dennis was a pudgy, balding man in his forties who was only in charge because this was one of the least important businesses in his daddy's portfolio.

"I don't know, Dennis, because the 'back room' is a two-square-foot stall in a bathroom that reeks of the three-hour shit you take every day."

Dennis handed a coffee to the woman, who looked at his hands like she was afraid he might not have washed them. It was a safe bet. Dennis walked past me, headed to the back. "I can't believe your hygiene," he muttered under her breath.

"Man up!" I called after him. I leaned back against the counter with a sigh as an espresso came into view. "God bless you, Benny," I said, taking it. "I hate this job."

"Then why stay?" Benny asked.

"Because it pays well, and I chose to give it up at homecoming. This job gives me the most time with her before my other job starts."

Benny sipped his coffee and eyed the door. The morning rush was headed our way—soccer moms, yoga enthusiasts—all coming at once. "You ready?" he asked.

I straightened my hat and put a smile on my face as the first customer approached. "Welcome to Jose's, what can I get for you?"

WELL LOVED

"How's it coming?"

Johnny came out from behind the bar and walked over to the man trying to save his piano. The man had taken over a table with various woodworking tools, glues, and several items Johnny didn't recognize. The keys were spread out on the table, one clamped in place.

"Not good, sir," the repairman said.

"I was afraid of that."

"When was the last time this piano was tuned?"

Johnny thought for a moment. "What year is it?"

"Nineteen eighty-seven."

Johnny let out a long breath. "Then probably forty-seven. My grandpa had it tuned when he came home."

The repairman's eyes widened. "Forty years? Jesus, and there are bullet holes in the side. I dug this out of the inside." He held out his hand and dropped a slug into Johnny's hand.

That doesn't surprise me. Listen, if there is any way you can get this thing fixed, I'll pay whatever you want and give you free drinks for a year. This piano has been standing here since before my dad was born. Hell, probably longer than that. It's been played for at least four hours a day all that time. The only tuning was the little adjustments my dad knew how to make, that I think I just made it worse.

It has held thousands of beers up top. The reverend and his wife conceived a child against it before he became a reverend. It is a very important part of this holler. We love this piano. I wish we hadn't moved it an inch to the left. I think that's what killed it."

The repairman sighed. "Let me call my wife."

THE FRAME

"What do you think?"

"The picture is lovely, Grandma, but the frame is a bit old. It looks tarnished," I said. "I could have gotten you a better one."

Grandma climbed off her step stool. She stepped back and looked at the old picture of my grandfather. He was in an Army dress uniform. The picture was yellowed black and white, like it had been hanging around for decades. It had been, according to Grandma, in the attic for a long time. "He sure was a looker, wasn't he?"

"Ew, Grandma, not cool. I said, "I don't want to think of Pop-pop like that."

Grandma smiled. "She doesn't think you look handsome, Ralph."

The picture turned so that it was looking at me. "I think I'm gorgeous."

My eyes went wide and I swiveled like I might pass out. Grandma caught me and said, "That's the secret of the frame, my love."

I cursed my lips, nodding even though I knew I had to be dreaming. "I'm going to go lay down."

"Okay, love you, sweetie," the photo of my grandfather said.

I walked up the stairs mumbling to myself, "I don't understand what is happening."

As I got to the landing, I heard Grandma say, "You will, if you outlive your soulmate."

COFFEE AND PEOPLE

"How do you do that?" she asked.

"Do what?"

"Take the coffee machine apart while you talk? It seems super hard.

I laughed. "I do it every single day. After a while you get used to it. I could probably do it blindfolded."

Her eyes widened. "I have to see that."

"Maybe some other time," I said. She had her mother's wavy hair. Two of her front teeth were missing. Large enough for the straw on her smoothie to fit through. I started washing a mug as she asked, "How come you work here?"

"I love working with people. This job lets me do that."

"Do you also love coffee?"

I nodded. "Coffee and people. That's why I take the machine apart every night, to make the coffee great and the people happy."

She took another drink and seemed to contemplate this.

I finished my work, untied my apron, stowed it behind the counter, and made my way to the time clock. "I already got you," Mckayla said, walking toward me.

"Thanks," I said. "I gave your kid a smoothie."

"I'll pay for it tomorrow."

I waved that away. "I got it. Go feed her."

Mckayla walked up to her daughter, and I saw them chat for a second before the kid turned to me. "Benny, would you like to get pizza with us?"

I looked at Mckayla, who gave an almost imperceptible nod.

"I would love to," I said.

FATHERHOOD

The tension didn't leave his shoulders until the truck door slammed shut. Twelve hours of dealing with people asking stupid questions, twelve hours of employees somehow not knowing how to do the job they were hired for. He only had about six hours until it got dark and he had to pick up the truck to start his side job. The rent went up and kids didn't come with money.

He started driving home. His eyes were fluttering, and despite all the soda and caffeine he'd had, he was still struggling to stay awake. A car behind him was laying on its horn, and he realized he'd fallen asleep at the second light.

"Fuck, sorry," he called out the window. When he pulled into the driveway, he took a minute to let the day's bullshit sink in. He didn't want to go back. He liked his job, but the hours he was working were too many. It was going to kill him.

He saw his eldest come running around the side of the trailer with a plastic bat. He saw the truck and turned to the side of the trailer he'd come from. "Dad's home!"

His other two kids ran around to see the truck. Waddled was a more apt term since his daughter was only three. He smiled at them. They were worth it. He dropped the stuff in the truck to pick up in a few hours.

He opened the door with a smile on his face. "Who's ready to play baseball?

THE PIANO

"**M**om, he's done."

Sarah waited at the couch, leaning against the back of it, scrolling through her phone while the guy looked over the big piano for the eighteenth consecutive minute.

Mother walked into the room, her hair wrapped up in a hankie. It was odd seeing her so frustrated. She was a normal mom, always calm, even when kids got injured or the bank called. But ever since they'd started going through Grandma's house, her mom had been frustrated and crying on and off.

"What do you think?" she asked, coming into the room.

"You could buy a house with this piano." The guy said, "It is a hundred years old and in perfect condition."

Mom nodded like she had expected this news. "You want it?"

The guy's jaw actually fell open. "What?"

"If you want to pay to get it out of here, you can keep it."

"I don't understand. This thing is in perfect condition. It's been,-"

Mom interrupted him. "It's been regularly tuned despite never having been played. It has been polished, never so much as a fingerprint on it. It is a brand new piano from 1912, and if you don't want it, I am going to take a goddamn hammer to it and throw it out the window in pieces."

The guy looked stunned and a bit like he was afraid to speak. "Yes ma'am, I want it. I'll have guys over to get it this afternoon."

"Thank you," Mom turned to Sarah, "Go upstairs and help your brother pack up Grandma's handbags.

> NOVELETTES

ROADTRIP

Clay's life is going nowhere until a violent encounter at a gas station pulls him into a hidden world of monsters, magic, and a talking dog with a criminal past. Swept onto the road by the gruff hunter Deacon and the enigmatic Fisnik, he trades his dead-end routine for a cross-country chase through unraveling magic and towns touched by something deeply wrong.

CHAPTER ONE

Clay was on his way to work, wishing something would fall from the sky and crush him. He worked at a supermarket. It wasn't a bad job, he actually liked the work. It was just the people he worked with who were garbage.

He rounded the corner of Third Street and saw an old-fashioned station wagon parked at the gas station. It was a cool-looking car. He had always liked station wagons. It wasn't old enough to be a classic, but it looked like it was from the seventies or eighties. Clay wasn't much of a car guy.

He could see inside the gas station as a man walked up to the counter. Clay watched for a moment. The man waved his hands at the cashier, and when that didn't work, he grabbed him by the neck of his shirt and pulled him over the counter. He held the cashier on the ground, his right hand starting to glow. He punched the man repeatedly until the man stopped moving. Clay walked across the street towards the station, unsure why his legs carried him towards danger. He reached the door when a voice from the car said, "I wouldn't go in there if I were you."

Clay turned around, but there was no one there. A wire-haired Vizsla poked its head out of the passenger seat of the car. "What?" Clay said.

"I wouldn't go in there if I were you," the dog said. Its voice was deep and sounded old, like a wizard from a movie. "He is taking care of something, and he has a tendency to attack without thinking once a fight has begun."

"Thanks for the heads up," Clay said.

"Absolutely. May I ask why you came over here?"

"I saw that guy beating the absolute shit out of the cashier and wanted to help."

The dog was very expressive, and Clay could tell he approved. "If it helps, the boy is a werewolf and he's been killing people two towns over."

"Damn," Clay said. "I guess—"

"Help me."

Clay turned to see the man from the gas station standing in the now open doorway.

"What the hell am I supposed to do?" the dog asked. "He looks like he weighs two hundred pounds."

The man grunted. "You then, come help me."

Clay followed him inside. The cashier lay in a puddle of blood. "Grab his hands," the other man said. Clay did as he was told and grunted as they picked the werewolf up and carried him towards the backdoor.

"How did you get to the station?" the man asked. He was a stocky guy, not much taller than Clay, maybe six feet, but he looked like he was made of bricks. His arms strained against his flannel shirt. His hair looked like it was usually kept neat but had gone too long without a cut. It was hard to guess his age; he could have been thirty-five or fifty-five. He wore jeans and work boots, looking more like a lumberjack than a werewolf killer.

They reached the back of the lot behind the station, where a shovel was digging a hole by itself. "Toss him in," the man said. "One, two, three."

Clay let the body go, only now realizing he was just as guilty as this man—but given the talking dog, and what felt like a magic prickly sensation in his brain, he didn't think he had much to worry about with the cops.

The shovel started to fill the hole, and the man held out his hand. "Deacon."

"Clay," he said, returning the shake.

His grip hardened, and Deacon pulled him closer, holding his left hand in front of his eyes as if to poke Clay's eyes out. He started humming, then switched to speaking in a language Clay couldn't understand.

A small golden light appeared at the end of each finger, and Clay was powerless to stop them from going into his eyes.

He could feel what he assumed was magic crawling through his brain, like it was slowly trying to make sure it didn't miss anything as it eliminated his memory.

Then it was gone. He still had his memory, but the feeling in his brain had vanished. "Do you know my name?"

"Deacon," Clay said. "You told me like thirty seconds ago." Deacon repeated the spell or whatever three more times, none of them working, before he said, "Fuck it, come on."

Clay followed him out front, and Deacon said, "Wait here."

He continued to the station wagon and leaned against the window, talking to the dog. Clay was once again unsure why he was doing as this strange man told him.

It was nearly three minutes of animated conversation, the man and dog both glancing at him from time to time, before Deacon walked back over. "Okay, so it seems you might have some potential, or maybe magic is just being hinky again, but if you want, you can come with us."

"Okay," Clay said.

"Okay? No deliberation, no pause?"

"Nope," Clay said. "I hate my life, I'm a nerd, and this seems like an adventure."

Deacon looked impressed. "Fair enough, kid, get in and we'll go grab you some clothes."

Clay lived in a boarding house, rented the room by the month, and had no attachments. He glanced at his room for less than a second as he grabbed his bag and started packing. He tossed in his most important notebooks, a couple of novels, and all the money he had stashed in various places so the landlady wouldn't find it.

He took a moment to look around to make sure he had everything important, his memory bag was already packed—that was everything. He flipped the light off and headed outside. His bed, computer, and other possessions would be sold or whatever, but he didn't care. "I just assumed my computer wouldn't be a good idea," he said as he put his stuff in the back.

"You read too many fantasy stories," Deacon said.

"But in this case," the dog added, "you are correct. It wouldn't likely last long, especially if we go where I believe we will."

"Where's that?" Clay asked.

Deacon looked at him from the rearview mirror. "Don't worry about it."

Clay got in the passenger seat as instructed, and the dog took the middle of the back bench seat.

Turning to look at him, Clay asked, "May I ask your name?"

"How kind, yes you may. My name is Fisnik. I am a very old talking dog who used to be a wizard."

"Cool."

CHAPTER TWO

They had been on the road for a few hours when Clays asked, "So, are we headed somewhere specific or just wandering like Sam and Dean?"

"Who?" Deacon asked.

Fisnik spoke from the back, half asleep, "It's a TV show about two brothers who roam the US hunting monsters and saving people. It's quite good, though I wish they explored lesser-known monsters more often."

"We're following signs," Deacon said. "Magic has been...acting weird lately, and from what I've been able to tell, most of the chaos has been centered in this country."

"So this is like a detective case?" Clay asked.

"Yeah, but one where there's almost no evidence, the suspect could be almost anyone or anything, and we have no help."

"Way to sound confident," Fisnik said.

Deacon looked at him. "Shut up."

"So why were you in Oshkosh?" Clay asked.

Deacon sighed, "We were in Green Bay trying to track down a wizard who used to stay there, then we were on our way to Milwaukee to visit a different friend when we saw the dead people in the paper—it fit the hunting patterns of a rogue werewolf, and you're caught up on the rest."

Clay processed the information and said, "So we're headed to this friend's house now?"

"No," Deacon said.

"Why not?"

It was Fisnik who answered, "He is dead, or at least the him we need is dead."

"What does that mean? The him you need is dead?"

Fisnik yawned, "In the world of magic, dead is not always dead."

He was soon snoring. Deacon reached his arm behind the seat and dug around for a minute before his arm came back up with a little leather bag. He tossed it onto Clay's lap. "Work on that, we'll see if you have any real talent."

He went back to driving without another word. Clay held the bag in his hands, inspecting it. It was leather, with a thick hide flap and a bone to keep the flap closed through a loop on the front. Two sets of strings ran through a flat piece at the front, one set to tighten the bag, another to form the loop to keep it closed. There was a thick belt strap on the back.

He opened the bag and inside he saw a small pocket notebook, a smaller pouch, and a few bits and bobs. A spool of string, a few needles in a case, a small knife the size of a finger. He opened the book and saw it was filled with inscriptions, diagrams, and words in at least three languages. The writing was small and cramped, appearing to be in three or four different hands. He brought it close to his face, trying to read some of it.

Deacon reached over, never taking his eyes off the road, and tapped the center of the book. It expanded until it was seven by ten inches. "Thanks," Clay said.

Don't mention it," Deacon said. "It shifts from time to time, but English is usually chapter three."

Clay nodded and turned to chapter three. He started reading, and it felt like his mind opened for the first time. He stayed on the first spell: How to levitate a pencil.

They were stopped under a bridge, seemingly in the middle of nowhere. From the chill in the air, he knew they were still in Wisconsin, though they couldn't be far from the border given how long they'd driven. Clay yawned. "Where are we?"

Deacon was outside on the passenger side of the car. He finished peeing and turned around. "Mason City, Iowa, or close to it."

"What are we doing here?" Clay asked.

Deacon raised an eyebrow. "So you read a spell book for a few hours, and now it's 'we'?"

Fisnik appeared from the tall grass, kicking behind him. "I told you I liked him."

Deacon smiled and looked back to Clay. "We got a call last night, just after you passed out. There's a small town just south of here, not many people and unincorporated, some fishy things have been happening."

"We're gonna investigate?" Clay asked.

"Yup. There's a bottle of water on the hood for you to brush your teeth, then we'll leave.

"I don't,-"

Deacon put a hand up. "I am not road-tripping with smelly, bad-breathed assholes."

Clay opened the door with a, "Yes sir."

The town was barren. When they said small, they meant small. It was one main street with a bunch of closed businesses and one open feed store with a sign that read, 'NOW SELLING NON-AGRICULTURAL BOOKS.'

"This is weird," Deacon said. "A town like this..."

Fisnik finished his sentence, "Someone should be around to notice strangers."

Deacon pulled the car into a spot in front of the feed store. "Clay, let's go shopping. Fiz, if anyone comes by the car, kill them."

"I'm a dog, dipshit."

Deacon rolled his eyes, "Anyone magical."

"Children have an inherent magical aptitude that doesn't fade."

"Holy fucking Christ, kill bad guys." He opened the door and as he got out said, "Jesus, every time."

Clay looked at Fisnik, who said, "I would follow him."

Clay got out of the car and caught up to Deacon. "This is just like supernatural. What're our covers?"

"Okay, forget the TV show, kid. We are here for dog food. That's all the cover we need."

Clay felt his face get hot. Deacon opened the door, and a bell chimed. They walked in and were hit with a smell of putrescence unlike anything Clay had encountered since a raccoon died in the walls of his house, and the landlady refused to call someone until the neighbors started to complain and threaten to call the city. "What the fuck is that?" Clay asked Deacon.

Deacon handed Clay a hankie, which he brought to his face, suddenly smelling freshly cut grass and cool sheets on a warm summer evening. "It's rotten human brain," he said. He didn't look as bothered as Clay but took a second hankie out of his pocket.

They walked past aisles of haphazardly stacked bags and the odd bits and bobs found in every small-town store, with unsustainable prices and a century-old feel.

They found the wooden kiosk raised a few feet off the ground at the center of the store. There were flyers, lost dog posters, and all kinds of community announcements tacked all around the window counter.

The man behind the counter was a deep grey, as if the actual life had been sucked out of him. His skin was saggy and looked ready to fall off. He stared into space like he didn't know who or what was there.

"Don't touch anything," Deacon said. He moved forward in a defensive pose, as if the man might suddenly turn from a rotten potato into a ninja. He started speaking under his breath, and his hand began glowing with a smoky light-green fire. He waved it over the counter, careful to keep anything not magic away from the man.

Clay jumped back, slipping on spilled grain.

The grey man darted forward and grabbed the fiery hand. Deacon pulled back, but the man held fast for a few seconds.

The fire spread up his arm, and in moments, the man was burnt to dust.

The dust continued burning until there was no trace the man had been there. Clay got up and went to Deacon. "Are you okay?"

Deacon examined his arm and hand. "I'm fine. Nothing got on me."

Barking came from outside. At the same moment, Clay saw a woman, looking the same shade of grey but more decomposed than the man had been, heading straight for them. He moved.

Clay shoved Deacon aside and grabbed a framing hammer from a pegboard. He threw it and turned. By the time it sunk into the woman's brain, Clay was already headed outside.

They got outside and saw the car surrounded by bodies. There were at least seventeen of them—male, female, even a few little grey kids. Fisnik was on top of the car.

"About time," he said.

"How did you kill them?" Deacon asked. "You can't do any harm."

I just knocked them out. You'll be wanting to burn them.

Declan closed his eyes for a second before his hands lit up with green fire. "Scaoil tine," he said. "Keep calm or you'll burn too."

He set to burning the bodies, and Clay closed his eyes. "Scaoil tine," he said. He felt nothing and thought he had done it wrong, but when he opened his eyes, he saw a familiar green flame covering both hands up to the wrist. He stepped off the porch of the store and went to a body.

It was a woman not much older than him, maybe thirty. He held a hand out and nothing happened. "Imagine it flying towards her," Fisnik said.

Clay pictured the fire leaving his hands and shooting to the body, and it happened. It almost happened faster than the thought could process. "Good job," Deacon said. His hands were clear, and Clay saw that the rest of the bodies were gone. Clay pointed a fiery hand down the street, and Deacon turned.

There were fifty people headed towards them, all of them grey. The one in front, leading the pack, was a little girl of about eight. "They're already dead," Deacon was at his side. "Throw the fire at them."

Clay closed his eyes. His heart was racing. "Is there anything we can do?"

"No."

Clay opened his eyes and let loose a thousand-foot spray of green fire. He closed his eyes so he wouldn't see the girl burn, and that was a mistake. His face felt hot, his hands started to sting, and he got double vision before he passed out and his head hit the asphalt.

Clay woke up with a groan. "What—"

He was staring at the sky, and Fistik's face came into view. "You did too much and passed out."

"I realized that."

Here," Deacon said, offering him a hand. He slowly helped Clay up, and Clay winced.

"My eyes hurt, and it feels like I'm going to vomit."

"Severe migraines are a side effect of magical exhaustion."

He walked over to the passenger side of the car and opened the glove box. "Is there a healing potion or something that makes it go away?"

"Nope," Deacon said, tossing him something. Clay caught it and read Acetaminophen. He took four.

They walked around town. Deacon had a small messenger bag over his shoulder. He seemed to be looking for something. Clay walked a few yards behind, next to Fisnik. "So, you used to be a wizard?"

"Indeed, about two hundred years ago."

"Wizards must live a long time,"

"Average lifespan is around six hundred years unless killed."

"Mind if I ask what you did to become a dog?"

"Oh, you name a crime, I probably did it. I was the darkest of dark wizards—murder, arson, black magic, enslavement, human sacrifice. I did things that haunt my dreams. Things that would certainly drive you to madness."

"Is that why you can't kill?" Clay asked.

"That's just one of my many punishments. There are seven hundred and thirty-nine years left on my sentence."

"Wait, are you—?"

"Indeed. I must live until I've paid my debts. I cannot die. Trust me, it's not a fate I would wish on anyone."

"Why not?"

"Because I still feel everything. I remember everything. I have watched loved ones die, and their descendants as well. I have also been injured thousands of times, starved, abused, run over, shot, thrown in a river. These times cherish pets for the most part, but that has not always been so."

"That's horrible," Clay said.

"I deserve it."

"Hey! Over here." They both looked up the road to Deacon as he rounded a corner.

When they caught up to Deacon, he was cutting a fence. The old red brick building said DEPARTMENT OF WA-TER AND SANITATION in big block letters faded from the weather.

They slipped through the hole Deacon cut and walked up to the building. Deacon tried the door and stepped back, "You mind?" he asked Fisnik.

Fisnik closed his eyes. Clay could almost see the wave of energy that emanated from the dog. Suddenly the door opened wide. Fisnik opened his eyes and wobbled. "Magic is exhausting and I've already done a lot today," he explained.

"Do you need to go back to the car?" Clay asked.

"He's fine," Deacon said. "Let's go."

He hurried into the building and Clay looked at the dog. "Don't worry about it," Fisnik said.

They walked past empty offices full of paper and computers that would probably never be on again, some straight out of the nineties and looking like they had been used hard in the last ten or twelve years. They heard loud noise like whirring and screaming, but machine screaming.

They went through a door labeled 'water works' and came to the source of the noise. A massive pump was echoing as it worked to provide the town with water. Fisnik whined from the noise and backed into the hall. Deacon took a breath and let out a thunderous, "Silence!"

The room quieted and Fisnik came back in. "Sorry, that was just too much."

"It's all right, man," Deacon said. He sat down with his legs crossed, he opened his bag next to the ledge. There were concrete stairs leading down to the well and pump, along with various equipment stored in the room. Deacon took out a couple of glass vials and small leather bags, small enough to be concealed by a palm. He took out a mortar and pestle and started grinding powders and flakes of things. He asked over his shoulder, "Is it three pinches of chili flakes or two for poison detection?"

"Three," Fisnik said.

Deacon nodded and returned to his work. Clay watched him with the calm of a seasoned chef. He retrieved a funnel from the bag and carefully poured the mixture into two vials. The resulting powder looked like a sand art bottle you give kids to keep them occupied in a waiting room.

Deacon handed Clay a bottle and said, 'Think of a time…you were lost. You can't find home or your mom or something. Think like you're a little kid lost in the woods. Picture that feeling moving down your arm and into the bottle."

Clay clutched the bottle in his hand, thinking of loss, of being lost. He felt himself start to cry and then he imagined an invisible rope coming out of the bottle and pulling that feeling down his arm. He looked down, and the grains of the vial were glowing a deep crimson.

"Drop it into the well," Deacon said.

Clay dropped the vial and nothing happened. He waited for a few seconds that seemed like hours before he said, "Kind of anti-climactic."

The bottles shot up out of the well, and Deacon stretched back to catch his. Clay's vial went further, and he had to dive backward, landing hard on his back as the vial landed on his chest, he slapped his hands over it to keep it from falling. "Ow," he said. "That fucking hurt."

"What color is it?" Deacon asked.

Clay inspected the vial and saw that the sand was now a muted purple, like a violet left out in the sun. Clay told Deacon, holding up the vial for him to see. "Shit," Deacon said. "Mine too." He reached a hand down to help Clay up. "I had to try it twice and thought it would be a good lesson."

"Why try it twice?"

"Magic has been behaving weirdly lately. Sometimes simple spells you've known for a decade won't work. Other times, spells that take a bit of work come out with twice the power they should have."

"What does purple mean?" Clay asked.

Fisnik answered, looking worried. "It means someone did this on purpose. That faded purple means the poison was magic in origin. If the magic had seeped in from a plant or dead creature, the soil would have absorbed most of it, and the result would have been the townsfolk getting a mild diarrhea or maybe a rash. Not zombies."

"Can we find who did it?"

Deacon shook his head. "Anyone who poisoned a town on purpose would have hidden their signature."

"So what do we do?"

Deacon looked at the dog. "We need the Rethari."

"She is not going to take you. She hasn't been there in years."

"So I'll convince her."

Fisnik turned his head, like a puppy watching TV. "Deacon,"

"It'll be fine," Deacon said. "I'm sure she's wanting to get back on the road for a while anyway."

"If she asks me, I will be forced to tell her the truth." Fisnik said.

Clay held up a hand. "I don't understand what's happening here, but I don't want to lie to anyone either."

"Fine," Deacon said. "I'll keep you both in the dark."

They had been on the road for a few hours when Deacon pulled onto an interstate.

In the front, Fisnik said, "You never use the interstate."

"We need a bookstore," Deacon said.

"Ah, I see -

"Are we going to an out of the way magic book shop?" Clay asked.

Deacon looked at him like he might be crazy. "Barnes and Noble."

They left Fisnik with the windows down and walked through the big doors. Clay loved the smell of a book store. Old, new, used, there was something magical about that smell. "What are we here for it?"

Deacon didn't answer him. He walked back like he owned the store, and Clay followed him to the language section. "Pick a language."

Clay stood in front of the shelf, looking at the books with the names of languages: Russian, Spanish, Latin, Irish, French. This store had a large language section. Clay wondered if it was a test, like one of them was supposed to speak to him.

He carefully went through every book until he found one with a label he didn't know. Underneath the name, it said, the language of Scotland. It had a colorful cover, and he thought herecognized the writing from his spell book. "This one," he said.

Deacon made no look to show satisfaction or distaste. "Get everything you need to learn that. I have a notebook in the car and pens and pencils. I'm going to get a few novels."

He walked away without another word.

They came out of the store with a bag of books for Deacon and a bunch of learning material. Fisnik looked at the bag and wagged his tail. "Gaidhlig. Wonderful choice."

"Is someone going to explain this to me?" Clay asked.

"On the road," Deacon said. "You hungry?"

"Starving."

They went through a drive-through and Deacon ordered. "Yeah, let's get seven burgers, three fries, a pie, strike that, four pies. Five cokes and a couple of those shake things."

"Good lord," Clay said. "Are we buying food for three more people?"

Deacon smiled. "Just us."

They got their food and continued on the road, getting off the interstate and stopping at a little wayside area. They set the food out and Deacon said, "Dig in."

What followed was a scene off a farm. Clay didn't know what came over him. He ate until there was no food left near him. By the time he finished one burger, he had another in front of him. The other two did the same, and if anyone drove by, it must have looked, Clay thought, like someone had just slopped hogs.

When they were finished, Deacon scooping the last of his ice cream, he explained, "Magic is tied to language. Words of power bind themselves to the energies of magic. It's how humans learned to harness magic in the first place. There is wordless magic, but in almost every case, the magic of a place is bound to the language of its people."

"So I'm going to learn Scottish magic?"

"No. America is a different case. The languages of the natives are stronger usually, but their magic is different and they don't tend to teach outsiders. America is a home of immigrants. No one, even Indians, is originally from this continent. That means any language that is not your first can become your language of power."

What about English?

Fisnik burped, "Boring, less powerful, and somewhat sapping of energy given what its people have done to harm both the human and magical worlds."

Clay nodded. "Okay then." He thought a moment, "I feel bad about those people."

Deacon frowned. "I know. There really was no helping them. I'd say they had all been dead at least a couple of weeks."

"If not a month," Fisnik said. He scarfed down the last of his burger. "If the town had gotten more traffic, we would have an epidemic on our hands."

Clay was silent for a long time. He knew they were right. He didn't understand why he was processing this all so poorly. He guessed it would catch up to him at some point.

It was a bit clichéd, freaking out at magic when you had seen it performed. He made a mental note to keep his surprise to himself as much as possible.

"Are you finished?" Deacon asked. Clay nodded, and Deacon started bagging up their trash. He piled it on the ground near their picnic table and closed his eyes.

From his shirt pocket, he took out a small vial and said, "Holy fire."

The trash burst into flames and was sucked into the vile, where the flames continued to swirl with a faint light. "What the hell was that?" Clay asked, aware he had already broken his rule.

"English is good for stealing the energy out of things," Deacon said. "Let's get some sleep. I call the back seat."

"It's the middle of the day - " Clay said.

"We're three hours from Chicago and need to get there at night. I also prefer traveling at night. It's a good idea to get some shut-eye; we'll be up late."

Clay shrugged. "Okay, I am tired, I guess."

"More than you realize," Fisnik said.

Deacon lay back on the back seat, Fisnik getting in the way back on the space between bags. Clay laid up front and fell asleep in seconds.

CHAPTER THREE

Chicago Fairies

They pulled into the parking space, and Clay stashed his book away.

It had gotten too dark to read a couple of hours before, but still held the book, going over the new words in his mind.

Deacon turned to look at Fisnik. "You wanna come?"

"No thank you, dear boy. The music is painful. I can hear it from here without the earaches."

"Very well. Clay, let's go."

They walked a few blocks to the club. Deacon showed the guy at the door a piece of paper in a little business card holder, and he let them cut the line. They stood in a doorway, the sound coming through in a muted barrage of noise. "We'll wait until the show is over, then follow me."

Clay nodded, and Deacon opened the door for him. The sound grew exponentially louder. Clay followed Deacon through the club to the bar when Deacon loudly yelled, "Laphroaig, two doubles!"

He put some bills on the counter, took the drinks, and led Clay to a table in the corner. After checking that no one was watching, he waved his hands over the whiskey and muttered something Clay couldn't hear over the music. Deacon handed him one of the glasses and mouthed, 'Shoot.'

Clay shot the whiskey. It was nice but burned a lot. He let out a breath, then heard Deacon in his mind. *Islay isn't for everyone, but peat is good for the spell.*

I can hear your thoughts.

Yes, it'll last about two hours. I thought it would be easier to talk this way. Just look like you're enjoying the music.

Clay didn't respond, just nodded. They both nodded to the music, not saying much for a while. The club was cool. It looked like an old jazz club. He guessed it had started hosting other events to make money. He saw a poster on the wall for a stand-up show, and tonight many tables had been moved to make room for the crowd. People danced to the rock music.

The band looked cool, and their music was good. Clay focused on the bass player and saw nothing else. She wore dark jeans, a black tank top, and a beanie that hung loose, achieving a laid-back cool look she was going for.

She was absorbed in her playing. Her eyes scanned the crowd, and sweat glistened on her chest. Her gaze returned to her bass, then suddenly met his. He jerked back, and a smirk lit up her face before she refocused on playing.

We're here for her.

Clay looked at Deacon and in his head asked, *Really?* Deacon nodded, and the music suddenly stopped. The lead singer, a girl with red hair, was very much not pulling off the rocker look, said, "Thank you and good night."

Deacon stood up and motioned for Clay to follow.

They went towards the stage and through a door in the back wall. The hallway was only about as wide as Deacon's shoulders and packed with random restaurant supplies, chairs, and other bits with no apparent storage area.

The walls were covered with cords and pipes like veins, channeling the club's energy where it needed to go. They found the dressing room and waited to one side of the door. Clay could hear the band discussing something. He couldn't make out the details. It wasn't long before the other three members of the band wandered out of the room.

Deacon stepped in behind the last one to leave, the drummer, and kept the door open just a crack. "Come on," he said.

The dressing room had one makeup table, a couple of chairs, and a dirty-looking couch with cracked leather. It was covered in costumes and leftover restaurant supplies like cups and bins of silverware.

They walked in just as the bass player was pulling her top over her head. She unclipped her bra and grabbed a wipe off the table, running it under her breasts. "Hello Deacon," she said. "I saw you staring."

"I wasn't staring," Deacon said.

She turned around, her bare breasts exposed to Clay. He looked away, and she giggled. "I was talking to him."

Deacon slapped him on the arm. "It's alright, Clay. She's just messing with you. She enjoys toying with men, don't you, Tara?"

Clay looked at her as she shrugged. "Sometimes, when I'm in a mood." She went to the couch and rifled through a bag. Clay couldn't help but notice her smile again. "So what can I do for you?"

Before Deacon could speak, she ran to a trash can and violently threw up. Clay rushed over and held her hair. She vomited three more times in quick succession.

She stood up. "Thank you," she said, reaching for a glass of water. She gargled, spat into the can, and resumed rifling through the clothes. She found a big T-shirt and pulled it over her head.

Clay wasn't proud that he hadn't noticed her head. Her perfect breasts had distracted him from the two horns on her head, an inch or so back from her forehead, arching slightly before turning again and curving up. They were black in this light, but he saw hints of a shimmering red in them too.

"I was thinking you might want to get back on the road," Deacon said.

Tara raised an eyebrow. "Oh yeah?"

"Swear," Deacon said.

"Are you still hunting this magic Messer guy?"

"I am, but I honestly know that you haven't been on the road in a good long while, and I was thinking maybe you might want to join our little quest." He pointed to Clay. "The new kid likes you, obviously. He has a boner."

Clay's eyes went wide, and he felt his face get hot. Deacon looked at him. "You were thinking really loudly."

Tara laughed, and it sounded like nature, like sitting in a field and just listening. "I'm flattered, uh—"

"Clay," he offered.

"I'm flattered, Clay. I'll come along as long as you promise we go to Vegas."

"Deal," Deacon said.

"Well, I'm gonna throw on some sweats and we'll go."

"Whole life in a bag. I knew you missed the road," Deacon said with a mischievous grin.

"Fuck off. My cat is fed and I'm paid until March on my apartment."

She unbuttoned her jeans and Clay's heart skipped a beat. Tara raised an eyebrow. "There's a bathroom in there if you wanna take care of yourself real quick."

He considered it for a half second before saying, "I'm fine."

Tara shimmied out of her jeans and withdrew a pair of sweats from her duffle. He saw her panties as she changed and felt like he would start a fire. "I'll be right back," he said, stepping into the bathroom.

They walked down the alley to the car, and Fisnik popped his head out of the window. "Lovely to see you, my dear."

Tara scratched him behind the ear. "Hey Fiz, how's prison?"

"A never-ending pain."

"Good. Slide up front, would you? I want to get some shut-eye. The new kid's my pillow."

Fisnik looked behind her to Clay and Tara turned. "What?" she said, "You jerked off to me, least you can do is let me rest my head on your lap."

Clay said nothing. He got into the back passenger seat and Tara laid across the bench with her head on his lap. She stretched out and yawned, "Don't worry about it. It happens with Fey in situations like this."

"Okay," Clay said. He tried hard not to notice her breasts falling to either side of her. Tara was soon asleep and they were on the road in minutes.

Clay looked out the window, watching the world go by. He didn't know how long they had been driving when Fisnik looked at him through the gap between the seat and the door. "Did you really masturbate?"

"It was like I didn't have a choice," Clay whispered. "I mean, yeah, she is the most beautiful girl I've ever seen, but it was like my dick had a mind of its own and needed the world to know."

"That is very interesting indeed."

"Why exactly?" Clay asked, still in a whisper.

"Tara is Fey, as in of the Fey folk. Sexual energy has many meanings in the world of fairies."

Clay raised his brows. "You wanna tell me what this means?"

"Tara will tell you when the time is right. Something tells me there will be more tests and interactions before her gods tell her the truth."

"I have no idea what the hell that means," Clay said.

"Good. You aren't supposed to."

When Clay's eyes opened, Tara was still in his lap but she was clearly awake, scrunching her eyes against the sun of mid-morning. "My head is killing me," she said.

"You must have drunk a lot before you went on last night."

She opened one eye to look at him. "It's my potion."

"Oh,"

"You have no idea what I'm talking about, do you?"

"I do not."

Tara sat up and looked at him, her eyes still squinting. "I'm fey, a faerie. That means I can't use technology created after around 1970, and nothing with more than a tiny bit of electricity. Basically, the car battery is the only thing my presence won't turn off.

Clay nodded his understanding and she continued. "I take a potion before going on stage that lessens the effects so I can play. The downside is after it wears off, it leaves my head feeling like I drank three bottles of vodka and no water. Like a hangover but a thousand times worse."

"Damn, why take it then?"

"Because I love to perform." Tara laid back down on his lap and looked up at him. "Tell me what you like about my body."

Clay's mouth moved without his permission. "I like that you're not skinny. You have a middle. When you put on that shirt last night and it made you look thicker in the middle, I lost it. Your breasts are fantastic, big fan of your tits. Your ass is out of this world, but ultimately I love the look on your face. I get the idea there's secret power hidden behind your eyes, but you might also be a bit insecure and lonely. When I look at you, I want to watch a movie on the couch, holding your belly because it's sexy. Then I want to help you belt on your armor and watch your ass as I follow you into battle."

Tara was smiling. Deacon was watching Clay through the rearview mirror. Fisnik watched him through the crack between the door and the seat. "What the fuck just happened?" Clay asked.

They erupted into laughter. "Don't sweat it, Clay," Deacon said. "You wouldn't be the first man to fall to Fae."

"Uh, I..."

Tara sat up again and kissed him on the cheek. "I liked it."

She leaned through the gap in the seats. "So Deek, where are we headed? Got any leads?"

Deek recounted the story about the zombies. When he finished, he said, "So we're headed to Kansas City."

Tara groaned, "You have got to be kidding me."

"He is our best bet for information on all the weirdness, and a possible dark wizard."

"I just... why didn't you tell me we had to see Laz? I would not have come if I had known we were going to go anywhere near that flaming asswipe."

"He is not that bad, Tara," Fisnik said.

"The fuck he isn't." She sat back against the seat and stared out the window for a few seconds before adding, "He ate a girl in front of me and then tried to fuck me. I still haven't gotten over the tit honk."

"He killed someone?" Clay asked.

Tara looked at him and waved that away, "He only eats the ones who have it coming, according to him. But it is still fucked up to do it in front of me. Plus he makes fun of my horns," she said the last part to the front of the car as if to punctuate her complaint.

"I'll make sure he's on his best behavior," Deacon said. "If he gives you shit about the horns you can stab him anywhere but the heart."

"Deal," Tara said.

They rode mostly in silence for a couple of hours. Clay was weirded out by his lack of control earlier and did his best not to stare at Tara. She had fished a novel out of her bag and read it sitting sideways, her legs spread out on the seat, not quite touching Clay.

In an effort to distract himself, he read his spell book and started working on pronunciations in his head. "When can I try a," he ran his finger over the page in an effort to sound it out, "fey micota."

"It's a simple enough summoning spell if you can pronounce the Gàidhlig correctly," Deacon said. "Next rest stop or wayside."

"Awesome," Clay said.

"That better be quick, D," Tara said. "I'm about to piss myself."

"There's a gas station up ahead. We'll do it there." Deacon told her, "So dramatic."

The gas station was clearly not well traveled. It had all the makings of a traveler's center were there, but the faded paint, duct tape over a window crack, and overall vibe suggested neglect. It was clear they weren't used to visitors.

Tara ran into the station to pee, and Deacon got gas. While it was filling up, he told Clay how to pronounce the spell. Clay said, "Feumaidh mi cota." Nothing happened. He tried again, putting the same energy he had into the fire spell. Nothing happened again.

"Perhaps he needs an example," Fisnik said, coming back from the bushes.

Deacon nodded. He tried and nothing happened. "The fuck?" Deacon closed his eyes, thrust out his arms, and said, "Feumaidh mi cota." A woolen coat appeared on him. Greyish blue with a high collar. "That was weird," he said, looking relieved.

"The issues with magic," Fisnik said.

"What?" Clay asked. "You mean I didn't do it wrong?"

"No, dear boy, Deacon's power is most likely the only reason it worked. Magic has been behaving strangely and it seems to be getting worse."

Tara walked out of the gas station, her beanie flapping in the wind. "I got some snacks," she held up a plastic bag. "What'd I miss?"

"Fisk, fill her in while Clay and I pee." Deacon said.

Fisnik nodded and looked at Tara, "What snacks did you get?"

Back on the road, Clay was eating a Hostess snowball when Tara said, "If it makes you feel better, I didn't do anything to you. These guys don't know anything about women or Fey, and certainly not Fey women. That happens on its own."

"Why?"

She smiled. It looked sympathetic, but there was a mischievous glint in her eye. "I can't tell you that yet."

"Can you tell me one thing?"

She considered a moment then held up a finger.

"You're... why do you have horns?"

Tara's posture immediately became defensive. She pulled her feet away and crossed her arms, trying to look tough. "They're not weird."

Clay's eyes widened, and his heart ached at having upset her. "No, no, I think they're amazing. I love them. It's just not every day you see a beautiful woman with horns, and I'm new to magic, so I was curious."

"You mean that? You're not gonna make fun of me?"

"I would never make fun of you for any part of your body. It's hurtful and uncreative. Now if you have a bad fart in public, I will loudly ask if you've shit yourself."

Tara smiled. She lowered her arms but didn't put her feet back. "The horns are my fey mark. Every fey has a thing that marks them as fey. Horns like a dragon," she motioned to her head. "Gills, cat eyes, plumage, colored skin, face flaps. We all have a thing."

"Where does it come from?"

Tara's mouth went straight, and she tsked. "I said one."

Clay smiled. Fisnik poked his head back. "The legends say that when Heaven and Hell ended their war, the angels who were neither damned to hell nor welcomed to heaven were forced to remain on earth. Their marks are a reminder of their failure to choose a side, or their rebellion. The mark is random, and families of Fey usually all have different marks. Genetic marks are not unheard of but are quite rare."

"Thanks, Fisnik," Tara said. "Here I was trying to be all mysterious."

"Women are mysterious enough. You don't need to try."

"Ain't that the truth," Deacon said.

"What would you know?" Tara said. The car immediately got quiet. "I'm sorry, D, I was,-"

"It's fine," Deacon said. "You were just kidding around." He moved to turn the radio on, and the car started sputtering.

Deacon cursed under his breath. He turned off at the next exit. "This is why I hate the interstate."

"That had nothing to do with the interstate," Fisnik told him.

"Shut the fuck up, dog."

The car coasted to a mechanic on the other side of the parking lot across from an indoor mall, and Deacon went in. He talked to the mechanic, and they could see him getting upset.

From outside, he looked like he was about to go over the counter.

Fisnik looked at both of them and said, "Perhaps you should go to the mall. The mechanic is certainly not going to make us a priority after that. I'll send word when we're ready."

Tara looked genuinely sorry. "I didn't mean to bring her up. I was just messing around."

"You did nothing wrong, my dear. Deacon was a tad emotionally unstable before Elanor died. The magical mishaps have only heightened his instability and emotional immaturity."

"I'm guessing that his wife died," Clay said. "And his being upset hurt the car."

Tara rocked her head side to side like she didn't want to admit something. "I mean, my presence alone was—straining it, but yeah. I upset Deacon, and that surge of emotion killed the car."

"Run along," Fisnik said. "Grab me something meaty." Tara popped her door open. "Come on," Clay followed her, and they walked side by side. "I think it's time for a new beanie," Tara said.

"Do you ever mix it up with a different type of hat?"

"They don't make them to fit me. Too wide."

"How come you hide? Surely to God the late-night rocker crowd would assume that,"He looked around, "you know,"

"I appreciate that," Tara replied. She loved that he looked around.

"Anytime. They would assume it was your rocker persona or something."

"A, that's more of a heavy grunge metal thing, and B, people are not nearly as accepting as they pretend to be."

CHAPTER FOUR

The mall

Tara did not like big spaces like the mall, especially in the Midwest. Chicago was in the Midwest, but it wasn't really part of it.

The mall looked like every other mall: big glass dome overhead, escalators, stores responsible for the destruction of the middle class and mom-and-pop stores nationwide. It was just a mall.

Clay followed her to a store that sold clothes for people too poor to shop at Hot Topic but who wanted to look like they did. He was following her a lot. She would have to test to see if he was willing to tell her no. His reaction in her green room had been a promising sign, but she didn't want a puppy. Elise had a puppy and Tara hated her brother-in-law.

"What's your family like?" she asked.

"Dead."

"I'm sorry to hear that."

He shrugged the way guys do when they're uncomfortable and don't want to show emotion. "It was a long time ago. I've been on my own since I was fifteen."

"If you ever want to talk about it, I'm a very good listener."

"Why do I want to tell you? Is that magic too?"

"I don't think so. I think you just genuinely like me. I have that effect on people."

Clay smiled. He had a nice smile. He was handsome in that rescued dog kind of way. His hair was raven black and desperately in need of a cut. His eyes were soulful and deep brown, almost looking hazel in certain lights.

Tara pulled a beanie off the rack and then another. She held both up for Clay, "Which one? Blue or black?"

He cocked his head in thought, "I think you should go for a lighter color. That green would be nice."

"What?"

"Why would it be nice? Your hair is red and those colors go well together. Ask anyone, or just look...literally anywhere during Christmas."

Tara rolled her eyes. "Why would I go with a lighter color?"

"Dark blue and black are close to the pitch black you've got. I just think a lighter color would show off your face more. You're beautiful." He shrugged his shoulders. "That's all."

Tara turned around and smiled, her face warming. The good feeling spread through her chest. "I'm gonna go look at clothes. Meet me at the changing room in a few minutes?"

"Yes ma'am."

Tara grabbed a handful of band T-shirts, some to replace hers that were almost threadbare, and one to sleep in because she had forgotten pajamas. She took it as a good sign. She was getting used to leaving some things at home.

Turning to make sure no one was looking, she grabbed a hanger marked as her size and slipped into the dressing room. She threw off her t-shirt and unbuttoned her jeans. It always excited her, seeing herself in a mirror like this. It made her think that maybe someday someone else might see it. She slipped the new bra on and thought it looked sexy. She moved to her other item and felt stupid when she looked around again.

The dress was green, the same shade as the beanie. It was a sundress that hung to her knees and showed just enough cleavage to be beautiful without looking trashy.

It made her feel beautiful. She took off her beanie and looked at herself in the mirror.

Red curls fell around her, brushing her skin in a way she wasn't used to. Her hair almost always fell behind her, with only a few strands ever touching her exposed arms a t-shirt.

She looked like a demon. She hated her horns, hated how isolated they made her feel, how ugly they were. They ruined how good the dress made her feel. It wasn't until her vision blurred that she realized she was crying.

She dropped the dress from her shoulders and stood there, a naked, teary mess, when there was a knock on the door. Tara threw herself to the floor, grabbing something. She covered her head and caught herself in the mirror, naked except for a green beanie, red hair everywhere. "Tara?"

Her chest dropped as she sighed in relief. Picking herself off the floor, she said, "Yeah?"

"Find anything good?"

She spoke as she dressed herself, her nipples hardening. She squirmed a little, enjoying talking to him naked. "A couple of band T-shirts and something to sleep in."

"Yeah?"

"Don't drool, it stains the already disgusting carpet." She felt like she needed a shower from her butt on the carpet. She opened the door and saw him standing there with nothing. "You didn't look for clothes?"

"Jeans, shirt, flannel over it. I'm good."

" Men."

They made their way up front, and Tara paid for her items. She realized she was wearing the new beanie. Carefully, she took the tag off so the woman behind the counter could scan it. "You can't leave wearing merchandise." she said.

"Can't I just pay you and you not worry about it?" Tara asked.

"No."

Tara read the screen on the little pad. One hundred. "Here," she handed the woman a hundred and fifty. "Keep it."

"Ma'am, it is store policy. You have to leave your items in the bag or I cannot complete the transaction. Just take the hat off. Bill!"

Tara turned and saw a slightly overweight man in his early forties walking over. She backed up against Clay. "I cannot take this hat off," she whispered.

"I know. Let me,-"

"These two are trying to steal this stuff. That bag she has—"

"I am not, I'm trying to overpay." Tara said.

Bill spoke into a little radio on his shirt. "I need further assistance on the east side."

"Ow," Clay said, pressing his finger and thumb to his forehead. He moved forward, and Tara was painfully aware of his pressing into her. "They're done. They're going to pick us up on the south end of the mall," he whispered in her ear, looking like he was trying to be sexy, but Bill and the irate little gnomish woman took it as conspiracy. "Run, pick me up on the west end," Clay whispered before moving around her and walking up to Bill.

He put his hands on Bill's shoulders and said, "Officer pretend cop, I am truly sorry for this—"

Bill did not have time to react as Clay whipped his forehead back into Bill's nose. Clay was off, and Bill turned to follow him.

Tara turned to the woman and threw the money at her. "Cunt."

Then she ran. She ran like her life depended on it, and it very well might. Humans did not have a good track record of finding fey. They usually made it look like something else, but it was almost always an officer-involved shooting or a car accident. They always died before the media got close. It was what humans did. They didn't need a conspiracy. Killing what they didn't understand was their nature.

Her lungs were powerful but burning when she made it to the car. She was certain she had a bruised rib and wished she had put the bra on. It wasn't athletic but it was necessary.

She opened the back door and threw herself into the seat behind Deacon. "West side, go!"

He sped off before the door was closed. Tara saw the side they were coming up on and opened the door as she slid over.

Clay dove into the car, landing with his head on her lap. She used magic to flick the door closed, and they sped off. Her mouth moved a million miles an hour as she apologized. She called herself stupid for forgetting to put the beanie on her head.

Clay smiled. He gently grabbed her face and kissed her.

CHAPTER FIVE

Laz

The house was most definitely not what he had been expecting for a vampire. It was an old colonial house with a magnificent garden and what looked to be a fresh coat of paint.

The garden was magnificent, and the house appeared to have a fresh coat of paint. They pulled into the driveway around six-thirty in the evening. Deacon told them to follow him and not dawdle.

Apparently, some of the plants that lined the brick path were special.

The path to the house was ominous, and they liked to sedate victims. They all stood on the porch, and Deacon rang the bell.

The door opened before the chime stopped, and Clay thought, *figures, Vampire speed.*

"What do you, - Deacon? Do come in, man. Come, come!"

He stepped back and opened the door for them. Clay couldn't see him clearly until his foot crossed the threshold.

He was suddenly thrown against the wall. His head hit a picture, and the vampire was millimeters from his face. "Who are you?" he asked, a British accent clearly tainted by time in America.

"My name is... Clay," he choked out. The pressure on his windpipe was worsening.

"I see. You smell, normal."

"I, uh, I don't know how to respond to that."

His head tilted in confusion. His skin was pale. Jet black hair falling to his chin. He was perfectly coiffed and well kempt. "Why is that?"

"Because I believe that people who profess their lack of normalcy are the most average and normal people. I also don't want to lie right now because I'm pretty sure you can take my heartbeat like a tiger."

Clay was released and fell the two feet back to the floor.

Laz was smiling. "I quite like you," he said. He held out a hand and said, "Lazlo Kentworth."

He shook the hand. "Clay, as I said."

"Lovely to meet you, Clay. Would you all like some dinner, or are you ready for sleep? I've made a number of new quilts this year, and they're all upstairs fresh on the beds."

Tara had her arms crossed. "Lazlo?"

Lazlo smiled at her. "Feychild?"

Tara's jaw shifted in annoyance. Fisnik stepped from behind her. "Nice to see you again, Kentworth."

Lazlo's head tilted again. "Fisnik? I seem to remember you being somewhat more bipedal."

"Makes sense, I haven't seen you since... I dunno but it was around here somewhere."

"I don't believe this was a state yet." Lazlo said, "Quite some time indeed."

"I need a nap," Deacon said.

"Same room as last time, dear boy. The rest of you, come and have a cookie if you're not ready for a meal."

He led them back to a well-lit kitchen. There was a gorgeous antique dining room table with a thick knit heat pad in the center. There were magnets on the refrigerator and notices. On the wall was an intricately designed calendar that seemed to show Lazlo was overly involved in the community.

He saw Clay looking and said, "Oh that. I do not sleep, you see, so I spend my time doing every conceivable thing. You can only clean the house so many times before you decide to learn knitting and watch all of Netflix."

"What's that?" Tara asked.

"It's a streaming platform, dear, television, movies, quite a lot of it was terrible, my god, those B-movie films; but it does pass the time while I'm working on my projects."

"You do charity work?" Clay said. "That's not what I expected from the first vampire I met."

Lazlo brought a tray of cookies and a couple of plates of pasta. "Well, what did you expect? A house run down with dozens of bodies in the yard? That's a surefire way to get found out."

"How do you hunt?" Clay asked, taking a cookie. Chocolate chip melted in his mouth, making his eyes roll back.

"Have you ever gone on a website and looked up homes in your area where sex offenders live?" Clay nodded. "Well," Lazlo continued, "they don't update that site, any of them. If they did, they'd know that there are around ten percent of the projected number

"Wait a second," Tara said. "That's who you killed in front of me? A pervert?"

Lazlo nodded. "I am terribly sorry about that. It is so rude to eat in front of a non-vampire. She was on her way out and I just had to kill her. She raped seven young girls from her class in Miami, then moved here."

"What about the tit honk?" Tara said.

"Can you blame a man? Look at those things. Am I right, Clay?

Clay looked at Tara, who was staring daggers at him. "I... uh... the pasta looks great."

Lazlo raised an eyebrow. "Are you—"

"Shut the fuck up, Lazo," Tara said.

They ate in silence. It didn't take long.

Clay hadn't realized how hungry he was, and from her expression, neither had Tara.

Lazlo guessed Tara felt the same. When they finished, Lazlo said, "Now, if you're both ready to retire, you may take the attic. I'm afraid I've dedicated the second-floor rooms, other than Deacon's current room, to my various crafts. Fisnik, care to join me for a movie marathon while I knit quilts for the senior center?"

"Love to," Fisnik said, hopping down from his seat at the table.

Tara took extra cookies and said, "Come on."

The attic was large. The steps were steep and carpeted. By the top, they were on all fours. Clay noticed Tara still wasn't wearing a bra as he climbed behind her. There was a room to the left of a small bathroom and a larger room to the right, with a bed against one wall. Another bed was a few feet further down on the opposite wall.

There was a large window on the far wall. The curtains were drawn, and a couch sat along the left wall, tucked into the corner near the window.

Tara set her bag, recovered from the foyer, down on one bed and pulled out of her oversized shirt she'd bought at the mall. His heart skipped a beat at this.

Being her sleepwear, she shimmied out of her jeans. She winked at him, turned around, and took off her shirt, soon replacing it with a big one that fell just below her butt.

Clay rushed forward, took her by the arms, and turned her around. "You need to explain what the fuck is happening to me," he said. "Right now."

"What's happening to you?"

"Why do I want to fuck you so much? I get it, you're beautiful, I'm a guy, but I'm old enough to control myself. I haven't had such uncontrollable urges in at least eight years, if not longer. I like your body. A lot, but right now I have this overwhelming urge to bend you over this bed, and my brain isn't interested in finding out if you're into it. Do you get what I'm saying?"

"It's taking all your self-control not to rape me?"

His arms fell down, and he motioned wildly, like a mute who had finally gotten someone to understand them. "Yes, that's awful, but it's so true. I have no idea what is happening to my body, but I just—" he made a frustrated motion at her and threw himself backward, running a hand through his hair.

"Okay, calm down," Tara said. "Do I need to leave for a moment?"

" Or I do."

"I'm going to use the bathroom. I will be right back." She went to the bathroom, and Clay felt control returning. His caveman brain seemed to turn off, and his blood cooled. When his erection subsided, he said, "Okay."

He sat on the other bed, and Tara came over, sitting down and crossing her legs. Clay sat opposite her, thankful the shirt fell so far down. "Look at me," she said. "Hey, I'm fey right? In their culture, magic is very mutable; it adapts to your tribe and their customs. A common thing amongst my people, there used to be a deliberate test for that kind of thing, and over time the test turned magic. The key is that your heart and your genitals are not linked. That means it matters who you give your heart to, not who you sleep with."

Clay gave an understanding nod. "Okay."

"When two people who are attracted meet, the test begins. I can't tell you any more than that, just know it doesn't mean you actually want to harm me. You're not a bad guy; you literally have no say in how you're feeling or how your body responds. Trust me."

His brow furrowed, "What does that mean?"

"It means I've soaked my underwear just looking at you, and it was really hard not to jump you after you saved me at the mall."

"So it's—"

She finished for them both, "It's not just you."

He nodded, and she touched his face. It was soft and made him smile.

"Good night, Clay."

"Good night."

Tara dreamt of her family. She didn't like them, but it was undeniable they could help with both tests yet to come. She was jarred awake late into the night and saw Clay turning over in his bed. She shot up and watched his form in the dark. Her beanie was by her bag next to the bed, and she started to reach for it but stayed her hand.

"No, mom, stop."

Tara got out of bed and stood over him. She reached out a hand, and he hesitated. He looked so upset, tears staining his face. He started to move again, and she picked up the covers, sliding next to him. She threw out all the calm feelings she could to try and soothe him. He shifted until she was the little spoon, painfully aware of his body pressed into hers. It was soft and nice, and neither were aroused.

CHAPTER SIX

C lay felt really good when he woke up. He didn't know why he felt that way, just that he did. He got the best sleep of his life. He breathed in and stretched wide. He looked over at the other bed and laughed to himself.

Tara was a tangle of limbs and sheets, like a hurricane had swept across just her bed. *She must be a rough sleeper*, he thought.

It was still early as he pulled on his jeans and headed downstairs, but there was already activity in the kitchen. Lazlo was in an apron, hunched over the stove. The counter was filled with breakfast dishes from all over the world: haggis, the fixings for an English breakfast, croissants, and a sawdust-looking thing that Clay thought was muesli. He saw giant pancakes and big sausages, oatmeals and crepes. It seemed like a cornucopia had exploded. "Wow," was all he said.

Lazlo turned around. His apron was impressive. It was black with red trim and a bunch of pockets so that everything he needed from spoons to measuring utensils to a few pencils where he made notes in a big notebook on a stand in the corner. "I do love to cook," he said. "I have an adventurous eaters club who come around once or twice a week to help with new recipes."

"So, you can eat?" Clay asked.

"No, but I can taste. Gives me terrible indigestion, and it often feels like torture. I loved to cook when I was alive. I had a restaurant in Edinburgh."

"Wait a second, how are you around in the morning?"

Lazlo held up his left ring.

The ring was a thin band of black metal with pronounced vine-like workings. It couldn't have been comfortable to wear. "Daylight ring. Take it off and I burst into flames."

"Do all vampires have one?"

Lazlo shook his head, turning back to the stove. He spoke as he stirred something in a big cast iron skillet. "Eat, eat," he said, pointing to a stack of plates and cutlery. Clay moved to start making his plate. "No," Lazlo started, moving over to deposit a strange-looking egg dish onto Clay's plate, "a daylight ring costs so much. Most vampires who even know they exist are probably still working toward it. I've only had mine a hundred years.

Clay dropped an enormous sausage onto his plate and asked, "How long did it take you to save up?"

"Oh, it's not just about the money, though that took three hundred and forty-nine years of continuous night work to save. It's all about the ingredients, the collection of which took me nearly seven centuries."

Clay's eyes went wide. "Seven?"

"Plants, ingredients that must be constructed under certain stars, travel back then was a nightmare. Getting a pirate to ship a coffin to the other side of the world during plague times is no easy feat."

"Are you talking about your stupid ring?" Tara entered the kitchen looking like she hadn't slept, in her big T-shirt, part of which was tucked into her underwear, her hair was wrapped up and around her horns and seemed to stand of its own accord.

"My my," Lazlo said, "I know whose pussy I want for breakfast."

Tara glared at him. "Your gift with subtlety has waned, you perverted degenerate."

Lazlo shrugged. "I haven't been fucking as much lately. Well, fewer humans—vampires quite like it when you plainly say you want to fuck them. There was this one fellow—"

Tara held up a hand. "Coffee."

Lazlo pointed to the stove. Tara held up a finger and said, "Pinch my ass on my way to the coffee and I swear to all the gods, I will pull your ring off. I do not care what we need from you."

Lazlo held up a hand as she passed so he didn't have one free to pinch her. "Fey do not make idle threats," he said to Clay.

Clay couldn't resist. He swiftly jutted out a hand and pinched Tara on the butt. She spun around like a Jedi. Clay smiled. "You didn't threaten me."

Tara smirked and went back to pouring coffee. "Want some?" she asked.

"Yes please," Clay said.

He sat down and immediately left his plate to go back to the counter. "Can I make you a plate?" he asked.

Clay couldn't see her face, but he thought he heard a cheer in her voice as she said, "That would be lovely. Lots of meat and bread."

Lazlo was leaning against the bridge, arms still open, eyeing both of them. "You two are lovely."

"Shut up," Tara said.

"Spiteful little sprite, aren't you? Meat and bread? Still..." He nudged Tara's shoulder as she walked to the table.

She sat down and glared at Lazlo. "Mentioning my family was a low blow."

"Quite right," Lazlo said. "I'm sorry."

Clay brought her a plate, and they ate in silence for a few long minutes. Deacon walked into the room and went over to start filling a plate. He took a little bit of everything and scarfed for a few minutes before looking at Tara and saying, "You look like shit."

"What the fuck dude? Is Clay the only nice man here?"

Deacon and Lazlo spoke in unison, "Yes."

"Anyway," Tara said, "I sent a lot of calm out and it meant a bad night's rest for me."

Clay's brow twitched at that, but he decided if Tara wanted him to know, she would tell him.

The meal progressed with some small talk but mostly a lot of eating. Clay noticed that Tara had her horns exposed but every so often would still raise a hand to check if the beanie was there.

When the plates were empty and the coffee all gone, Deacon sat back and said, "Laz, I need to speak with you in—private. Clay, Fisnik says he'll give you some pointers outside."

He stood and walked out of the room without another word.

Tara leaned into the rest of the table. "Does he think he's our colonel?" Lazlo laughed and she said, "I'm going to shower. Breakfast was great, Laz, thanks."

CHAPTER SEVEN

Tara got out of the shower and toweled off. She preferred to air dry but didn't want to ruin Laz's floors. She unzipped her toiletry bag and brushed her teeth.

She took out the salve she liked and applied it to her itchy horns, sighing in almost orgasmic relief as they subsided in their attempt to drive her to madness. She put on her moisturizer after washing her face and wrapped back up in a towel in case Clay came upstairs.

She hadn't been lying about how much he aroused her. They were paired, it seemed, though he could fail the test, or she could. It was rare, but it had happened to her aunt back in the nineties. She put on her new bra and a band T-shirt. She chose the jeans she thought made her look best and headed downstairs, pulling a beanie on the way outside.

She saw Fisnik running and jumping around Clay as he looked more and more frustrated. Anyone around would think a guy was hanging out with his yappy dog, not that a nearly millennia-old criminal was teaching a wizard magic. It helped that Lazlo's hedges were high and soundproof so no one could see.

"Uck!" Clay said. "Why can't I get this v—"

"You are making progress," Fisnik said. "Just try and calm down. Find your center. It's a simple levitation spell."

Clay shook himself out like he was about to start doing improv. He closed his eyes, and she could see his mouth moving, though she heard nothing. Tara took a seat in a cast iron patio chair.

Clay was trying to levitate a potted plant he had dragged into the middle of the yard. She watched as it lifted a few feet into the air. "Good job," she called out.

His eyes flew open, and the planter shot straight into the air. "Grab it!" Fisnik yelled.

Clay threw his hands up, and his magic caught the planter. A split second before it crashed into the lovely fountain just off center of the yard, he had a look of boyish shock on his face as he moved the planter back where he'd gotten it originally. She smiled to herself because she just knew he was making Jedi comparisons in his head.

Fisnik galloped over to her and asked, "Would you mind terribly to go? I'm afraid you're a distraction."

"Think I'm getting his goat, Fiz?"

"Why don't you just test him now? Find out for sure so the poor lad can have some blood sent back to his brain."

Tara stood up, bending over to scratch the dog behind the ear. "It happens when it's supposed to."

She walked away without another word, started to wander through the garden, but decided against it.

She wanted to snoop through Lazlo's house and maybe find something to read. He had so many books that it would be a decade before he knew it was missing. She walked back through the kitchen and down the front hall. "So where do we need to go to find the source?" It was Deacon's voice.

I" think you know, dear boy," Lazlo said. Tara looked at the wall, tilting her head as she searched the grains of wood. She could sense the trees they used to be and asked them to speak to her. In response, a seam glowed faintly gold, visible only to her.

She pressed it, and a door opened in the right wall, under the stairs.

The room was small, with a desk and some shelves, basically a large closet that made the two men look larger than they were. The wall behind Lazlo was lined with books, except for a cork-board. The cork-board was crowded with bits of paper, like a serial killer's collection.

Deacon was in front of her before she could blink. "Cadal," he said, touching her forehead, and the world went black.

Tara woke up on a horse. She blinked several times, still groggy. It felt like she was dreaming when she heard, "This is wrong."

"Clay, you knew I was going to do this," Deacon said.

"Bullshit. I did not know you were going to knock her out for three days and drag her into the middle of nowhere. We need to go back."

Tara finished waking up. "You knew?" she said. "What does—" She took in the scenery and her heart beat faster. They were in a forest. It had to be fairly deep. The path was not well defined. They were provisioned, each of the three horses outfitted for a full trail ride.

She shook her head, her voice breaking like a little girl's. "No, no, you can't take me back there. Deacon...this is... no!"

Her hands were tied to the pommel of her saddle. Deacon stood next to her horse and untied her hands. "This was just so you wouldn't fall off," he said. "Stop crying. I am sorry. I need this, I need their help. I will fund an entire weekend in Vegas."

"Four days."

"Deal." he said.

"Why is this so important, why them? Deacon, I hate them—"

"I know you do, Tara, I know. If there was anyone else on this continent that could help me track the source of the magic problem, I would go to them."

"How do you know they'll even help?"

"I don't, but I can't even find them without you."

"You're a fucking bastard, Deacon Caldwell."

"I'll let you hit me when they find us."

He walked up front and mounted his horse. Clay moved his mount, a pretty red thing that Tara thought was a mixed breed, though she was less accustomed to horses than she once had been. "I had no idea what was going on," Clay said. "I swear.

I knew he was looking for the Rethari. But I didn't know that meant you. I knew that Fisnik told him that if questioned, he would have to tell you the truth, but I honestly didn't put it together until Deacon was loading you into the car."

Tara let a breath out through her nostrils. "I need you to do me a favor."

"What? Anything."

"Avoid talking to me for the next two or three days so I can figure out if I'm angry with you."

Clay thought a moment and said, "That's fair. Can I ask one last question before I shut up?"

Tara took a long blink and kind of rolled her eyes, but she said, "Yes."

"Who are the Rethari?"

Tara took a dramatic breath and let it out, trying to ease some of the tension in her shoulders. "They are my family."

CHAPTER EIGHT

The Rethari

Clay had been silent for two days. He kind of liked it. He picked up a lot just by listening. He listened to Deacon. Deacon talked about magic and the feelings it gave when it started to falter. He read his book while in the saddle and even practiced a few simple spells, like throwing emotions, that didn't require him to speak.

On the second night, he brought Tara coffee in a tin cup. He sat away from her, eating his dinner of bacon and beans. Tara took a big drink from her cup and said, "If I had to guess, I'd say we'll wake up in camp. It's been long enough for them to find us. The trees have been talking since we got here."

Fisnik cocked his head to the side. "So they'll just make camp around us while we sleep? Or will they take our camp and put it in theirs?" Everyone looked at him, and he said, "I've not had many dealings with Rethari before. All the Fey folk I've met have been loners, exiles, or from other tribes."

Tara nodded like that made sense to her. "We'll wake up in their camp, no doubt my mother will have breakfast ready, along with a lecture."

"I appreciate this." Deacon said.

"Fuck off. I'm partying my tits off in Vegas." She stood up and walked to her tent.

She turned back and said, "Clay, I'm not mad at you. I believe you when you say what happened, and given that you had known about magic for all of thirty-six hours, I believe you were led by this dick nozzle. I appreciate you giving me time to think, and you may speak again."

His voice cracked from disuse and he said, "Thank you."

They exchanged their goodnights and Clay went to his own tent. He liked the woods; it was peaceful and easy to fall asleep. Just as he was about to drift into unconsciousness, he heard Deacon and Fisnik by the fire.

"Think it'll happen for him?" Deacon asked.

"With all the luck around, I imagine so," Fisnik said.

"Lucky bastard."

"Don't be a jerk, Deacon. You know it's not what happens during, but after, that's the real test."

"Yeah," Deacon said, "but that doesn't mean it won't be fun."

Clay woke to small children with feathered faces staring at him. His eyes went wide and he said, "Hello,"

"Ese fastious go sa," said one. She had white feathers all around her head and face. She did not have a beak and sounded like a little girl.

One of the others started to talk when Tara appeared at the flap of his tent. "Rik sa isa von do ba do ba." The kids skittered away and Tara said, "They think you're cute."

"What'd you say to them?"

You're mine, and if they don't find their mothers, I'll feed them to the hounds."

"Jesus," Clay said. "Little much, don't you think?"

Tara gave a half shake of her head and smirked. "These are wild Fey. They'll lock you up with a curse and keep you as a slave until they're old enough to use you."

"They looked like they were seven or eight."

"They are, and they would have fed you cursed food so you couldn't leave their side until they could claim you as a husband and get a baby or two from you. Then, if they like you, they'll let you tend to the animals. If they don't, they'll feed you to something and find another baby daddy."

Clay couldn't help the horrified look on his face. "Does that happen a lot?"

"Ever wonder how many hikers go missing in the US and are never found?"

"Holy shit."

"Yeah, and the sexual age of maturity for a wild fey is creepily low, so do not, under any circumstances, take anything offered to you by someone under fifteen."

"Got it."

There was some shouting from outside the tent, and Tara opened the flap. "Jzuana dos at tks ariksa ma'ama i." She turned to Clay and said, "Our language sounds really weird. Most of them are going to refuse to speak anything else to you."

He nodded. "Got it." He got up and felt the air hit him, realizing without looking down that he was exposed.

Tara cocked her head to the side. "Two questions: are you at all hard right now, and did you go to bed with pants on?"

"Weirdly, no, and yes, I did."

Tara nodded, considering more than one thing, then opened the tent flap enough to slip out. "Put some pants on," she said from outside. Then he heard, "Whoever took his semen better give it back!"

Clay emerged from the tent and saw a tiny village.

It was a large circle of old-fashioned wagons and wooden caravans. One open space between wagons was a pen with sheep and goats. Chickens roamed everywhere. People were cooking, sleeping in hammocks connected to trees.

Caravans were parked, kids ran around, and teenagers huddled in groups. They all had a fey-mark, visible even from a distance.

Not far from their camps was the central fire.

A group of people sat around it, causing a commotion. Clay found Deacon and Fisnik sitting near the fire and saw the enormous skillet that had a hundred things cooking at once. It was at least five or six feet in diameter and he saw one lady with green skin and fish ears turning pancakes on one side while bacon cooked next to sausages in the middle and about six dozen eggs fried around the edges.

Tara was on the other side of the fire, looking like she might strangle the woman she was speaking with. The woman resembled an older Tara, with the same skin and general body shape.

Her body seemed slightly altered by childbirth. She had a long monkey-like tail she was using to stir a large cauldron of oats.

He couldn't understand the language, but he didn't need to.

There were certain body marks and movements that children and parents used to fight, transcending languages and cultures. Parents drove you crazy, and kids never learned. It seemed true for fey as it was for humans.

Clay sat next to both of them, and Deacon handed him a plate. He ate breakfast while watching Tara argue with her mother. The food was good, tasting pure and more satisfying than usual. A girl with her left eye surrounded by scales like a dragon had given her a black eye and left its skin behind, handed him a cup of red liquid. He shook his head. She pretended not to understand and kept offering, clearly knowing he was refusing.

He kept his hands firmly on his plate as she dipped the cup, spilling the drink on his food.

Fisnik was at his side and growled at the girl. It rose into a bark until she slinked away, her white robe trailing behind her. "You are quite the commodity, Clay," Fisnik said.

"Why aren't they bothering Deacon?

"Your body is young and you're handsome," Deacon said. "And my soul is tainted."

Clay started to ask what that meant, but Tara walked over to them, looking furious. "My cunt of a mother says the only way they will help us track the magic problems is if I have my ceremony."

Clay didn't know dogs could gasp, but Fisnik did. "You do not have to do that."

Tara did not respond. She looked at Deacon, her arms crossed over her chest, and it was the first time Clay would have described her as truly vulnerable. "How important is this?"

Deacon looked ashamed. "I've gotten word from fifteen friends that they can't do magic. Another thirty people I've tracked can't do much more than the kid, and they're old."

Tara turned to Fisnik. "Is he lying?"

"I do not know, child. I know that the problems are bad and only going to get worse. You and your people are more removed from the things that taint the blood of wizards, but it will eventually reach them too. I can feel it, but I also will not ask you to do this."

"Goddamn motherfucking,-" Tara closed her eyes, pinched the bridge of her nose, and Clay thought he heard her start to cry. "Fine, fuck it."

The circle cheered, except for their group. Tara marched off, then stalked back to Clay. "After the ceremony—you will be tested. You can say no, but you will lose me and any opportunity to know me other than how we know each other now."

"I'm in for whatever means I get to know you more."

Tara looked proud, but there was a deep sadness in her eyes. She sighed. "I hope you have fun."

"What's wrong?" Clay asked.

Tara walked away, her head held high, shoulders back, clearly refusing to show any of her people how upset she was.

Fisnik sat next to Clay. "She is afraid of the results. Some people fail the test the magic brings, and if you pass, then she will be tested, and that scares her even more."

"Why?" he asked.

Fisnik looked at him with deep soulful eyes that probably had been there before he was a dog, but were certainly deeper because dogs just generally looked like they knew the secrets of the universe. "If you come out of your test she is nearly positive of her reaction, but her test will test you both, and she isn't sure about that."

"Why is everyone so fucking cryptic about this?"

"Have you ever heard of the observation effect?"

"Yes."

"Well, it holds true in magical tests given by nature."

A gong sounded. The sun had set hours ago, and Clay had been standing around for almost an hour. A pit of dirt lay inside a rectangular area fenced off with bark fencing. It stood just high enough that you had to step over it to get inside.

He'd watched as they cast fire spells to consume the dirt. Two people in white robes with bird-like faces, save the beaks, their hair braided down past their waists, lit torches until it was almost as bright as daytime. The crowd gathered until Clay felt the entire tribe must be in a circle, surrounding the pit. The younger people sat around it, likely to see what it would be like for them one day.

Finally, from behind some caravans, Tara was led by her mother on one side and a man with horns on the other.

She wore a white robe like the torch lighters and was brought to the short end of the rectangle, away from Clay.

Her mother took her robe, and she walked naked to the middle of the pit. She knelt down in the heated sand and the man with horns said a lengthy monologue in their language that no one bothered to translate.

After they finished their magic words or whatever, Clay tried not to roll his eyes. He didn't need to know the man with Horns blared, but he didn't even know what he was saying. He was long-winded and sanctimonious.

Tara was quiet the entire time. Her head was down, her hair glinting in the firelight like a mane. It barely concealed her face, but the set of her shoulders told Clay everything he needed to know.

The torch lighters brought out a small barrel, careful not to spill a drop. They came forward, one on either side of Tara, and at the horned man's signal, dumped what appeared to be thirty or forty gallons of fresh blood all over her.

She was covered, head to toe. Not a drop seemed to get on the sand. Nowhere was skin visible on Tara.

He stepped out of the pit just as Tara stood. The blood moved on its own, flowing upward to cover her completely. She made eye contact with Clay. He didn't need magic to read her thoughts.

She was scared.

The horned man picked up the torch and lit the blood.

Strong, iron hands wrapped around Clay from behind, restraining him as Tara erupted into flames. He struggled, but it was like being bound in chains. "Look," Deacon said in his ear, "she's fine."

She didn't look fine. Tara wasn't hurt; she didn't even have blood on her anymore. She was soaked with sweat and started to cry as people rushed forward to help her.

Her eyes found Clay, and she mouthed, "Have fun, please." She was taken off in the direction she'd come from and Clay felt Deacon release him. He turned to say something, but Deacon had already turned away.

Clay saw the tears streaming down his face.

"So you're Tara's beau."

Clay turned around to see five scantily clad women standing around him. Their fey marks ranged from a tail to a kitten nose to kelpie hair, but they were gorgeous. They oozed sex appeal, each in different ways. One was tall and busty, with a figure most men dream of, the next lanky and coy-looking. One of them, with green hair like dry kelp, took his hand and said, "Come with us for the test."

They took him to a tent big enough for all of them and laid him down. He wanted to get up but somehow knew this was the test. One of them pulled his jeans off, followed soon by his underwear, while the others undressed themselves.

He looked at the kelp girl who took his penis in her hand and smiled. "This is going to be fun." The one with the massive tits and a kitten's nose said, "Tara's lucky to have you." She leaned over, her bare breasts grazing his legs as she kissed him under the belt. The skinny, sly-looking one stepped over him.

She began to lower herself onto his face and said, "Relax. This is gonna be fun."

He worked on the skinny girl, briefly wondering if her giggles were real or fake, while two of them put his hands to work and the others worked on him. He was inside every hole in the room, and a couple of things went inside him. He lost all track of time and meaning, lost in a heap of naked ecstasy. But Tara never left his mind, not for a moment—not even when he was resting, watching all five girls service each other in an effort to bring him back to life. He missed Tara.

CHAPTER NINE

T he morning after

Tara woke up feeling raw, both emotionally and physically.

Part of the ritual was a scrubbing to remove the blood and the dead flesh of your old body. It was less a spa scrubbing and more like brushing down a wet horse. Every part of her body was pink from the rough brushes her mother and younger sisters had used. Hilda had scrubbed hard enough to draw blood from Tara's inner thigh.

The emotional rawness came from having moved further into the culture she had been trying to escape her entire life. A ribbon two fingers wide of pinkish-red skin, unmistakable as a Fey mark. It couldn't be confused for a burn because it swayed from the tips of her index and ring finger on her right hand, all the way to the top of her shoulder. It wouldn't even be mistaken for a tattoo because no one got weird tribal swirls in the same shade as a shitty sunset. It was ugly and gross, and she wanted to cut her arm off.

Tara stood up and violently shook her head, as if that would make the memory go away. She dressed in jeans and a t-shirt, ignoring the fey clothes her mother had set out. She left the tent and saw her mother peeling potatoes on the steps of their caravan. "Where's my bra, Mother?" Tara said.

"Burned it. Fey do not constrain their breasts that way."

"You had no right to burn my property."

Her mother threw another peeled potato in the pot. "You should stay here."

"Give us what we want and I'm leaving. You made a bargain."

"I shouldn't," she said with a sneer. "A bad bargain is no bargain."

Tara rolled her eyes, her blood ready to boil. "Typical Fey bullshit, just a way to justify your dishonesty."

Her mother pointed her knife at her. "Careful, you are Fey and not too old for a lesson."

Tara's mouth quirked into an angry smile. "I would love you to try. Remember, there are laws and I'm a born member of this tribe. You just married in from a bunch of godless heathen stone Fey."

Her mother charged her, but Tara stood her ground. Her mother was cut off at the last moment when her father stepped in front of her. "Calm down," he said.

Her mother looked down, and Tara felt momentarily sorry—not for what she'd said, but for the berating her father would get later. Fey women were no pushovers, nor were they submissive, but you did not fight with outsiders in camp. Her mother turned back to the caravan, "How could the gods curse me with such a daughter?"

Rising to her tiptoes to look over her father's shoulder, Tara said, "I guess the gods don't like you any more than they like me."

The slap was swift and biting. Tara landed on her butt, looking up at her father. "Too far," he said.

Tara rubbed her face. "I'm sorry, Papa."

He helped her up and said, "I know how you feel about your heritage, but cursing your mother is not acceptable. Don't think I didn't hear that Stone comment."

Tara looked down, "I did not mean to insult you."

"And your mother?"

"I fully intended to insult her."

He smiled at that one. "Your man's test should end soon. The girls have not been with someone for a while, so they may have prolonged it, but the results will be known at daybreak."

"What if he fails?"

"If his heart lies in his cock, then he was no man for my daughter."

Tara rushed to hug her father. "I love you."

"And I you," he said, squeezing her. "I know better than to ask you to visit, but would it kill you to write me every now and again?"

Tara gave a small nod. "I will. I promise."

"Here," he handed her a neatly folded map made from thick brown leaves. "You should say goodbye to your mother."

"Not worth the beating."

Her father shook his head. "I love you, my willful child."

Then he walked away without another word, and Tara turned away to seek out Clay's tent.

Clay woke feeling rested, but still tired. His muscles felt relaxed, but his brain was foggy and yearned for sleep.

He felt a tugging and heard a slapping sound. "Tara," he said in a low mumble.

The giggling brought him awake. The girls were all still naked, giggling as the fifth one, the slender girl, rode him. As she bounded, looking as if racing to beat a clock, she said, "I had to have you one last time."

Clay came, and she lay against him for a moment. "You passed," said the kelp-haired girl.

They did not make their goodbyes, only left the tent. Still jaded, Clay heard them talking outside but couldn't make out the words.

Clay lay back, trying to decide how he felt. On one hand, sleeping with five beautiful women multiple times each had been a true sexual highlight, but all he could think of was Tara. He wondered how she would feel, what she would think.

"Put your pants on, lover boy." It was Tara calling to him.

He stood up off the furs he'd slept on and looked around for his pants. "I think they took them," he said.

"Mother fu—wait, hold on." His pants flew into the mouth of the tent. "They left them near the fire." Tara said.

Clay emerged from the tent a moment later, and Tara tossed him his shirt.

"Just wanted a look at ya," she said. Clay laughed. "The girls talked about you."

"Oh yeah?"

"They said you're a great lover, but your tongue is positively magical."

Clay looked away shyly. Tara was leaning against a wooden stand where hides were laid over some small logs to dry or for storage. He wasn't sure. She looked cool and calm, her hands down in front of her. "So, uh, how're you feeling?"

Clay didn't approach her. He wasn't sure if he should yet. "It was awesome. I've now had sex with seven women. But my sole concern right now is what you think of me."

Tara's face softened, and Clay realized the calm air had been an act. "Really?"

Clay nodded. "Yeah."

"So, do you want to do that again?"

Clay shrugged. "I mean, if you wanted to have an orgy, I wouldn't leave the room, but honestly, I couldn't care less if I ever see anyone else naked."

"Are you fucking with me?"

Clay shook his head. "No ma'am. My heart is racing at the idea that you'll leave or be angry because I did that."

Tara smiled and rushed forward to hug Clay.

He loved the feeling of her face against his chest. She wasn't much shorter than him, so he didn't have to adjust his head to kiss her horns. "So, if I am allowed to ask, what was the result of the ceremony or whatever that was last night?"

Tara stepped back and rolled up the sleeve of her T-shirt. Clay looked at the swirl going down her arm. It wove down her arm all the way to the middle two fingers, leaving bits of exposed, unmarked flesh. It trailed down her arm like a river snaking around a mountain. "That's fucking hot."

"What?" Tara sounded surprised and maybe a little wounded.

Clay's eyebrows raised. "Is that like a religious mark or something? Was that a terrible thing to say out loud?"

Tara stared to tear up. She dropped her hand, leaving her sleeve rolled up. "No but, you think it's hot?"

"Do you not?"

She was crying fully now. "No! I hate it. hate being Fey. I hate these fucking horns and having to hide them. I hate me!"

Clay placed his hands on her biceps and ran them down to her hands, taking them in his as he pulled her closer. "I know you feel this way, and you have your reasons, but without a doubt, you are the most beautiful, sexiest, hottest—"

She wiped her eyes and asked, "You mean that?"

Clay held his hands up in defense, "Not that you wouldn't be hot without your marks. I mean, with a face like that and tits like those, you'd be a ten."

Her eyes narrowed. "What am I with them?"

"I don't know. I threw the scale in a ditch. I don't need to measure anyone anymore."

Tara smiled. She touched the side of his face and brought him in for a kiss. Their lips touched and a feeling spread through Clay like being next to a fireplace on a cold night, or being in a soft bed after a hard day's work.

They broke the kiss and Deacon spoke before either of them could. "Tara, I, uh…" They both turned and saw him standing there like a kid after a mess-up. "I'm sorry," Deacon said.

Tara handed him what looked to be a folded leaf. "There's your map, let's go."

Clay didn't know how and was a little afraid to ask, but they were very near the car. It was a few hundred yards' walk to where the station wagon was parked. They got in, and Deacon looked at the map. Fisnik was over his shoulder.

"Well, I'll be damned," the dog said. "We're going to Vegas for two reasons."

CHAPTER TEN

Vegas

"No, no."

Clay jerked awake, and Tara was staring at him. "You need to talk about the nightmares," she said.

He let out a deep sigh. "I was responsible for the deaths of my entire family."

He sat up a little in the car and stared a hole through the floorboards, refusing to look at anyone. He could feel their eyes on him. He knew if he looked up, he'd even see Deacon in the mirror. "We were camping...when I was fifteen. My family was crazy about the outdoors. We were rock climbers, rafters, all that. We were doing a huge rafting and camping trip for spring break, and I was pissed they made me go because I wanted to stay home.

"My first girlfriend had let me cop a feel, and we'd done some hand stuff once. Fifteen-year-old me was convinced that if I stayed home, we'd have sex, or at least I'd get blown. So I acted like a complete asshole the entire time. I pissed my dad off so bad, causing fights and just being a prick, that we took the wrong route. They went over a waterfall. I was able to get out in time, nearly drowned, and they all died."

The car was silent. Clay refused to look at anyone until Deacon said, "I chose magic over my wife and she died for it."

"What?" Tara asked.

"I, uh," he swallowed hard, "I had the opportunity to save my wife by giving up magic, but I told her medicine would. ..She was ready to deliver our daughter, and they both died."

"What kind of situation would—" Fisnik started, but Deacon silenced him with a look.

Deacon continued, "I was messing around with inter-dimensional travel. I made a bargain to get the spell I needed to learn to travel between worlds. I had no idea at the time. When I promised my joy, I thought it meant the emotion joy. I had no idea it meant I would lose the only people to ever bring me joy."

"Is that why you're fighting to save magic?" Tara asked. "Because it's all you have left?"

Deacon nodded.

The car was silent for almost a mile before Tara said, "Thank you both for sharing. You know our stories. I hate myself and my people, and Fisnik is a piece of shit who tried to take over the world."

"Technically, I tried to destroy the world," Fisnik said. "I wish that was the worst of my crimes."

A few miles in front of them, Las Vegas came into view.

They pulled up in front of a hotel and casino. Tara and Clay got out, retrieved their bags from the back, and Deacon handed Tara a card through the front window.

"Rent two rooms and have fun. Leave my name at the desk so we can go up later."

"Where are you going?" Tara asked.

Deacon put the car into drive. "Don't worry about it," he said as they pulled away.

They watched him go, and Clay said, "He really does think he's in an action movie, doesn't he?"

"Yup," Tara said. "Let's get rooms and then we have a decision to make."

"What's that?"

Tara smiled, "Do we have dinner before partying or after?"

They dropped their bags in a room and immediately headed out, catching a cab. Tara gave the address to the other end of the strip. In the cab, Tara took off her beanie and stowed it in Clay's bag. He was reading his spell book, noticed her, and asked, "Why no beanie?"

Tara was all smiles and giggly energy as she said, "Vegas is the one city in the world where people don't care. They don't even look twice at them."

Clay thought for a moment and said, "That makes sense."

The cab let them out at a club. There was no one outside save for a man who looked like he was chiseled out of marble, his arms crossed as they walked up. "Tell Monty I'm here," Tara said.

The man took a step inside. Clay heard loud music and saw lights flashing through the edge of the door. Coming back out, the man held the door open for them, and Tara led the way inside.

Clay saw lights flashing through the edge of the door. Coming back out, the man held the door open for them, and Tara led the way inside. The music was loud, the lights were dark red and swirling more than flashing, and the dancers were very naked. Clay had never been to a strip club before; it had always seemed like a people zoo.

He also never had money to spend on strippers.

Tara led him to the back of the club, past a bar on the left and some booths set up to watch strippers on the right. Tara led him to the back of the club, past a bar on the left and some booths set up to watch strippers on the right.

He was momentarily distracted by a woman who seemed to be suffocating a man with her breasts. Tara tugged gently on his arm.

They walked into the office, and a white-haired guy with frosted tips and cat eyes looked up at them. He wore a white suit with a green shirt and socks. His feet were on the desk, and he ended his call with, "Hey, I'm gonna have to call you back, family just came in."

He got up from the desk and came around to hug Tara. "How are you? I heard about your ceremony. Oh, look at that." He touched the mark on her arm. "I dig it."

"Thanks, how did you hear?" Tara asked.

"You know word travels fast through the fey. There may not be trees, but we aren't short on nature here." He looked at Clay. "You must be the beau. I heard about you too, man." He held up his first two fingers on his right hand and flicked his tongue.

Tara slapped him on the arm. "Clay, this is my cousin Monty. He isn't on speaking terms with the tribe, but he does a lot to help outcast fey like me."

"Hey, the unloved have to stick together, right?" He held out a hand, and Clay shook it. "I hear you're one heck of a wizard, holy fire on day one?"

"How'd you hear about that?" Clay asked.

"I follow Fisnik on Facebook."

"That brought up more questions than answers."

Monty smiled. "It always does, so what can I do for you both? I assume this isn't social, otherwise you would have gone to the house."

"I'm here to blow off some steam," Tara said.

"I don't blame you," Monty said. "If I'd just seen Aunty, I'd be doing coke right now."

Tara gave a little half-smile. "Thing is, I'm a little bit broke."

Monty raised an eyebrow. "You work like a dog."

"These guys picked me up at a club. I've got money, it's just all in the back of my sink cupboard in Chicago."

"Oh, that's fine. You can just owe me. I'll be in Chicago in a couple of months on business. Tell the dancers I'm covering you. I'll let Fiaria know at the bar. You gonna hit up town?"

Tara looked at Clay, "Monty owns a dance club too." Turning back to Monty, she said, "Hell yes."

Monty smiled, and Clay found it both comforting and unsettling. "Go have fun, and if I don't see you again before you leave, I'll meet you on the road."

"And then we'll dance," Tara said. She led Clay out of the office, whispering in his ear, "Rethari blessing."

"Cool." Clay said.

Tara smiled at him. "Let's party."

They did shots at the bar, of what Clay wasn't really certain by the fifth. Tara kept going until they found themselves in a booth, both getting lap dances.

Clay hummed a spell in his head that worked to clear his mind a bit, but he still had a hard time focusing on anything.

Tara rubbed the woman on her lap, reveling in the drunken warmth spreading through her. It had been a really long time since she had cut loose, and all the memories and feelings her parents had dug up had piled on the need to relax. "I fought with my mom," she said to the stripper over the music. "She's a bitch!"

Why am I saying this? she thought to herself. *I need to shut up.*

When their time was up, Tara looked at Clay. "You wanna go?" she called out. He nodded, and she moved closer to him, slipping and banging her hip into the edge of the table. She slid against Clay, enjoying the feel of him.

It wasn't entirely sexual; it was just comforting to have a solid body next to you that you could hold and count on.

"Let's go dancing," she said.

Outside the club, they hailed another cab, and Tara told him where to go. Sliding in next to Clay, she leaned against him, her face smooshed into his arm. "It's gonna happen," she mumbled.

"What is?" Clay asked. Was he not as drunk as she was?

"My turn," she said. "It's coming."

"Don't you think we should get some sleep?" Clay said. He was slurring a bit, but she guessed he'd probably done magic to sober up at least a little.

Tara whined like a kid. "No, I wanna dance. I'm hot when I dance. I'm not even wearing a skirt."

"Nope," Clay said.

"You wanna make me one?"

"What?"

Tara shook her head too many times. "I can't make clothes change. All my magic is nature-based. Put me in a skirt, a hot one."

Clay shrugged. "Okay." He straightened up and Tara slid.

"I'm going to try English," he spoke under his breath. Tara narrowed her eyes, trying to read his lips through her double vision.

She felt warmth like oatmeal and leather. She looked down dispassionately, as if she were an outside observer. "Clay,"

"Yes?"

"My vagina is touching the dirty cab seat."

"No sex please," said the driver.

Clay closed his eyes and Tara smiled. His face scrunched up when he concentrated. Warmth enveloped her again, and when she looked down, she was wearing a sexy plaid skirt that fell to her knees. "Great job, babe," she said.

The cab stopped at the club and they got out. Tara felt a kiss from the gods and looked at Clay. "Why am I not wearing underwear?"

He smirked. "I'm drunk and bad at magic?"

She cuffed his ear. "Pervert."

The club was packed. The dance floor was raised and covered in screens projecting lights upward.

A catwalk-like balcony ringed the room where VIPs could watch the dancing. Tara heard Clay in her ear but didn't comprehend what he said. Her body moved on its own. She swiped a shot from a passing tray and downed it, tossing the glass.

She swayed, gyrating to the thumping bass, when she felt a man on her. She reached up, running her hand down his neck. She couldn't see him from that angle, but it didn't matter.

Another man was soon in front of her. He was dark-skinned with chiseled abs, clearly spending too much time sculpting at the gym. Tara ran her hands over his chest, a primal growl escaping her lips.

Ordinarily, neither this man nor the one inappropriately rubbing against her would be her type. But the test had begun. Even though she was drunk, Tara knew the magic flowing through her was guiding her actions.

Her body was not her own. She found Clay standing at the bar, and they locked eyes. She couldn't read him and was too lust-filled to try.

She could feel herself, blood rushing to her groin. Reaching behind her, she ripped the man's crotch and looked at him from the corner of her eye. She gave a nod, turning back to the man in front of her.

She lifted her skirt, heedless of the other people in the room.

They took her, rocking her back and forth. She felt filled but not whole. Neither of them paid her any attention, so she reached a hand down and did it herself. Her mouth found the man in front, and soon all her holes were filled. The magic surged in her blood and it felt like she would die.

There was no love involved in this. It was animalistic, brought on by the test the gods had sent her. She closed her eyes and saw Clay, a vision of the two of them together. She pictured lying with Clay, and her heart her eyes and saw Clay, a vision of the two of them together. She pictured lying with Clay, and her heart felt whole.

The magic reached a peak that was almost too much. Both men came at once, a split second before Tara did. She yelled out in ecstasy. Then all the lights blew out.

CHAPTER ELEVEN

We went out last night.

Clay woke up wishing he was dead. He had no idea where he was. He raised his head and saw Tarş lying at the head of the bed. They were top and tail, and judging by their bags near the window, they had made it back to their rooms.

Tarş groaned and raised up on her elbows. "What, uh—"

"Your orgasm blew up every electronic device in the club. I have no idea how we got here."

"That would be me," Fisnik said, phasing through the door joining this room and the next. I found you and brought you here. How did the test go?"

Tara sat up with a grimace, gripping her head. "We haven't had a chance to talk about it."

"I see. I'll order some food to your room and be just in there if you need me." He phased back through the door, never breaking stride.

Tara sat cross-legged on the bed, her hands fidgeting in front of her. Clay lay back down and said, "So explain this to me now that it's over. Why did you fuck two guys at the same time?"

Tara shook her head. Clay was starting to get frustrated with this test stuff. "You have to decide how you feel first," she said.

Clay looked at her, thinking of getting upset, but lay back down, staring at the smoke-stained ceiling. "Not threatened. I mean, I probably should be, but both of those guys were hotter than me and looked tougher than me, but I was not threatened. When I caught your eye, I thought, this is fine. Her heart still belongs to me."

Tara made a noise and Cleo looked at her, wincing from the sudden motion. She straightened up, trying to look calmer than she clearly felt. "What if I am pregnant?" she asked.

"What do you mean?"

Magic coursing through your blood makes for good sex but terrible prep. I was not safe. I mean, it would be the black guy, the other one was in my ass, but what if I'm pregnant?"

Clay thought that over. When he didn't speak, Tara said, "Be honest. You have to be honest."

"Honestly?" He raised up on his elbows to look at her. "I don't know if I'm ready to be a dad. I know I wouldn't have much of a choice, but I'd be really scared."

"But it wouldn't be yours," Tara said.

It was difficult to shrug with his body weight on his elbows, but he managed. "Mine now."

The next thing he knew, Tara's body weight was on his. He grunted a little at the attack, but it was nice having her weight on him, like a comforting blanket. She looked at him, a smile in her eyes as well as on her face. "Do you mean that?"

"I do."

Her smile widened. "The test was naturally adapted into Fey kind, more so for Rethari, because Fey believe sex and love to be separate. That doesn't mean I'd cheat or you would, or that it would have to be okay. The test was originally because Fey grew inbred from never going outside the tribe. The test was developed to see if a couple could survive the often necessary intercourse with outsiders needed to provide healthy babies for Fey,"

"So wait, humans can become Fey?"

Tara shook her head. "What happens, if the woman does not have a slave to give her a child, she wanders into a human settlement and gets pregnant, her body makes the child fully Fey. It's like how you are half Jewish if your dad is the Jewish one, but if it's your mom, you're fully Jewish because you came from a Jewish vagina."

Clay nodded his understanding. "So now that we know our relationship isn't built on our junk, what happens?"

"Now we can move on knowing that we are meant to be."

"I'm lost again."

"When the test was adopted into magic, meaning that magic itself now controls the test, it became between two people who are meant to be together instead of two people who just happen to be together. That's why we were so ready to jump each other. Our hormones will even out, and we can move forward together."

"Well, in that case," Clay said, "will you have dinner with me tonight?"

Tara tilted her head, and the most adorable smile spread across her face. "I would love to."

There was a knock on the door, and Fisnik's voice came from the other room. "That's the food."

Tara stood in front of the mirror, looking at herself in the dress again. She still hated the way she looked, but knowing Clay liked her gave her a sense of confidence and admiration she had never felt before.

She ran a hand over her left horn. It was hard and smooth from the salve she used to keep them from itching. She couldn't help but recoil at the touch. She tried to shake off her self-loathing as she went out the door.

She headed down to the restaurant to meet Clay.

CHAPTER TWELVE

He yawned and looked at the sun. Sunlight streamed through the window. He didn't want to go to work. He hated work. "Fuck!" he said, throwing his head back on his pillow.

His shower was hot, which was something. He knew it was bad for his skin, all the showering and hand washing, but when you constantly smelled like gasoline and meth from customers breathing on you, showering twice daily was a must.

He put on his work shirt and slogged to work, dragging his feet. Even the chime on the door pissed him off.

The day was normal. Customers took their bullshit out on him. One woman called him a faggot because they didn't have her brand of cigarettes, and a guy threw his slushie against the plexiglass when he was told the price had gone up by a quarter. Retail sucked.

Right before his shift was about to end, a guy walked in wearing a long coat with the collar popped, looking like it was from the Civil War. He had long black hair that fell to his shoulders. It was pushed back behind his ears, and he looked around wildly. "Clay," he said, approaching the plexiglass.

"Do I know you?" he asked.

"What, shit. Yes, you know me. Lazlo? Vampire? Ringing any bells?"

"Vampire? Those aren't real, my guy."

"We met a month ago. You were in my home in Missouri."

"I've never been to Missouri."

"Yes, you, fuck." The doorbell jingled and a lady walked in, her pink coat and brown trousers making her look like a medicine bottle. "Ma'am," the guy said.

"If you're a vampire, how are you out in daylight?" Clay asked. He was bored, so why not play along?

The man put his hands on the counter, leaning in with an emphatic look on his face. "I have not the faintest idea. I don't even have my ring." He held up his hands to show his lack of a ring.

"I'm sorry, man. Did you lose it outside?"

He rolled his eyes. "I don't know. I woke up on a park bench. I just know it smells wrong."

"It's a gas station, bro. They always smell like this." He closed his eyes and sighed.

The woman stepped up behind him, and he turned, grabbing her. He threw her neck back and sank his teeth into her. Clay saw the veins working in his neck as he sucked on the woman. She was soon out of blood, looking like a withered husk. Throwing her away, he said, "Well?"

Clay started to speak, but his head felt like it was struck by lightning. He saw an aura and had spots in his vision. Falling down to the counter, he groaned. "Fuck me."

"Are you with me?"

Yeah, Laz, I'm here. My head is killing me. Where are we?"

"I haven't a clue. What's the last thing you remember?"

"We were in Vegas, Tara and I were about to have a date. Wait, we need to find Tara. Have you seen her? Is she here?"

"Safe bet she's here somewhere," Lazlo said. "Whoever or whatever took us would have doubtless taken the others."

"Let's go look for her," Clay said. "First, though, I am going to take an entire bottle of Excedrin."

They looked all over town, cafes and shops, finally discovering there was a mall. Clay did not know how long he had been here, but since recovering his memories, he had lost any idea of this place.

It was just a little off. The air felt wrong, houses looked somehow off-center, or like their paint was a shade that shouldn't exist. He couldn't put his finger on it for certain, but he knew this place was wrong.

They stood on the upper floor of the mall, looking around at all the people. "Shouldn't we be looking?" Clay said.

"Have you ever been a bounty hunter?" Lazlo asked. "Waiting in an area the target has to cross is a far better method than searching every home or tavern. There, isn't that her?" Clay followed where he was pointing. Sure enough, it was.

It was Tara. She was beanie-less and hornless, with a couple of girls who looked like friends, laughing and talking. "Should we go get her?" Lazlo asked.

"Let's follow her," Clay said.

They watched from a distance as the girls went to the food court. Clay and Lazlo got a table a few away. Clay tried to use a spell he'd read about to enhance his listening, but it failed. There was no feeling, like before he learned magic, though it was worse. This time he felt the absence.

"Fine," Clay said, rushing Tara.

He came across the table until she backed up, knocking over her chair, and they ended up in a heap on the floor. He kissed her.

He saw her face snap into recognition.

"What the heck?" Tara said.

"I'm really sorry about that. Lazlo says cops are coming, and he was going to get really weird before they got here."

He scrambled off her and helped her up. "Who are they?" she asked, pointing to the other girls standing away from Lazlo but not yet fleeing.

"We're your best friends," the blonde said.

Clay could see the sadness on Tara's face. She winced. "I feel really bad that I don't remember you."

"You don't,-"

Lazlo stepped in closer and said, "Unless you want to kill a bunch of people, we need to leave. He wanted to leave you here to be happy without magic, but I said we should wake you up. Let's run."

Tara winced. "My head is killing me."

They saw the cops coming and took off. As they ran, Clay looked at Tara and said, "I know that was what you wanted."

Tara jumped over a bench. "I love you for being willing to leave me."

Exiting the mall, Tara said, "What about Deacon and Fisnik?"

Clay replied, "Well, I have a feeling we know where to find Fiz."

Tara was the one to find the pound—they were still evading the cops, so she didn't have time to process the day's events.

Her heart hurt. She had friends, normal friends.

They didn't bother to stop at the reception desk. They pushed through the back door just in time to see the vet with a needle in Fisnik's neck. Lazlo was there in a blink. He snapped the vet's neck and threw him across the room.

Tara carefully removed the needle. "You okay, Fiz?"

He nodded. Tara cocked her head and Clay said, "No magic in this dimension. He can't talk."

"Shit," Tara said. "Well, come on, buddy."

They exited through the back. Looking around, Tara saw a grocery store and a couple of other businesses. She looked back to the others and said, "What about Deacon?"

"He could be anywhere," Clay said.

Fisnik whined, "He is definitely in town," Lazlo said.

They turned to Laz. "How do you know?" Tara asked.

Lazlo pointed, "He's over there."

Tara turned and saw Deacon across the street, loading groceries into the station wagon. She started across the street, not waiting to see if the others would follow. She reached him and Deacon looked at her, "Can I help you?" he said.

Tara started to speak but saw a woman carrying a baby on her way to the car. "I, uh—"

"Are you in trouble?" Deacon asked, seeing the group behind her.

"Sorry," Tara said, "I thought you were someone else."

She turned and walked away, the rest of the group following her. They stood off to the side of the parking lot, near a bus stop with a homeless man sleeping on the bench. "We have to leave him," Tara said. "He can't go wherever we're going."

"I agree," Lazlo said.

"Was that woman,-"

Tara nodded, answering Clay's question. "It's his wife, or at least a copy."

Clay nodded. "When we leave him. The next question is how the hell do we get out of whatever dimension or world this is?"

They all leapt back as the homeless man jumped up. He was nondescript, of average height, with blown bushy hair. Nothing special or notable about him. Tara couldn't even tell his age. "I can help with that," he said.

He wore a dirty winter coat that looked like it was made from sleeping bag material. He looked as if he was waiting for applause. "Really? Nothing?" he said.

Fisnik buried his face in his paws, and the man pointed a finger at him. Fisnik's voice came back mid-sentence, "Magic."

"What?" Clay said.

"This is the god of magic," Fisnik said.

"Right you are, dog friend," the homeless guy said. "I've got a lot of names, but most people just call me god of magic."

"Why did you bring us here?" Clay asked. "And why isn't Lazlo burning? He's still a vampire."

Tara cocked her head and looked at him. "Really? Those were your questions?"

Clay shrugged, and the god continued. "Looks like we have a friend coming. Come here, young man."

Tara turned to see Deacon walking up to them. He was...a good man. Even with no memory of who she was, he still came to make sure she wasn't in trouble. She looked at the tire iron in his right hand and smiled.

The god snapped his fingers, and Deacon got his memory back. Tara could see the change on his face.

His brow set harder, lines returned, and tension made his shoulders rigid. "Magic," he said. "You've been the one messing with magic."

The god made a gesture like an actor receiving a compliment, complete with a little bow. "It is my domain. You're a smart one, Deacon."

"Giving me a replica of my wife was cruel," Deacon said. "Even for you."

"No, no," the god said, wagging his finger. "That is your family. When you didn't save them, I took them and put them here, in my little menagerie."

Tara saw the anger flash across Deacon's face. "You motherfucker, I'll,-"

"What? You will what? You are a mortal without magic in a dimension I control as a god, because I am a god, remember?"

The tire iron hit him square in the face and he fell. holding his face as blood ran down from his nose. He rubbed the back of his sleeve across his nose and smiled. "Good one."

Tara stepped in between Deacon and the god. "Why are you doing this?" she asked.

He shrugged. "I am bored. Even the magical community doesn't worship me anymore. Eternity is a long time."

"You've been killing and torturing people as entertainment?" Clay said.

"Yup," said the god of magic.

"Why am I here though? Lazlo said. "I don't believe I'm your jurisdiction."

"I needed a catalyst to start the show, see if these ones would choose to leave. You seemed better than her mother."

"Good call." Tara said.

Thank you. He clapped and started walking in a circle around the group. "Well, time to kill all of you."

"No." Fisnik said.

"What? the god said, cocking his ear as if he'd heard wrong.

"I know your name."

"You don't know my name."

Fisnik narrowed his eyes and slapped a paw on the ground. "I demand you give us choices, otherwise I will speak your name."

Tara leaned into Clay and said, "If a magic user knows someone's full, true name, they can hold power over them."

"Got it, thanks," Clay whispered back.

Fisnik and the god were locked in a staring contest. Finally, the god relented. "Fine, you may choose to stay or leave," he groaned. "You could have demanded I let you go."

Fisnik did not reply. He looked to Deacon. "Here is your second chance."

Deacon looked ready to cry. He walked over and grabbed Clay's hands. "Look in my eyes."

Deacon chanted, and Tara watched as all of his magic, a thick reddish-gold aura, flowed into Clay. Clay collapsed on the ground, and Deacon turned back to everyone. "I love you all."

Without looking to the god, he walked back in the direction of his wife and child.

The god looked shocked. "I did not authorize that."

"It had to have entertainment value though," Fisnik said. "You can monitor the boy as he learns. All that power, he's bound to mess up in a way your ilk would enjoy."

The god narrowed his eyes at Fisnik. "If you were not protected, I would kill you for millennia, Fate's beast."

"Fuck off."

"No, no, we have one more choice to hear. Fey child, what say you?"

All eyes were on her, and Tara swallowed hard. She felt her lack of horns and looked to Clay on the ground. Tears filled her eyes, and the god smiled. "Everything you've ever desired," he said.

She shook her head. "I choose him. He loves me as I am."

"So cliché," the god said. "Very well, you may go. Boring."

He waved his hand, and a portal opened—a perfect circle of orange and red light.

They didn't hesitate to run through. At the last second, the god said, "Here," and tossed Lazlo his ring.

They emerge from the portal in front of their hotel in Las Vegas. "What's your room number?" Lazlo asked. "I need a bloody nap." Clay gave him the key, and he walked inside.

"Are you ready to learn?" Fisnik asked.

"Yeah," Clay said.

"I imagine you have a lot of spells running through your head. Deacon was quite powerful. I will help you learn to control them."

"Thank you, Fiz, but first I have a pressing matter."

"What is that?" Fisnik asked.

Clay looked at Tara. "I have a date."

> PREVIOUSLY PUBLISHED

This section is three novelettes I published under old pen names that I wanted brought under my current name. I hope you enjoy them!

WE'RE NOT SUPERHEROES

Dereck never wanted to raise a teenager, let alone one with the same dangerous strength he's spent years trying to control. After a devastating accident leaves his cousin Katelyn in his care, their lives collide with a world of vigilantes and powers they don't understand.

CHAPTER ONE

Dereck was sitting at his desk reading a very poorly written book about some sort of alien teenager when the phone rang. "Hello?"

"Mr Marlin? This is Candice Jones from St Josephine's Memorial hospital. We need you to come down right away, I'm afraid there has been an accident."

Dereck didn't even wait. He just ran. He hung up the phone without another word and popped his head into his boss' office and before he got a reply he was running down the hallway.

It could only be his Uncle and Aunt. He'd spoken to his parents this morning and they were still in Missouri. His Aunt and Uncle and Younger cousin were driving up to see him and vacation in the city.

He hit the door so hard he thought it might shatter. But thankfully it just swung back and hit the side of the building. He'd been to St. Josephine's before so he knew the way to go. He was so worried that he didn't even pay attention to the fact that he was running at his top speed in front of civilians. He didn't care that anyone who saw him would think they were seeing an Olympic runner's faster brother running down the sidewalk at the speed of a car.

With a top speed of thirty miles am hour he made it in only about ten minutes. He burst through the doors and asked, "Where's my family?"

A very large woman with bright red hair looked at him holding a group of folders. "I'm gonna need a name." she said.

"Marlin, Theodore and Gale Marlin, and I think their daughter Katelyn was with them."

Something must have clicked in the nurse's head because she got a sympathetic look on her face and she said, "Please come with me."

She led him to a room with a glass window. There was a figure being operated on by a couple of doctors. The nurse turned to Dereck and said, "I'm sorry to have to tell you this, but your family was in a car accident and your Aunt and Uncle were killed. Katelyn is being operated on right now but,-"

She didn't need to finish. Dereck could feel tears in his eyes. He had always been close to his family. Before Katelyn was born his father and Uncle Teddy had taken him fishing a lot and to games and things all the time. He remembered baking cookies with his Aunt for the entire night when his mother had to go to the hospital for a surgery, and going around town the next day to give them away because they had made twenty dozen.

He turned away from the nurse and looked in at his cousin being operated on. She was only fifteen, and she had lost her parents,. He suddenly felt like he couldn't stand up. He melted into a nearby chair and the nurse looked at him with one more look of pity before walking away.

He sat in that chair for hours. He didn't even realize that it had been that long until the doctor was standing in front of him. "Dereck?" He looked up and saw the doctor. He knew Doctor Bill well, he'd been fixing up people like Dereck for a very long time. He was a short, stalky man with salt and pepper hair and sun burnt wrinkles all over his face. He looked more like a small town mechanic than a big city doctor for super powered people.

"Yes sir?" Dereck asked standing up.

"We have Katelyn in a room now. She's still asleep but she did very well in surgery. Luckily she heals fast. Did you know she she was like you?"

The shock on Dereck's face gave Bill his answer Dereck had never heard anything about Katelyn having powers. "From what I can see," Bill said. "She has the same powers you have. Her muscle tissue is so strong that I practically had to get a meat cleaver to cut the shrapnel out."

Dereck had to sit back down. "That must be why they were coming here. They were going to tell me about her powers."

"Even with her powers she's lucky to be alive." Bill said. "They had to cut the car to pieces it was so compacted. They said that she was asleep in the back seat, half the door metal was inside her legs."

"Oh my god." Dereck said. "I can't believe she survived. Will she be okay? No like, permanent damage?"

Bill shook his head. "She'll have scars for a while, but with how fast you people heal I don't know if they will stay or not."

Doctor Bill showed him to Katelyn's room before going off to deal with some 'Normal Emergencies' as he called them. Dereck felt like he was in someone else's home without permission. Katelyn was in the bed, her face so cut up that she was barely recognizable. He didn't know her very well. He was fourteen when she was born so they had only been baby sitter and baby when he knew her. She was still family though, and he didn't want to see her hurt.

He dreaded telling this poor girl that her parents were dead. He didn't even know what he was going to do with a young powered girl. He just sat down in a chair and covered his face with his hands.

Over the next several days Dereck got to know the hospital staff well. Katelyn stayed asleep, but he refused to leave her so he let BlackBall know to cover for him and told his boss he wouldn't be in.

Katelyn woke up on the ninth day. Nurses rushed in to check on her and take her vitals. As the nurse was getting ready to leave Katelyn asked, "Where are my parents?"

Dereck exchanged a glance with the nurse and she nodded, walking out to leave them alone. Dereck looked down at his cousin and felt like he wanted to cry. He had to tell her that the only guardians she'd ever known were dead. How did he just come out and say that? "Your parents are dead." He told her.

"What?"

He realized his mistake and sat down in the chair near the bed. "I'm sorry, but Uncle Teddy and Aunt Gale, they didn't survive the crash you were in."

Her face made his heart break. The tears ran down her face and when they hit the cuts on her face she cried more. "Do you want me to leave you alone for a while?" Katelyn shook her head and reached for his hand. He took it and sat there silently while she cried.

Katelyn didn't care if it made her look like a child to ask to hold her cousin's hand. She was sad and her entire freaking body hurt. She didn't remember the crash. She remembered her mother telling her to take a nap before they got there. Then she woke up here. "Are my powers why I survived?"

"Yes." Dereck said.

She took in a shaky breath and cried some more. "I didn't even want them. They died because I got these powers."

"Hey hey," Dereck said. "Your powers are not why they died. They died because of an accident."

She shook her head. "No, you don't understand. I punched a hole in the barn and they brought me up here to see if you could teach me how to control them...I'm why they died." He didn't have to tell her anything else. The look on Dereck's face told her that she was right, and that any protests would be a lie. "Can I have some food?"

Dereck rushed out of his chair and towards the door. "I'll go get you something."

As he was nearing the door, Katelyn asked, "Am I going to live with you now?"

He paused, looking like he wasn't sure what to say, but a moment later he said, "Yes. You are going to live with me."

CHAPTER TWO

I t took Katelyn another week to get out of the hospital. Every day she had to go through physical therapy supervised by doctors who knew about her powers, which was good since she left a grip in the steel railing of the stairs.

When she was finally released Dereck caught them a cab to his apartment. Katelyn had never been in a taxi before. It smelled like ball-sack and cow manure. She couldn't help but be mesmerized by the city though.The buildings seemed to go up forever. They twisted in shapes that she didn't know steel could be made into. It was wonderful to see all of this, but she was scared and sad.

Her knew home was a red building that looked really old. There was ivy going up the side and it reminded Katelyn of something she'd seen in an old movie. They went inside and had to climb up seven flights of stairs to the top floor, and down a hallway that was so small they had to walk single file. "Tomorrow we will have to go to the court house to get the paper work done so that you are allowed to live with me." Dereck said as he opened the door.

"Why are there so many locks?"

Dereck smiled. "Welcome to the city."

Dereck's apartment screamed single guy. There were dishes in the sink, and in the drying rack. The counter was stacked with papers and books, and so was the coffee table. A large set of weights was in the middle of the living room floor. "Your room is down that way." Dereck told her walking to the other end of the apartment. Katelyn followed him and saw that she had one end of the apartment to herself.

"There's only one bathroom, I'm sorry for that, but I am at the other end so you'll have plenty of privacy most of the time."

Her room made her sad. It wasn't that it wasn't good enough, it was great. The colors were gray and blue, everything. The paint on the walls was gray, the bed spread was gray with a blue stripe. It had her crying for her purple room and bright pink bed spread. "Do you mind if I take a nap?" she asked.

"Oh yeah, sure…I'll just be out here." He left and Katelyn laid down on the bed and cried.

She didn't know what time it was when she heard the knock on the door, but she said, "Come in."

"Hey," Dereck said, "I forgot that you don't have any clothes. Do you feel like going shopping?"

She shrugged. "I guess so."

The store was enormous. It made Katelyn feel like more of a country bumpkin than she was… She had never been inside a store this big. It was like three clothing sections of Walmart in one, and that was just women's wear. Dereck said it was one of the smaller and more affordable stores in the mall.

Dereck left her alone to try on jeans and shirts to make sure they fit and he came back with underwear and bras, far too many. It was a bit weird, but she got the feeling that he was uncomfortable and was trying to find something to do to help. "How many boobs do you think I have exactly?"

He laughed. "I wasn't sure what size you wore so I just guessed...was that weird?"

"A little, but this whole thing is weird." She pointed to each item in turn. "Too big, too small, way too small. One of my ass cheeks is bigger than that. "

"Are you allowed to say ass?"

Katelyn rolled her eyes. "I'm fifteen, not ten."

"Fair enough."

Katelyn ended up with about a week's worth of clothes and under things. As they were walking through the mall Dereck asked her, "Do you need tampons?"

She was a bit shocked that he spoke so casually about it. "Uh, yeah." she said.

As they walked down the aisle of the pharmacy Dereck asked her about other toiletries and she asked him, "Why are you so cool talking about stuff like that?"

"What do you mean?"

"Most guys would rather loose an arm than talk about tampons."

"Unlike most guys, I'm not from an eighties TV show."

"I don't understand."

"Lots of eighties TV shows had scenes where an older guy, usually a Dad, had to buy a bra or tampons for a girl and would be all uncomfortable about it, and it was always supposed to be super funny."

"Never was?"

"Not really no."

They got everything they needed and headed to the apartment. When Dereck unlocked the door Katelyn saw a man in the living room. She screamed and Dereck put his hands on her shoulders. "It's okay, he's a friend of mine."

She tried her best to look at him like he was crazy, though she wasn't sure exactly how to give that look. "Do your friends always break into your house while you're not home?"

Dereck thought for a moment. "Mostly just him."

The man was tall and dark. He was a white man but his hair was black and so were his clothes. He seemed to pull the light in from around him. He was a handsome man, angular sharp facial features that made him look like a Greek statue Katelyn had seen in one of her mother's art books. Walking closer she could see that his blue eyes were so bright they almost glowed.

He extended his hand. "Hello, you must be Katelyn."

She shook his hand, "You must be an intruder."

He smiled. "You can call me BlackBall. I thought you would be needing some of your things after what you've been through." He looked very sincere when he said, "I'm sorry for your loss."

"Thank you." She started to turn away and then she remembered what he'd said, "Wait, this is my stuff?"

He nodded with a smile. "I had to assume which room was yours but I think I got it right."

"Do you make it a habit of breaking and entering?"

"Yes. I can show you how if you like."

Katelyn looked over at Dereck. "I like him." She grabbed a box of her stuff and went to her new room.

"Thank you." Dereck said after Katelyn had left the room.

"I'm glad I could help. I didn't want the poor kid in a brand new place without at least some of her stuff to make it home."

Dereck and BlackBall walked over towards the kitchen and he got them a few beers. As they cracked them open. BlackBall asked, "So what do we know about her powers?"

"We haven't had time to talk about them with all that's happened."

BlackBall looked down the hall and called out for Katelyn. His friend moved fast and by the time she had come down the hall he already had the test set up. "Please don't destroy my apartment." Dereck said.

BlackBall looked at him with a conspiratorial look, "Remember your first apartment?"

Dereck sighed. "Okay fine, just be careful."

"What's up?" Katelyn asked as she came into the room. She looked at the cinder block on the counter and asked, "Do you just have cinder-blocks lying around?"

"Yes." BlackBall said as he came back from the fridge with an egg. "I want to judge how much control you have with your powers, so I want you to punch the concrete without hurting the egg inside."

Dereck almost laughed out loud at the look that Katelyn gave his friend, a look of sheer terror and incredulity at the nutcase before her. BlackBall turned to him, "Show her."

Dereck hated this test. He did it every couple of weeks to keep himself sharp on control, but it always made such a mess. He threw a punch and the air filled with concrete dust. BlackBall, always prepared, got the dust buster from under the sink (Dereck hadn't even known it was there) and started to vacuum the air.

When they had scraped all of the chunks from the counter, BlackBall picked up the egg, spotless, and present-ed it to Katelyn. "Holy shit."

"Foul language is the mark of the unintelligent." Black-Ball said.

"Your turn." Dereck said as he put another block on the counter.

Katelyn wound up and Dereck ducked. She had enough force behind that blow that he knew what was about to happen, and he was right because when he stood up there was a dent in the wall and a chunk of concrete on the floor.

When the dust cleared he saw that not only was the cinder block gone and the egg a pile of goop, there was a dent in the counter. "Wha...what was that for?" Katelyn asked through a fit of coughing.

"As I said before, I wanted to see how much control you have over your powers. " BlackBall said.

"How does he know I have powers?" She asked turning to Dereck.

"Who do you think taught him to control his?" BlackBall said, answering the question directed at Dereck.

"So what are you? Some kind of Yoda?"

"Something like that."

Dereck could see the wheels working in Katelyn's head. They had told him she was smart, but he didn't expect her to get it so quickly. "Are you some kind of vigilante?" she asked.

He momentarily considered lying to her, like he did to all the normal people in his life, but he decided that it wasn't going to work, what with them living together. "Yes." he said

Katelyn started to smile. "Can you teach me? I want to be a super hero."

Dereck and BlackBall spoke in Unison. "We are not super heroes."

She rolled her eyes. "I want to be whatever special name you've given yourselves then."

"No," Dereck said. "You just focus on being a kid."

"Screw that, I'm not a kid, you're just a dick." Without another word Katelyn grabbed another box and stormed back to her room.

BlackBall laughed. "Welcome to teenage girls my friend."

"Shut Up."

CHAPTER THREE

Katelyn had been to a court house before o But this building was at least three times the size of the one she'd went to with her mother. Dereck told her that this one building housed most of the important offices that the city needed, including child welfare.

He went inside and she was made to wait on a bench outside the door. She noticed that not very many people in the city paid attention to anyone else. She sat on the bench and where as in her home town where someone would have asked if she was okay, no one so much as looked at her here.

Another girl was led out of a big set of double doors several feet down the hall. Her guard went back inside and the girl caught Katelyn's eye and walked towards her.

She was a small girl. She could have easily played a fairy or something in a play. Katelyn could tell that she had been made to wear her best clothes because she looked extremely uncomfortable in a plaid skirt and expensive looking sweater.

The girl tucked a strand of shoulder length light brown hair behind her ear and asked, "What're you here for?"

"My cousin had to get permission for me to live with him. My parents died a few days ago."

"Sorry about that," she said sitting down next to Katelyn on the bench. "My parents are in there arguing over who gets me."

"That's nice that they both want you so much."

"Not really. They've been arguing over who gets everything since the divorce, right down to the crap in our fridge."

"Really?"

"They split half a carton of eggs."

"Wow."

"Yep. They don't like me, either of them. They just want to make sure that the other one doesn't get me." She extended her hand, "I'm Juno."

"Katelyn." she said, shaking.

"What're you into? Guys, girls, both?"

"Isn't that a bit personal?"

"You told me your parents were dead within thirty seconds."

"Fair enough." Katelyn said. "Guys, though most of them are too stupid so I mostly just ignore people in general. What about you?"

"I don't want anyone. Seeing them mostly ruined love for me." She motioned to the room her parents were in. "Guys turn out to be assholes, and I can barely handle my own crap, I couldn't imagine having to deal with another woman."

Katelyn laughed. Before she could say anything else she saw the guard come out of the room down the hall. Juno got up and walked backwards down the hall saying, "See you 'round Kate." before turning around and walking to meet the guard.

That day she had a meeting with a court appointed shrink to ask her if she wanted to live with Dereck, and then they discussed a bunch of other crap when Katelyn's immediate 'Yes' didn't satisfy her.

At the end of the day they were set to live together. They would have to get a few visits from a social worker and if they signed off then everything was good.

Dereck sent Katelyn to the store a few streets over for a loaf of bread. At least that's what he had told her. He really just wanted to give her a chance to go somewhere on her own so that she could get comfortable in the city.

"I think we need to test Katelyn's full abilities." BlackBall said coming in through the door.

"You know sometimes I regret giving you that key."

"No you don't."

"No I don't."

He came around and sat at the counter while Dereck was cooking. "Seriously though," BlackBall continued, "We should see just what she can do."

"Why?"

"Who's to say what she could do? I mean, if she has a second power that is activated by stress wouldn't you like to know about it? Or are you just worried that she might be stronger than you?"

Dereck looked at his friend with a blank face. "Why would I care about that?"

BlackBall shrugged. "Come on then, let's go to the facility and test her."

Katelyn walked in the door and sat the bread on the counter "Does he even have a house?"

BlackBall laughed. "Actually I'm here about you."

"Don't." Dereck said, knowing he was going to anyway.

"I want to fully test your powers, and I was asking your cousin here."

"I want to do it." Katelyn said.

Dereck sighed loudly, he pointed the knife in his hand at BlackBall and said, "You have to stop doing that."

Black Ball put his hands up in defense. "Fine, fine."

BlackBall's facility was huge. He tried to throw her off by calling it 'The facility', but Katelyn wasn't stupid, it was his.

It was enormous. The ceilings went up for what seemed like miles, like an open air skyscraper. In the far right corner there was some sort of strange apparatus that had a silver platform underneath what looked like massive sheets of weights. Across from the weights was a wall with large targets painted on it, some human shaped, some large bull's eyes.

On the left and right sides, about mid way through the room, were stairs that led up to scaffolding that wound up to the ceiling. There was a gym set up with large heavy bags and treadmills and things in the front of the room, and there was a mid sized car and a forklift parked to the right of the entrance. Katelyn looked around in wonder, trying to hide some of her shock, then she saw BlackBall and Dereck treating the place like just another room they had walked into.

"Where do you want to start?" BlackBall asked. It was only just then that she realized he was dressed like a ninja.

"Is that normal workout wear?"

"Helps to work out in what you fight in."

She gave him a look that said, 'Fair enough' and walked over, looking at the giant weight thing." I want to try that." she said, pointing.

He smiled. "I was hoping you'd say that."

A few minutes later Katelyn was standing under the large sheets of weight with a large belt on that was connected to two bungy cords on either side, if a safety button was pressed she would be flung out to avoid being crushed.

"Ready?" asked Dereck.

Katelyn nodded. Dereck signaled to BlackBall, who was standing nearby with the control switch extended to it's full length. A large black sheet started to descend and Katelyn braced herself like Dereck had shown her, shifted hands up and legs to support the weight.

It was heavy, more weight than she was used to, but after the initial shock of it, which lasted about three seconds, she was fine. "I'm going to add another every ten seconds until you tell me to stop." BlackBall said.

"Shouldn't you have said that before I got under here?"

"More fun not to."

About ten minutes later the weight had started hurt.

Katelyn didn't know how many weights were up there, but she knew it had better be a lot. She was sweating buckets because of it and it was only like three tons, she was gonna be pissed.

"How're you feeling?" Dereck asked. Katelyn didn't have the brain power to answer and not get squished, so she just gave a nod and a grunt. "Maybe you should ease up." Dereck said to BlackBall.

"Stress is the only real test." Was the response, as well as another batch of weight. Ten seconds later was more and Katelyn couldn't help but choke out, "I. Can't. Take. Any. More."

"Ten more seconds."

She felt like she was going to give out and would be crushed. The weight literally felt like she was lifting a thousand tractors, and she would know. She'd done reps with the tractor to show off when she'd discovered her powers.

The weight lifted and Katelyn fell to the floor. Her entire body felt like jelly. She was breathing heavy and felt like she might have a heart attack when BlackBall looked down at her and asked, "Wanna know your limits?"

She gave a pained nod. "One hundred tons with discomfort, seventy five without breaking a sweat. That's more than your cousin."

Katelyn smiled. Her chest still felt heavy as she breathed but it was starting to ease up. "What's next?"

"That's the spirit." BlackBall said reaching down to help her up.

That night they found out that Katelyn could jump five hundred feet in any direction, including straight up, could stop a car if it tried to run her over, and was in general more powerful than Dereck. As they were wrapping up BlackBall must have seen the look on his face as he was thinking about her powers because he said. "Don't worry D, you're still the better trained one."

"It doesn't bother me."

BlackBall gave him a smirk. "Sure it doesn't."

Katelyn's adrenaline kept going the entire ride home, she was bouncing up and down and looked as giddy as a kid after their first kiss" "What're we going to do now?" she asked. "I'm so jacked up I want to try and do something else."

"How about adolescent social interaction?"

"What?"

"You've got school tomorrow."

That killed her buzz. "Well crap." She turned in the seat and curled up, going to sleep almost instantly.

Katelyn stood outside of the brick school wondering what it was going to be like in there" Her last school had been in a town so small that there was only about one hundred kids total. She'd seen several times that many go inside already, and most of them were around her grade.

Just as she was about to walk inside she saw a familiar face walking up the sidewalk. Juno had seen her first. "Hey Kate."

"You go to this school?"

"As of today." she said with a sly smile.

"What's so funny?"

"Oh my Mom wanted me to go to a very different school but I played the Dad card. Her reaction was funny. Basically I go to this school because my Mother hates my Father."

Juno started to walk towards the school and Katelyn stayed. Juno looked at her and asked, "What's wrong?"

"Nothing." Katelyn said. "It's just that, well I'm from a small town...I've never gone to a school this..."

"Rough?"

"Yeah."

Juno walked back down the steps to Katelyn and put her arm around her, "Stick with me Kate, I know my way around a tough crowd." They walked into school and Katelyn felt a little bit better with her new friend there.

Dereck struggled to get the front door open with the stack of manuscripts he was holding. He'd told his boss that he may need to find another job so that he could be home with Katelyn and she had said that she didn't want to loose her assistant, but that he was too good to loose, so she made him an editor so he wouldn't have to come to the office so much.

He looked at the stack on the counter and sighed. This stack needed done by the end of the week. He could get it done, but not a whole lot else. He refused to give up patrol and he had other responsibilities now. If he could only make a dent tonight he could intersperse the others throughout the week. He got an idea and picked up the phone. When BlackBall picked up Dereck said, "I need a favor."

"Thank god, I am so bored."

"You know you could get a job."

"I own things and hire people dude, What's up?'

"Can you hang out with Katelyn tonight? I need to make a dent in these manuscripts and it would be better without anyone else here."

"Yeah, I'll take her to work out tonight."

"Great, that'll give me several hours to work."

"If you get overwhelmed you should go on patrol for an hour or two, you know, beat out your stress on some muggers."

"That's not a bad idea."

Juno was a great friend. They didn't have all of their classes together, only a few of them, but they'd talked a lot at lunch and during free period. Katelyn noticed that Juno didn't like to talk about herself much, she spent most of the time asking about Katelyn. So she told her about Bellview and their farm. Juno had gotten excited hearing that Katelyn had gone to a parking lot Nashville Panic show. They actually found out that Nya's song was both of theirs favorite song. All in all it was a good first day.

When she got home she found Dereck sitting at the coffee table with a stack of papers that came as high as her breasts, and BlackBall watching television. "Seriously Dude, do you have a home?"

BlackBall looked at Dereck and the two of them shared a smile that make Katelyn feel like there was something she was missing. BlackBall got up and walked over to her. "Go pack a bag with some workout clothes."

"Um...Okay...why?"

"Your cousin needs to work and I'm bored. Hurry up, I want to eat first."

A half an hour later they were sitting at a booth in a small retro diner decorated like it was still nineteen fifty three, Katelyn ordered a burger and BlackBall said, "You're going to want more, trust me."

"I'm not very hungry."

He shrugged. "Okay." BlackBall ordered a small burger and the endless pancakes, of which he ate five plates.

They ate and sat there until it got dark. BlackBall checked his watch and said, "It's time, let's go."

He took her to a strange part of the city that looked more like it belonged in a small town. There were tall buildings on either side of the street, much lower than the tall buildings near her school. There was suddenly a long strip of low buildings that advertised seven different businesses, one of them a gym.

They got out of the taxi and walked around to the alley. BlackBall walked up to the back entrance of the gym like it was no big deal to be prowling like burglars at a closed business. He knocked three times, then twice, then three times again. The door opened and BlackBall looked at her, "Let's go."

They walked through the back and she saw that the large windows had sheets over them so that no one could break in.

Though she suspected that they had more to do with people seeing inside than with burglary.

They went to the dressing rooms and changed. Katelyn and BlackBall were dressed very similar with black shorts and a gray T-shirt, though she suspected he wasn't wearing a sports bra. "I thought you worked out in costume."

"Shoosh, The owner runs the gym for powered people, but he doesn't need to know about our other night time activities."

Katelyn held up her hands defensively. "Sorry."

He came forward with a fist, "Fist bump on the unintentional matching."

She bumped the fist, "You are a very lethal dork."

"Why thank you."

They went over to the weights first and she noticed that they all said more than the average. Five hundred, two thousand. "Is this gym for body builders?"

BlackBall laughed. "He has a couple of guys switch the equipment out after hours. He makes quite a bit of money catering to a powered clientele."

BlackBall set her up with a thousand pounds and showed her how to do squats. She did a thousand. Then they moved on to dead lifts, bench presses, and a bunch of other weight lifting. Then they hit the treadmill, running so far that she couldn't even look at the number she was so focused on not falling down.

The strangest part of it all was that BlackBall kept up with her. Dereck had said that he wasn't a powered person, she had no idea how he did it. He couldn't lift as much weight as she could, but he did just as many reps, which probably should have caused muscle failure.

Katelyn got off the treadmill and saw a man in the far side of the gym that she swore hadn't been there a moment ago. He looked to be in his late twenties to early thirties and he was lifting a normal amount of weight with his arms, above for a human but not particularly heavy for this gym, and thousands more pounds were floating all around him. Katelyn could only stare as the weights floating moved in time with the ones in his arms. Finally she went into the smaller other I room where BlackBall was doing upside down sit ups on some monkey bars. "You have to come see this."

He let his legs fall forward and she thought for a moment he was going to hit the floor, but be flipped again and landed in almost a sitting position. He stood up like it wasn't amazing and walked towards her. She thought he would look at it with amazement, but he just waved. "Hey Flink!"

The weights went slowly to the ground and the man blinked out of existence, appearing just in front of them. Katelyn jumped back and yelled, "What the fu-"

"Dude, with the cursing?"

The man named Flink calmly looked at BlackBall. "Who's this?"

"Dereck's cousin."

He held out a hand, "Nice to meet you." She shook his hand and he continued. "I just popped in for a bit of exercise but I've got to be going. See you soon?"

BlackBall extended his hand and they shook. "Just come by the next time you're in town."

"Will do."

Then he blinked out of existence again. Katelyn turned to BlackBall. "Who the hell was that?"

"Flink."

"What are his powers exactly?"

"Flink is...complicated." BlackBall said. "Let's go work out some more." And he walked back to continue his workout. Katelyn gave another look at where Flink had been and turned to follow him.

Dereck had his gear unzipped and down, trying to reach his back. Thankfully he'd one most of his bleeding in the kitchen where it was easier to clean up. The door opened and Katelyn came in. She was still in workout clothes and drenched in sweat, her shirt a darker gray than it had started. She didn't say anything, just walked stiffly into her room. He heard a thud and suspected that she had missed the bed on the first try.

BlackBall walked in and saw what he was doing. "Want some help?" he asked.

"Please."

He shifted on the couch so that his friend could sew him up BlackBall was an expert, he could talk and sew at the same time. "I think you should train her to patrol."

"I've told you, I don't want her out there. I mean, look what I did tonight."

"I tested her tonight to see what she could take."

"Didn't you see that the other night?"

"Last time I tested her powers, this time I tested her Will. I met her rep for rep and she never quit. She saw me doing it and she didn't even complain."

"Hurtin'?"

"It literally feels the same as the time I got him by a truck."

"Ouch."

"Yeah, but even if you don't let her go out, she should still learn the control, the dedication. I mean, what would happen if she got into a fight at school and didn't know the difference between beating someone up and killing them?"

Dereck winced and sighed when the sewing was finished. "Okay, fine. You can train her. I will help but I think the job should be left to the one who's better at it."

BlackBall chuckled a bit, "Thanks. I really do think this is a good idea."

"I hope so..."

When BlackBall had left and he had cleaned up his mess, Dereck thought about what he had agreed to. He loved his life. He saved lives and helped people. But he wasn't sure if Katelyn would be able to take it. It was not easy. He got very little sleep, worked a lot, and lived in near constant fear that if he slipped up even one time, he would spend the rest of his life in jail because he was in fact, a criminal.

He knew she didn't have to go on patrol, just learn the control like BlackBall had said. But he knew she would eventually get tired of just training.

CHAPTER FOUR

Dereck was on patrol, but before hell left he'd given her the news that she could start training. While he was talking she kept her composure, even when he'd said that she wasn't allowed out on patrol, she could always change his mind on that right? But then he'd told her that he was sticking her with a baby sitter, "What?"

"BlackBall will be here in an hour, he's going to hang out while I'm working."

"So you trust me enough to give me superhero training but you can't trust me to be alone?"

"It's not like that, I-"

She interrupted him, "I do not need a baby sitter."

"Katelyn," He said calmly, "It's not like that" It gets lonely around here and I just thought you might like someone who knows about you to hang with. Someone you don't have to lie to all night about your powers the way you do in the real world"

She immediately felt awful. "I'm sorry. That's nice."

"Alright then."

Dereck had left for patrol before, but for some reason she had never seen his gear. She'd been expecting something like what she'd seen in superhero movies, but this was just a leather jumpsuit like a mechanic would wear, black and durable. "That's what a superhero wears?"

"Not a superhero...and yes, this is what I wear. But BlackBall wears a ninja outfit that I always forget the name of."

"That reminds me, what's his story? I mean, he has no powers."

"No, but he is a traditionally trained ninja and a really great detective."

"So he's Batman?"

Dereck laughed. 'Except he's a lot scarier and he doesn't need all the toys."

BlackBall arrived and Dereck left. Presently they were sitting on the couch, neither of them really watching TV. Finally Katelyn said, "So you're a ninja?"

"Yes"

"Like you were trained in Japan?"

"Also raised there."

"Think you could beat me in a fight?"

"Of course."

Katelyn was a bit shocked at that. Was he really so cocky that he thought he could beat someone with super strength? She got up and motioned for him to come at her.

BlackBall raised his eyebrow, "Are you serious?"

She motioned again. Finally he stood up, stepped out from the coffee table, and motioned for her, "Come on then."

She took a single step forward and everything went fast. In a split second she was on her back in the remains of what had only a moment ago been the coffee table. Breathing hurt but she managed to roll onto the carpet. "Ouch." She groaned.

"We will start on control, then move to combat." BlackBall said lending her a hand up.

"No, I want to try again." She took a deep breath and tore the chunk of wood out of her back. She was thankful that her powers had her already healing from her relativity minor injuries. She would be fine in a few seconds. "I wanna make a bet. Let's fight in more space and if I land a hit, even just a single hit, then I start fight training and we do control and stuff along the way."

BlackBall stared at her for what seemed like an hour, like he was a big cat studying which member of a herd he would kill. She got the feeling that he already knew in that instant exactly how he would beat her, "To the roof." he said.

Dereck came through the window and saw BlackBall reading in the chair. The entire couch was taken up by Katelyn's sprawled out body. She was drenched in sweat and completely asleep. "Did she even come close to landing a hit?"

"Not really. How about you?"

"Stopped a mugging and I,-"

"What?"

"I had to kill a guy."

BlackBall looked at Katelyn and then back and Dereck, "What happened?"

"I, this parking lot. I could hear the guy talking rom the roof across the street, he uh...his friend left and he was going to wait until this woman came out and he was going... I grabbed him and pulled him around the corner seconds before he...I snapped his neck and got rid of the body."

BlackBall was a hardened killer. He didn't do it for fun but he had never seen a problem with taking a life that was better off not in the world, Dereck knew that. But his friend also knew that Dereck didn't like killing. He got up and walked over, putting his hand on Dereck's s shoulder, "It was justified. He wouldn't have been prosecuted, you had no proof of intention, and he would have just done it again."

"I know, I'm fine, I just-,"

"I know."

They stood there in silence before BlackBall said, "I'll see you later, I'm going to go on patrol for a bit Katelyn and I will start training tomorrow."

"Thanks man. Good night."

"Night."

Katelyn awoke to shaking. It took her a moment to realize that it was Dereck shaking her awake. "Time for school."

"I can't go, too tired."

"This is the life kiddo," he said. "I went to bed at three and got up at six. You wanted to train and this is part of it. Come on."

Katelyn got up with a lot of groaning and complaining, but she finally managed to get out the door. She skipped the shower, deciding to do it after gym.

"Jesus you stink." Was the first thing Juno said.

"Yeah, I didn't have time to shower."

"All weekend?"

"Haha, come on. I've got third period gym, I'll shower them."

Juno stopped her in the hall, giving her the most concerned look that she'd ever seen her friend give. "Are you okay? I mean, like, no offense but you look like shit rolled over."

"I'm good. I promise."

School was hell and she wouldn't have made it through at all but for Juno. Juno repeatedly stabbed her in the fatty part of her back with a thumbtack to keep her awake during the classes they shared, making a strange face when she had to do it harder a second time for Katelyn to notice. And she lied to a teacher fifteen minutes into a class they didn't share to get her out and Juno kept watch while she napped in someone else's unlocked car in the parking lot.

Dereck was just finishing up a call with an author when his boss came into his office. She walked in and stood in front of his desk, "Yes ma'am?"

The look on her face told him something was about to happen that wouldn't be good. "I'm sorry Dereck but I'm going to have to let you go."

"Can I ask why?"

"I just haven't got the money to pay this many people. You and the three editors hired before you are all being laid off."

Dereck sighed. He wasn't about to beg. Especially when it wouldn't go any good. "Well I know the drill. I will get my things packed up and be out of here by lunch."

"Nah, make it the end of the day. Corporate is making me fire you, they might as well give up another day's pay."

Dereck laughed and his boss bid him goodbye.

Katelyn had another training session later that night so she was hoping to score a nap. She and Dereck met in the stair well as he was lugging a box up the stairs. "Are you really having trouble with a box?"

"Not the weight, the damn thing's about to bust at the seams. I've got three more in the hallway upstairs."

They made their way up to the apartment to find a short woman with a clipboard and a pantsuit standing in front of the door. "Can I help you?" Dereck asked as the woman turned around, hearing them walk up.

"I was beginning to think I had the wrong apartment." The woman extended her hand. "Shelly Long. I'm with social services."

Dereck's face lit up and Katelyn knew he was hiding something. "Can we make this quick?" Katelyn asked. "I want to take a nap before I go work out."

Both Dereck and the social worker looked at her. Dereck's eyes were pleading for her to shut the hell up. "What do you mean?" The social worker asked. "Are you not sleeping well?"

"No ma'am., I've just had a long day at school. My cousin was nice enough to get me a gym membership and I like to work out. I was just hoping to rest up a bit first."

Shelly smiled. "Then I will try and make this quick."

Katelyn unlocked the door and they went inside. Dereck set the box down and they both stood awkwardly in the hall while Shelly walked around the apartment, She looked at everything, occasionally making notes on her clip board. "I'd like to see Katelyn's room and talk with her alone for a bit." Shelly said after what seemed like a much too thorough snooping.

Katelyn led her into her room and cleaned some things off the bed as she sat down. Shelly took the desk chair, which was also blue and gray. "So I have a list of questions I have to ask you. I know that some of them are strange and uncomfortable but you'll have to stick with me."

"Okay..."

"Are you happy here?"

"As happy as can be expected giving the circumstances."

"Are you being beaten or mistreated?"

"He won't let me go out after eleven but I think that's called parenting, not abuse."

Shelly laughed. "That's true. Um...does he or do any of his friends sexually abuse you in any way? Have you been inappropriately touched?"

"No ma'am, I am only being touched in the right ways." Shelly looked at her shocked and Katelyn burst into laughter. "I'm kidding. Nobody touches me in any sexual ways...like at all."

"Really?"

"This isn't Arkansas lady."

Shelly laughed and nodded her head. "Okay, I believe you. I only have a few more questions."

Dereck was going through the boxes he'd brought home when he saw that he had accidentally taken the slush pile. He looked at the box of discarded manuscripts form the whole office and an idea began to form in his head.

The door opened and Katelyn and Shelly came out of the room. Katelyn walked up and he whispered, "Give me a minute." She eyed him and then turned around, walking back into her room. Shelly looked concerned but Dereck walked close and said, "I need to tell you that I lost my job today."

"That isn't good. What happened?"

"They just couldn't afford so many editors. It was me and three other people."

"You will need to find something else quick" She said. "If you don't have a continued source of income you could loose custody."

"I will have something by the time my unemployment runs out, hopefully before."

"Okay, well we'll talk again at our next meeting."

Shelly left and Dereck said, "You can come out now." Katelyn came out with her gym bag. Her nap apparently forgotten.

"Will you be on patrol tonight?"

"yeah."

"BlackBall and I are going to work on my punches. It's really hard not to break the paper."

Dereck smiled to himself, remembering that particular lesson. "It helps though. You wouldn't want to punch someone in an honest way and accidentally kill them."

"I guess that's true." Katelyn said as she was leaving soDereck decided that he was going to take a nap and headed for his room.

Hours later he was sitting on a rooftop watching the street. A group of kids bit a younger than Katelyn were walking up the street followed by older kids. Dereck waited to see if this was just kids bullying or if it was something worse.

The younger boys headed down an alley. Dereck wondered why people always thought going down an alley would be a good idea. The older boys ran down the alley and started to hit the younger boys.

Dereck had no problem with boys being boys. Or girls being girls if you wanted to be inclusive. He did, however have a problem with seven against five. Especially when the seven had forty pounds and half a foot on the younger five.

He started to get off the roof, but before he could the boy moved. He moved with super speed as he ran around, tripping the bigger boys. He grabbed the one who looked to be the ring leader and he punched him over and over.

His super fast fist soon had the bully's face pummeled into a mess of blood and broken bone. He dropped the body and zoomed off.

CHAPTER FIVE

Juno looked pissed. Katelyn wasn't sure if she would need her powers, or if they would even help. As she got closer to he steps Juno jumped down and got in her face. "I thought we were friends." she said.

"We are." Katelyn said trying to figure out what was going on.

"Then why don't you ever want to hang out? We hang here at school but I'm getting tired of asking you to do stuff after school and you saying no. If you don't want to spend time with me that's fine. But I want to know if I need to look for a new best friend."

Katelyn felt like she might cry. Over the last three months she'd spent so much time training that she'd neglected the only friend she had. "I do want to be your friend." Katelyn said. "But,-"

"What? You just don't want to spend anytime outside of school with me?"

Before Katelyn could reply Mr Gilmore, the history teacher, came out of the front door. "Get to class ladies. Now."

"Can't let fifteen year-olds know that you're a smoker?" Juno said.

Mr Gilmore was not amused. "Inside. Before I give you both a month's detention for being out after the final bell."

The girls started walking up the steps and Juno looked at Katelyn. Katelyn knew there would be hell to pay for what was about to come out of her mouth, but she didn't want to loose her friend. "Do you want to come over for a sleepover this weekend?"

Juno's face lit up. She smiled and nodded. "Back Inside!" The two of them hurried through the door and to their classes.

When she got home that afternoon Dereck and BlackBall were standing at the counter looking over a bunch of papers. It must have been something secret because they started to it cover it up when she came near. "Can I have a friend over this weekend?"

"No...wait, since when do you have friends?"

"I have a friend. I met her at the courthouse. Why can't I have her over? Are you planing on bench pressing a car in the living room?"

BlackBall cleared his throat and they both looked at him. "Speaking as her trainer," he said. "I think she's earned a bit of time off."

Dereck sighed. "Okay. You can have her over so long as it's okay with her parents and you keep your mouth shut about all of this," He motioned to the papers and the three of them.

Katelyn smiled and she hugged Dereck. Running around the counter she hugged BlackBall and he gasped. "Little too hard dear."

She dropped him. "Sorry." She ran to the living room to call Juno.

Dereck and BlackBall sat on the roof as the giggling sounds of a sleepover drifted up from the window. He handed his friend a beer and said, "I did this right, right?"

"What do you mean?"

"Like, I'm supposed to just take her word for it right? Or should I have called her parents?"

BlackBall shrugged. "I think asking was good. I don't think you were supposed to meet them or anything."

Dereck took a sip and spoke without looking at BlackBall. "I don't like this, what is something slips out?"

"Like a body part?"

"No dumb-ass, like what if she tells this girl?"

"I personally think we should investigate her and see if she can be trusted." B1ackBall said, "Katelyn could use a friend."

"She has us." Dereck said, a little bit offended

"yeah, her guardian cousin and his weird ninja friend. You're family and I'm *your* friend. She needs someone close to her age to be friends with." He stood up and started to stretch. He went into a hand stand. "I don't know how we' re going to find this boy. I've been talking to every person in the city with powers. I also called Mac, just to let him know."

"How is he?"

"Same old same old. He took in a younger girl like you did. Her name is Maggie and she's-"

"Barbara's daughter, right."

"yeah," BlackBall said. "They've been going around and helping people get control of their powers together. He said he'd keep an eye out for a boy with super speed."

"I hope we find him before he kills anyone else. I just hope nobody believes those boys if they decide to tell I someone what they saw."

"I talked to them," BlackBall said. "They won't talk."

***

Katelyn felt someone shaking her awake. She looked around and saw Juno on the bed and she almost peed her pants when she saw Dereck standing over her. "BlackBall needs help. I'll be back in the morning, Do me a favor and make up something for your friend." Katelyn gave him a thumbs up and flopped her head back down on her pillow.

Juno woke up before her and Katelyn found her friend in the kitchen. "Where'd your cousin go last night?"

"Um..." Katelyn blanked. She hadn't thought of an excuse for Dereck yet. "I don't know." Katelyn said.

"He might have a girlfriend or something."

Juno's face told her that she wasn't buying the girlfriend story. Katelyn didn't look at her as she went to the fridge to get the milk out. She was hoping Juno wouldn't be able to read the truth on her face like most people had been able to all her life.

Katelyn made herself a bowl of cereal. She went to get a spoon and as she turned around she heard, "Think fast!"

She didn't have time to think, only react. She punched the object flying at her and a cloud of black dust covered the kitchen. "Oh. My. God." Juno said slowly.

Katelyn didn't know what to do. She got the dust buster and started getting rid of the dust. When she was done she looked at Juno, "What exactly would you have done if that had hit my skull?"

"I was pretty sure it wouldn't."

"Pretty sure?" Katelyn said raising her eyebrows.

Juno shrugged. "I was in the bathroom and saw your cousin come through the window in a super hero costume. He tripped over a cinder-block and smashed it with his foot., I went back to bed while he was cleaning up the dust."

BlackBall came in through the window and Katelyn saw Dereck come up the hall. BlackBall looked at Dereck. "I told you she was smart."

Dereck had a smile on his face. "I made it a bit obvious though didn't I?"

"Not really." Juno and BlackBall said in unison.

"So does this mean that Juno is part of the team?"

Dereck nodded. "We thought you deserved a friend who knew what you are."

Katelyn ran over and gripped her cousin in a hug. Smashing her face into his chest she said, "Thank you."

BlackBall clapped his hands to get everyone's attention., "So, you want to go show off a bit?"

The girls dressed and BlackBall took them all to the facility. As they walked in Juno said, "Okay, show me your powers."

Katelyn walked over to one side of the wall and jumped up to the last level of scaffolding. The rest of them looked like ants from five hundred feet. She and BlackBall had practiced landing, but she still wasn't very good. Though she had to try. There was no way she was walking all the way down.

Falling through the air was a wonderful feeling. It was even better than going up. It did not feel good however, when she landed and shot forward, by landing wrong, scrapping up her legs and leaving a dent in the left wall.

Juno ran over and reached out a hand as Katelyn climbed from the ruble. "Is that supposed to happen?" she asked.

"Thanks. No that isn't supposed to happen. I haven't got landings down yet."

They spent the rest of the day showing off for Juno. Katelyn, Dereck, and even BlackBall. Though he didn't take off his mask. Katelyn didn't say anything about that. He would let her see his face when and if he wanted.

When they were getting ready to leave Katelyn saw Dereck and Blackball share a look. She looked at both of them and asked, "What is it?"

"I decided it's time for your first night on patrol." Dereck said.

Her eyes lit up. "Seriously? We're going out?"

Dereck shook his head. "No. I'm staying home. Later on BlackBall is going to teach me how to not worry about you in the field. Until then I'm not qualified to work with you

"Do I get a costume?"

BlackBall and Dereck sighed. "It's not a costume." They said in unison.

"And yes," BlackBall said. "You get one."

CHAPTER SIX

BlackBall took her to the local college campus. "They were kneeling on a roof when she pulled at her costume again. It was just like what BlackBall wore. Black pants and a shirt that cinched in the front with a belt. It was pure black ,and seemed to pull in light and make her invisible. The front was lose enough to let her hide things in it but she felt the need to keep pulling it in place.

"For the love of God stop fidgeting." BlackBall said. "It's fine."

"It feels like it's going to fall open."

"It will if you keep fidgeting. It is made to hide your body and figure, you'll be fine."

"Why am I dressed like you?"

He sighed. "So much talking. You and I are dressed for stealth That's why you can't tell us apart. We are not Man and woman, we are ninja."

"Dereck doesn't dress like this."

"That would be why I call his gear his bondage outfit.

She laughed and he looked at her with daggers. They both turned and looked over the edge of the roof at the sound of a distressed girl.

The girl was walking away from five guys. They kept up with her and they pulled at her clothes and body. "Oh goody," BlackBall said. "I love gang rapes."

Katelyn really hoped she'd heard wrong due to the hood. "Why?"

He looked at her, "Because I get to beat the hell out of a bunch of rapists instead of just one. Pull your mouth cover back up."

Katelyn did as she was told. Nothing but her eyes were visible as she and BlackBall jumped from the roof. He slid down a pipe and jumped from a height that wouldn't hurt while Katelyn landed in the grass, leaving only a small crater. He was still closer when they confronted the group.

As instructed she didn't speak. She simply punched the first guy she came up on, careful not to kill him. When she looked over, three more men were on the ground. There was a loud bang and she saw BlackBall look over at her. What was he looking at? She looked down and saw the black suit getting wet. She touched her stomach and it came away red. She didn't have time to think about what it was before the world went black.

"So what do you do for a living?" Juno asked.

"Currently I am trying to become a literary agent."

"That's pretty cool."

The two of them had been at the apartment for hours. Dereck really hoped that no one came here to find him home alone with his cousin's friend and K no cousin. There was nothing going on, but he didn't want to try and explain that to a social worker. "Juno." He said. "Couldn't you rather go somewhere else? I know you were supposed to spend the weekend here but Katelyn won't be back for hours and she'll not be much fun tomorrow."

"I'm fine sir. If you'd like me to go,-"

"No, no, I just thought it might be weird for you and I to hang out here."

Juno shrugged. "My parents are busy this weekend so I'm glad for any kind of company."

Dereck started to say something but the phone rang.

"Hello?...what?" He hung up and ran for the counter. He grabbed his keys and said, "Let's go." As he headed out the door without stopping to wait.

Dereck knew the gate password. They drove up the driveway to the large house. "This place is insane." Juno said.

It was. The house was taller rather than wide, eight floors. The right and left wings had octagon shaped trim around the roof, making it look like a castle.

Dereck skidded to a stop and jumped out of the car. He ran up the steps and hit the large double doors with almost enough force to break them down. He looked around the marble foyer for BlackBall, "In here!"

He turned to the right and went into the large living room. There was a small living area set up in front of the fireplace large enough to stand in, and an entire wall of books at the far end of the roof on either side of the large windows. Though he knew these weren't the impressive ones, those were in the study upstairs.

This was a grand room that felt like a museum or Buckingham palace and was strictly for show. Katelyn was laying on the couch, her stomach bandaged. BlackBall came out of the doorway on the far wall holding a tray with juice and other breakfast supplies. Dereck rushed over to Katelyn. "Are you okay?"

"I'm fine," she said wincing only slightly. "BlackBall got the bullet out and he says I should be completely healed in a few hours."

"One thing she doesn't have on you," BlackBall said. "She is not bullet proof inside one hundred feet."

Dereck was ashamed that he felt relief at hearing that. He should be thinking about the fact that his cousin was shot, not being proud that he had at least one ability over hero "How did this happen?" he asked "Weren't you watching her?"

"She was taking down her first guy and I took the other three," he said. 'The last guy pulled out a gun just as I turned around."

"I hope he's dead."

"He will be."

Katelyn looked horrified. "You're gonna kill him?"

"Yes." They said in unison.

"I didn't know we killed people."

Juno walked into the room from where she'd been waiting. She came in without paying much attention to the inside of the house. "I don't see how you'd not kill," she said to Katelyn. "I mean, if someone was about to kill a baby and you didn't have proof, they wouldn't go to jail just on your word. You'd have to kill them to save the kid."

BlackBall raised his hand and pointed at Juno. "I like her."

"Well regardless, you won't be in the field again for a while." Dereck said.

"What?" she said getting up. "That's crap, my first time goes bad and you bench me?"

"Goes bad? You. Got. Shot."

"So? I'm fine." She tried to get up but winced the entire time. Finally, when she was in a sitting position she motioned to herself. "See?"

"Yeah," Dereck said nodding sarcastically. "It's like you weren't even hurt at all."

Katelyn turned to BlackBall. "Will you try to talk some sense into him?"

"Sure, as soon as he stops making sense."

"What?"

BlackBall crossed his arms., "I have obviously not trained you well enough to be in the field. With your cousin's permission we will continue training until you are ready."

"Which will be in a long time." Dereck added. "You should have never been out there. I let him change my mind."

Katelyn's face was red with anger. She stood up and stormed out of the room without another word. Juno looked at the two men and said, "I don't know about you but I'm not going to follow her."

BlackBall laughed, "Breakfast anyone?"

Dereck laughed despite the fact that he was still incredibly angry. She could have died and it was his fault. He sat down with the others and took a bagel from the tray. Juno was sitting across from Dereck. She turned to look at BlackBall sitting in the chair at the end of the table and said, "I know who you are."

His mask no longer needed, he took it off. But he wasn't fazed. "I know who you are too. And I know why you aren't with your parents right now."

Her eyes went wide and she looked at her hands, only occasionally taking a bite from her muffin. Dereck looked at Black-Ball and wondered how many people's secrets he knew.

Katelyn didn't really know where she was going. She just left the living room and went up the stairs. On the eighth floor there were only two doors, one on the far right corner away from the stairs and another on the opposite corner at the left side.

She picked the left since it was closer. The door stuck and she pushed. The hinges broke and she was suddenly holding the door. Setting it aside she made a mental note to find some way to pay BlackBall back. Inside she found a large room. The floor was wood with a large square of mats in the middle. Four heavy bags hung in the corner in a tight circle, barely a man's body between them. Weapons racks lined the far wall. There were a couple of body dummies against the wall the door was on. Katelyn smiled to herself, an idea forming in her head.

CHAPTER SEVEN

...Three Months Later...

Dereck sat in the living room with the social worker. Katelyn hadn't gotten home yet and he was really hoping she would soon. They were running out of things to talk about. "So when do you think you will land your first client?"

"I've sent letters to several potential authors." he said. "I am hoping they will all agree to sign with me."

"That's good, that's good" Why letters? Surely there are better ways to contact them, more business efficient ways."

He couldn't tell if her judgment was meant as an actual question. "Um, well I thought it would be more official and inviting than an email. And more than one of them don't use computers."

She laughed. "Chose some of the more eccentric writers did you?"

He laughed with her, "Yes ma'am."

Katelyn thankfully walked in at that moment and tried to head to her room. He instantly saw the black eye she was trying to hide. "Katelyn come here." She kept going. "If you don't come here I will drag you back out of that room."

She turned and walked back into the room. He moved her chin and got a better look at the nasty looking black eye. "What happened?"

"Nothing."

"Not nothing. Nothing doesn't have you coming in here looking like you just got in a fight with Spider Ricco"

"Who?"

"Never mind. What happened?"

"I saw some kid getting bullied and I intervened."

"Who hit you?"

"Some douche. I beat the crap out of his friend and when I turned around he decked me. The kid got away clean though."

He looked at her for a moment, she averted his gaze. "What aren't you telling me?" he asked.

"I beat the crap out of the guy who hit me too."

Dereck sighed. "Are you in any trouble at school?"

"Seriously? I protected a kid and you are worried about whether or not I'm in trouble?"

"Just answer the question."

"No!" she yelled. She stormed off to her room and Dereck looked back at Shelly. "Was that bad?"

She shook her head. "Not when a kid is fifteen. I'm honestly surprised that you don't fight more often when I'm here."

Katelyn was doing her homework on the couch when BlackBall came through the window. She didn't get as surprised as she had in the beginning, but it was still disconcerting to look up and suddenly a dude was coming through the window. "Where's Dereck?"

She pointed to his room. "Having a call with a writer."

BlackBall slumped down into the couch. "I need to talk to him."

"What's going on?"

"Just some business."

"I get it. I'm still a trainee so I have to be in the dark right?"

"Pretty much."

"This is such crap," Katelyn said turning to look at him better. "I mean, how many times have you or Dereck been shot?"

BlackBall thought for a moment. "Never."

"Seriously?"

"Well Dereck and I have been shot at, but he's mostly bullet proof. And he's fast enough to move away to the point where he is bullet proof. The only time I've ever been shot was in Tibet, not while working so it doesn't count."

"Where did you get shot?"

"Left shoulder."

"How did it happen?"

"I don't want to talk about it."

As if his tone didn't shut down the discussion enough Dereck walked out of the hallway. "Oh hey, everything okay?"

"We need to talk." BlackBall said.

"I'm going to go to bed." Katelyn said walking away.

When she was gone BlackBall turned to Dereck. "I found him."

"What? How?"

"There have been several instances of pick pocketing throughout the city where someone found their money missing but there was no one around. An old woman was walking down an empty street and felt a breeze, then her purse was gone."

"That's weird, but how do you know it was him?"

"I hid several high speed cameras in the areas around where the robberies took place. The idiot robbed the same convenience store twice. So I traced him back to where he was staying."

"So do we go get him?"

"The problem is that I don't know how to catch him."

"You? Really?"

"The kid moves so fast the cameras were only just barely able to catch him. Even with you and Katelyn in the fight I don't know how to catch him. Mac is out of touch right now but he's going to call me when he can."

Dereck ran a hand through his hair. "Man, this is insane." There was a knock at the door and Dereck called out, "Come on in Juno."

Juno walked in. She was wearing a white under shirt with a flannel and jeans. Over the last little bit she had taken more to dressing like the rest of them. From what Dereck had learned of Juno he knew that she probably felt more comfortable now.

"Hey boss," she said. "Still okay that I'm here?"

BlackBall shared a knowing glance with Dereck. "Always okay that you're here Juno." Dereck said. He turned around and said, "Katelyn went to bed and he and I have to go out. So you'll have the place to yourself."

"Thanks for letting me hang out."

"No problem." Derek said and he went to get his gear on.

***

"They're gone." Came Juno's voice.

Katelyn opened the door. She was wearing her gear, ready to go out. "Thanks."

"I'm nothing if not gifted at lying to adults. Though I technically didn't lie."

"Well let's hope that they don't call. Otherwise you might have to."

Juno waved that away. "Just keep your earpiece in. I get bored and when you're not actually fighting we can talk."

Katelyn saluted. "Yes ma'am."

She left through the window. Juno told her that the guys had went to the left, so she went right. Hopping from roof to roof she made her way far enough to find crime, but enough that Dereck and BlackBall would be working somewhere else and wouldn't notice her.

She crouched on top of the roof and waited. After ten minutes of seeing nothing she pressed the side of her hood and said, "Call Juno."

"You've only been gone for twenty minutes."

"yeah well, there isn't a lot of ass to kick tonight."

"Nothing on TV either. Hey do you think BlackBall would teach me to be a ninja?"

"I doubt it, but you should ask."

"Why do you doubt it?"

"He just doesn't like normal people being in the game I think. I might be wrong, he and I don't get personal."

"What do you do?"

"He mostly just hits me until I learn a new way to not get punched."

"How's that working?"

"I have so many bruises on my chest my boobs are purple." Juno laughed. Katelyn looked over and saw a fight breaking out amongst a group of college kids, but they seemed to just be handling private business.

"Can I say something?"

"What?"

"Why do you hate your parents? I mean, can they really be that bad?"

"I'd rather not talk about that if you don't mind."

Katelyn laughed. "What?" Juno asked.

"You sound exactly like BlackBall. Maybe he will train you." She saw a figure in black following an older woman down the street. She didn't like the look of the figure. She interrupted Juno mid sentence. "I think an old lady is getting mugged. I gotta go."

"Call me when it's over."

"Will do." She hung up and stood. Getting a running start she jumped over to the roof on the opposite side of the street. She looked over the edge and saw that they had passed the building she was on, so she ran to the next one, and jumped down to the alley.

She slid up against the wall and saw the old lady pass. Katelyn went out, grabbing the figure and pulling it into the alley. It's head went back, hitting her in the nose, and then she had a gun on her again.

BlackBall had taught her how to get out of this. She swept her legs out and the figure went down. She was on top of it and saw that it was a girl not much older than her. She said nothing. Katelyn didn't see the knife.

It came up at her and she panicked. She snapped the girl's wrist and she cried out. Katelyn put her hand over the girl's mouth and she bit her. The girl recovered the gun and fired. Katelyn was instantly afraid. She shrunk back and the girl started to leave the alley. Katelyn jumped up and sped over, grabbing her from behind. "Please stop or I will have to hurt you." she said, trying to disguise her voice.

"Go to hell." She said, pressing the gun to Katelyn's leg. Katelyn panicked and pulled away, taking the girl's neck with her. The body slumped down, dead, and Katelyn stood there terrified.

CHAPTER EIGHT

"Hello?" Dereck said knocking on the office door.

"Yes, come in."

He walked into the classroom and sat in the chair on the other side of the teacher's desk. "You wanted to talk about Katelyn?"

The teacher, who he saw was named Mrs Hailey, wasn't that a first name? She was an older lady, past fifty, and she was dressed like she was seventy. She had on a floral dress with a white collar and big glasses that could have fit two or three people's eyes. "Katelyn has been very late. She often gets to class ten or fifteen minutes late. She behaves as if she doesn't ever sleep. She falls asleep in class and generally looks a bit like a zombie, glazed over appearance and big bags under her eyes."

"As far as I know she's been sleeping well and she always leaves the house before me so I have no idea why she's late."

"It's not just that Mr Marlin," She said. "Katelyn is also failing almost every class."

Dereck's eyes went wide, "Excuse me?"

Mrs Hailey handed him a piece of paper. It had Katelyn's grades from the last few months. She had Ds or Fs in every subject."Why am I only just hearing about this?"

"We sent notes home several times and they came back signed. We expected you to come in and talk about the contents of the notes but when nothing happened we assumed you had handled it internally."

"But when things didn't get better you thought to actually call until you got to me."

"Yes sir." she said nodding.

"Madam, you have my word that this will be handled."

"Good. Katelyn is a smart student. I'd hate for her to fall through the cracks."

"She won't be falling through anything so long as I'm around." He thanked Mrs Hailey once again for letting him know and he left the school, very angry.

He burst through the doors of BlackBall's house. The girl's had left a note that they would be there. "Katelyn!"

She came out of the left wing of the house, followed by BlackBall and Juno. "What's wrong?" she asked.

"You're failing all of your classes? You are walking around like a zombie, haven't been sleeping, and you're late everyday?"

"Oh, you talked to Mrs,-"

"Yes, I talked to Mrs Hailey. What the hell is going on with you?" He turned to BlackBall, "Have you been taking her out?"

"Absolutely not."

"I've been going out alone."

Both men turned to look at her. BlackBall somehow looked more angry than Dereck. "Are you fucking insane?"

He didn't know what was more shocking, that Katelyn had been going out alone, or that BlackBall had cursed. "That's why I've been late," Katelyn said. "I've been catching naps in the park."

"Why are you failing then?"

Katelyn looked down at her shoes and Dereck inhaled dramatically. "You'd better get talking before I throttle you girl."

"I killed someone and I've been having nightmares."

He felt his face soften. "We will talk about that later. Until then, you are forbidden from going out. If you go on patrol alone I will call a friend of mine and he will temporarily take your powers away."

"That's not a real thing."

"Try me then. And don't interrupt. You will have a bed-time until you get your school life in check. Training will be done only after your homework is finished. When your grades are back up and you have gone through a metric crap ton of new training, we will discuss you going back out on patrol."

"No."

"Excuse me? Did I preference that with if it pleases you? This will happen. Otherwise I will send you to live with my parents. You think I'm strict, go live there."

Katelyn shut up and BlackBall looked at everyone and said, "Why don't we work out for a while? Get everyone's stress down a bit?"

"Good idea." Dereck said.

They went to the gym and Juno held the pads while Katelyn hit. Juno took the pads off and shook her hand after the first punch. "Sorry." Katelyn said.

"Remember," BlackBall told her. "Concentrate on not using your full force. Just enough to get the job done."

The girls went back to work while Dereck sparred with BlackBall. As Dereck ducked a punch BlackBall said, "Should we tell her about the kid in the basement?"

"Not yet."

"Okay," BlackBall landed a hit on his stomach and he gasped. "Must have been hard to act all fatherly and crack the whip. But I think it will be a good thing."

"I hope so." Dereck said.

He thrust outward and caught BlackBall's shoulder. His friend staggered back. "You know we're going to have to rehabilitate the kid, or kill him."

"Can we talk about this later? I would rather not think about possibly having to kill a twelve year old boy."

"And potential super villain....."

"Seriously dude?"

"Alright alright."

So they trained. They forgot about all the things they would have to do soon. They forgot about protecting the city and the fights, both physical and internal, that they would have to get in. They trained their stress away. They would go on protecting the city. They would do what they had to do...even when it was hard.

BANDMATES

Amber has spent her life hiding behind her music, but when she's forced to step into the world, she finds herself leading a band that feels just as uncertain as she does. What starts as a desperate attempt to stay afloat grows into something louder, messier, and impossible to walk away from.

PROLOGUE

The night club was packed tonight. It was a cross between a honky-tonk and a jazz club, but they just called it, 'the club'.

Ronda looked around for another waitress, they could only afford to pay one waitress and it was her night off, but someone else was supposed to be here. Ronda took a tray of glasses to the bar. They didn't even have time to get them to the kitchen so Mark, her husband, was just sweeping them behind the counter's edge so the customers couldn't see. "Where is she?" she asked him.

"Where do you think Babe?"

She spoke as he handed her a pitcher of beer to go around and give refills to those who'd ordered them. "This shit is getting old. She has only been here a handful of times in the last year."

"I know. Tables three, eight, twelve and fifteen."

"I mean, I got it when she was still in high school, but this is beyond crap."

"I know, and we will deal with it. But for tonight, go give people their beer." With a huff, Ronda did as she was told.

Miles away, Amber was in the garage, where she had spent the majority of her time since leaving high school. She left for meals and showers, but that was it. that and when her friend Nya came over but even then they would end up in the garage. She played piano, worked on a song, practiced guitar, and she ended up crashing on the couch after her favorite I movie was over.

Ronda and Mark got out of their car, the early morning sky still gray as they walked up to the house. They stopped by the garage and saw Amber through the window, asleep on the couch, the light from the TV casting a glow on her face. Ronda huffed, she wanted to wake the little bitch up. But they were both tired, and it wasn't smart to hit your children when you were tired, they might get the jump on you. So Mark put an arm around her and they went to bed.

Amber woke up because of the banging on the door. She jerked awake and saw her mother, standing outside and look-ing like she was about to melt the door with the sheer fury in her eyes. Amber walked over and opened the door. Her Mom briefly looked like she was going to wring her neck, but all she said was, "Come with me." She turned around and walked away, Amber knew better than to stay where she was, so she followed her mother into the house.

Ronda walked in, went to the edge of the counter, and stood. Mark was making breakfast as Amber walked into the house. "Mark finish up, we need to talk."

Amber instantly grew nervous. Anytime her mother said that they needed to talk it wasn't good. Growing up with Musicians as parents, they were always very cool, but they could be strict and scary when they needed to be. Amber briefly thought she was going to get a spanking.

Mark turned around and set some eggs out of his pan onto three plates. Then he set the pan in the sink, ran some water over it and, as it steamed, turned around with his Dad face on. "Amber, why didn't you come to the club last night?"

"I got an idea f or a song and I wanted to get it down."

"And then?" Her Dad asked.

"I got tired."

"That's bullshit and you know it." Mark said in a tone that he seldom used with Amber. But even he was mad now.

"I just don't like all the people, the crowd freaks me out."

Ronda was three seconds away from strangling her child, grabbing her favorite guitar, and settling in for a life on the run, husband optional. She took a deep breath.. "Just because you don't like something, does not mean that you just get to not do it Amber., We needed help last night, what if Dad or I had had to get onstage and help out with the band? That would have left us with no one to wait tables, or no band, and either one is going to have people leaving us. We can't afford that."

"I'm really sorry mom." Amber said.

"Not sorry enough that you showed up! You haven't been to the club in weeks, Jennifer can't work every day, and I am getting really fucking tired of paying for you to sit on your ass all day in that garage."

Amber was hurt. She looked to her Father for help but he just nodded" "I'm with Mom. Sitting in that garage all day isn't healthy Amber. You need to get out, meet people, do some thing."

"But my music."

Her mother scoffed. "What good is your music if you never let anyone listen to it? You're not a musician Amber, you play instruments."

"What's the difference?"

Ronda motioned back and forth between herself and Mark. "We are musicians. We play for people, between the two of us we have played over twenty five hundred times for an audience. You sit alone all day and play for your poster of Ryan Reynolds. That's the damn difference."

Amber got off her stool and started to leave. Her mother told her to stop in a tone that brokered no argument so she turned around, pissed. "What?"

"Your Dad and I have made a decision."

Amber motioned angrily when she spoke, "And?"

Ronda squeezed her fists tight. "I'm going to hit her Mark. I swear to god I'm gonna hit her."

Mark came around the counter, he put his hands on her shoulders and gently moved her back behind him. "Amber, you have one month-"

"Three weeks!"

"Three weeks, to either join or form a band. Otherwise you will have to move out."

Amber and her father stared at each other for a while, neither sure what the other was going to say. Amber couldn't tell if they were serious. "What?" Amber asked finally.

"Find a band or we're kicking you out"" Ronda told ·hero Amber opened her mouth as if she was going to say something but her mother put up a hand to stop her. She pointed to the door, Amber turned and marched out in a huff.

CHAPTER ONE

Amber was sitting on the couch in the garage, the door up so that the summer air could come in when her best friend in the entire world pulled up.

Nya got out of the car. She was a lanky girl, she had short dark hair and pale white skin. She was wearing typical Nya attire, a dark sun dress that ended just above her knees with a leather jacket, and at the end of her mile long legs, combat boots. She had on bright red lip stick and a big black sun hat. She looked like she could be on her way to a church picnic, or to stomp somebody's face in.

Amber ran to meet her friend and wrapped her in a hug. The two of them hugged for a long time and when they broke Nya asked, "How are you baby?"

"Fine, thanks for coming over."

"No problem, it's been too long since we've hung out anyway."

"Totally, how's the new job?"

Nya took off her sunglasses and stuck them in her jacket. She walked over to the couch and layed with her legs over the back, somehow showing nothing, still looking like a lady. "I lasted three days on that job."

"Made you wear a uniform?"

Nya nodded and Amber puckered her lips, mocking sympathy. "Poor dear. Are you not hot?"

"Very, why do you ask?"

"Well I know we've been here before, but why don't you wear more summer like clothes? Maybe ditch the jacket?"

Nya waved that away. "The dress is enough. If I wore something else I would still be hot only I wouldn't look as fabulous."

Amber sighed. It was sad that that made sense. But that is what made them good friends, they got each others crazy. Nya sat up and looked at Amber. "What's so urgent? I mean I would have come over anyway but you sounded like you'd been given a terminal diagnoses."

Amber took her seat on the couch, fidgeting with her hands for almost a full minute before speaking. "My parents are making me start a band. Well, I have to start or join one in three weeks, or I'm out."

Nya jumped off the couch. She put her hand on her friend's shoulders and smiled. "And you want me to be in the band?"

"No, I wanted to know if I could move in with you,"

"No, sorry." Nya said with a disappointed look on her face, "Nan said it could only be me there, and also, your mom called me last night and said that if I agreed to let you move in, well let's just say that it was something very bad involving my rectum."

"Oh..."

"Plus, there is the other thing."

"What?" Amber asked confused.

"I want to be in a band!"

"Then you join one. I can't do that."

"Why?"

"You know how I get around people."

"Come on Amber, your parents are right. You've got to get out of this garage, Remember how much time you spent here in high school?"

"yeah," Amber said under her breath.

"And how the only time you ever really left was when I made you leave? Consider this the same thing. We're going to do this, you will be the leader, and I will be the leader's rude ass friend who refuses to let you bow out because you're scared."

Amber shrugged her shoulders, she let them fall in defeat. "Okay."

A half an hour later they were sitting on the couch, their legs touching as they faced each other. Amber had her old composition notebook out, looking over material for the band. They both went back and forth with different names. Nya had the computer on her knees trying to find the other instruments. She went down the list. "So we've got a guitarist," She said and Amber raised her hand. "Two piano players, me, and you as a back up."

"So all we need is a base player and a drummer." Amber said.

"I think I've got a few prospects." Nya said. They moved so that they were sitting correctly on the couch, scooched close together so they could both see the screen. Nya pointed to one name. "This guy has been playing for a few years," She pointed to a name farther down. "This girl won four different talent shows every year for five years, and this…"

Amber frowned. "That's not legal."

"What did he draw on that guitar?"

Amber looked closer. "That's gross."

Nya closed the computer. "So tomorrow we'll go and meet them?"

"I guess so." Nya looked at Amber with sympathy all over her face. It made Amber hate herself that she was so weak. "I'm nervous."

"Why?"

"No one has ever heard or read my songs except for you and my parents, I just….I don't know if I can do this."

Nya hugged her. "This will be great babe, I promise. And besides, you're the fuckin' boss. Just say that if you feel nervous."

"I'm the fuckin' boss."

"What's that?" She said cupping her hand to her ear.

Amber almost yelled. "I'm the fuckin' boss!"

"Yeah you are."

CHAPTER TWO

Amber was woke up from a nightmare. She wasn't entirely sure that's what it was, but it was the only thing that came to mind as she walked over to the counter in the kitchen.

The house was an old sixties house, so the kitchen and dining room were open and straight past them was the living-room. It made getting around the house a lot easier when you were still half asleep. She got herself a glass of water and splashed some on her face. She was hot and sweaty.

In her dream there had been a girl standing in the garage with hero The two of them had been kissing she thought. Amber had realized what was going on, that she was kissing a girl, and backed up, but the girl had said, "Come back." Then Amber had woken up.

She drank her water and laid her head down on the counter. It wasn't so much what had happened in the dream. Everyone had weird dirty dreams now and then. Her Mom frequently told her Dad about a dream involving some female musician or another.

What worried Amber was when the girl had said, "Come back," she'd wanted to.

Amber didn't know how long she had been leaning against the counter with her head down when Nya spoke, but it jarred her out of a thankfully dreamless sleep. "Still nervous?" Nya asked.

"Wha? yeah, a little bit,"

"It will be okay. I promise."

It occurred to Amber that she'd been leaning there for god only knew how long, but Nya had only just spoken. "How long were you watching me sleep?" she asked.

"About five minutes."

"Why?"

"I dunno." Nya shrugged. "You looked peaceful. Listen, do you wanna get on the road? We have quite a drive and I don't think I can sleep anymore."

Amber laughed at her friend's weirdness. "yeah, but you drive cause I want to try and sleep some more."

"Okay. I'm going to pee." Without another word Nya left the room. Amber walked around the counter, realizing with a bit of a shock that she had went to bed in her underwear and a tank top. She went back into the living room, not quite sure when they'd even come in here from the garage, to find her jeans. When Nya came back from the bathroom .Amber had found her jeans and thrown an ACDC T-shirt over her tank top. Nya spoke as Amber was lacing up her boots.

"See, I told you combat boots are the best form of foot wear."

"I was going to argue, but these are amazing" Amber said. They both grabbed jackets, Amber left a note for her parents and they went to the car. The sun wasn't even up yet. The sky looked the color of a bad charcoal drawling she'd done in ninth grade.

"When did we go inside? Last thing I remember was passing out in the garage." Nya said as she walked around to the driver's side.

"I have no idea, I was going to ask you the same thing."

"You know, you'd think we did drugs or something."

"My Dad says creativity is like a drug. It gives you a great high and leaves you exhausted afterwards., The only difference is that it's normally healthy."

Nya stopped, looking at her over the top of the car.. "I love that. I absolutely love that. I write songs all the time, I am very creative,-"

"And you frequently look like you've just come off a binge in the mornings." Amber finished.

They laughed and got in the car, Nya's ancient nineteen sixty four dodge dart that she had affectionately named 'Bert'. Nya had lived in him before Nan took her in, the old woman who owned most of their town. She had. even helped her parents buy the club. Amber settled into the warm leather seat as Nya started up Bert, and they drove to their first appointment.

CHAPTER THREE

Their first appointment was in a suburb somewhere in Tennessee. As they pulled up to the house they saw two boys, just a bit younger than them, standing there with a base and one of them behind a set of drums. "Did they see us coming, or have they been standing there since yesterday?" Nya asked.

Amber laughed. "Probably the second one."

They got out of the car and walked over, introducing themselves and telling the guys to start playing. Immediately they started waving for them to stop. Amber had been around music her entire life. She had helped her parents audition new bands and she had heard the good, the bad, and the very bad., These guys were awful., They played out of sync, if you could call it playing., The base player was just playing the same chord over and over again. The drummer looked like he was going to have a heart attack they way his face was getting red.

Nya was waving her arms for them to stop. "STOP! Stop ruining music for me." They stopped and Nya began, "Um...."

Amber could tell she was trying to be polite, but it was not going well. "Have you guys ever played together before?"

"Of course." said. the base player.

"In front of someone else?" Amber asked.

"No."

Amber looked at Nya, "Maybe if they played separately?"

"That could work."

"Oh no. We play together, never separately. Take us or leave us."

Nya and Amber spoke in unison. "Bye."

They left, hoping for better the next time. But the rest of the day ended up with similar results. They drove over most of South East Tennessee, but every musician they saw was a dud. The two most promising prospects turned them down when they found out Amber wasn't going to pay them.

Their last visit was to a house with a note on the garage that said to open the door. When they opened it up they saw a band wearing death metal makeup and covered in blood. They both put up their hands and walked slowly backwards to the car. They sped away and didn't slow until they were two streets away.

They were on their way home when they stopped to get something to eat at a place Nya liked. As they sat there Amber was staring into space, having only eaten half her burger. She jumped when Nya touched her arm with her cold skin. "Are you okay?"

"Yeah, I was just thinking about everything."

Nya nodded like she understood. Though Amber couldn't figure out what exactly it was she understood.

"What?" she asked.

"Oh nothing, I was just wondering why you were staring at the chick behind me's rack, but if, you were staring into space then you probably didn't even notice."

Amber suddenly felt like electricity had shot through her. She was fully awake. "No, I definitely was not staring at her. I didn't even know she was there."

Nya looked quizzically at her. 'Why so defensive?"

"I'm not."

'Okay." Nya said in the same tone that Orderlies use so as not to upset mental patients. The two of them were silent for a while until Nya slapped the table and spoke, her mouth full of burger. "Shayline!"

"What?"

"She's a friend of mine. We went to music camp together. Her family moved to Ashford a few months ago. I haven't been to see her, I've been a bit busy, but I got a letter from her a while back. I can't believe I didn't think of it."

"I'm still confused, think of what?"

"She's a kick ass base player!" Nya said after swallowing her food. She stood up, took her trash to the can, and came back to the table."Are you finished?"

"Yeah."

"Okay, you drive. I'm going to eat the rest of your burger."

They drove to Nya's place, a little apartment above Nan's store. It was just big enough for one, maybe two people, but Nya absolutely loved it. Ever since her parents kicked her out she'd been looking for a true home. Living in Bert had been okay for a while, but when Nan had taken her in, let her live here in exchange for a few hours a week work at the store, that was when she had found a home.

There was no bedroom to speak of. There was the kitchen as you walked in,with a dining room table in the middle, and a few feet in from that was the carpeted living room. There was a bathroom in the corner, just off the living room. It was just small enough for a toilet, tub and sink.

There was a closet where she kept her clothes on the same wall as the bathroom. Her favorite part was the door on the far wall, in between the couch and the fridge. It led out onto the gravel covered roof of the store. She frequently went out there to think and play her guitar.

Amber had been to her apartment before, but for some reason she looked like it was the first time. While Nya messed about looking for the letter Shay had sent her. Amber just stood there. "You know you can sit down if you like."

"I'm fine."

"Dude, why do you look like you've never been here? I know I didn't clean up my bed on the couch, but I mean come one, it's not like this place is a sty."

Amber looked shocked at her p "Oh no, I was just looking at your place...I mean it's cool. You live here, you get to do what you like, I'm jealous."

Nya was listening at the same time that she went through the top of her entertainment center she'd found on the sidewalk. She moved the VHS tapes and Records and DVDs and all the other crap. but she couldn't find the letter. She checked the coffee table where she had a bunch of papers and things, but nothing. Where was that damned letter? "Yeah, but I also have responsibility. I have to work a certain amount of hours at one job instead of rent, I have to work another job, which I still haven't found, in order to pay the rest of my bills, and I don't have parents who love me."

Before Amber could respond Nya remembered where she had been writing the other night. She wondered how she could have been so stupid, walking right past it. She went back over to the kitchen table. "Is that a typewriter?" Amber asked as Nya went through the papers that surrounded the machine. She lifted up the old Royal Aristocrat she had bought from the store downstairs.

"It's the best thing to write on when you write letters and, well if you just want to have fun writing."

"Can I try?"

Nya found the letter underneath her typewriter. She loaded two sheets of paper in and motioned for Amber to try her hand at the old machine. Amber sat at the table and started to write, Nya sat across from her and started to read the letter. Everyone thought it was weird that she liked to write letters, but all she would say is, "I like old shit."

"Me too." Amber said typing away. Nya hadn't realized she'd said that out loud. She went to her phone on the counter. She thought once again that she had been born in the wrong century as she turned the rotary dial.

"Hello?"

"Shay? It's Nya."

"This is her mother, but it's nice to hear from you."

"I'm sorry I haven't been around yet. I sent Shay a letter but I've been job hunting. You know how that goes."

"Oh don't I know it. Shay is at the park here in town. She should be there until around seven, then she'll probably get something to eat before coming home."

"Thanks so much Estelle."

"No problem sweetie."

They hung up and Nya looked over at Amber, who had now typed almost a full page She looked up and said, "I want one."

"Then we will get you one. But first we have to go meet the base player for your band." They got up, Nya locked the door, and they headed on their way.

CHAPTER FOUR

As they walked along the paved section of the park they came to a sort of intersection and saw Shay standing with her back against the brick wall that curved in either direction, It was smart. She would catch everyone as they went to different sections of the park. She was jamming away on her base, getting traffic from both directions as they threw a few dollars, some spare change, whatever they had, into her open case.

They stood several yards away, not yet in the open, still in their own lane of paved brick path. They sat on a bench at Nya's insistence and let her finish her show.

Nya had never felt an attraction to Shay, not since they became friends. But she had to admit the girl was attractive. She was Latina and had lovely caramel brown skin, a breath taking ass that stuck out in an oh-so-sexy way, and a good sized chest that made Nya's B-cup jealous for more than one reason. Follow up the amazing body with long black hair and a face that was some how sharp and angular, but soft and welcoming at the same time, and you had someone who just seemed to scream 'love me.'

Truthfully, all you needed to do was look into Shay's deep brown eyes and you would love her. Why were they just friends again? Nya shook that notion out of her head before she got any foolish notions of love that might screw up a friendship. The same notions she had decided to shake out when she was thirteen and decided her friendship with Amber meant more to her.

Amber thought the Hispanic girl looked extremely beautiful, and not in the normal way that she noticed a girl's beauty, like she actually thought that Shay was beautiful. She might have been the most beautiful girl Amber had ever seen.

When Shay saw Nya sitting on a bench with a red headed girl she decided to end her day of playing. She put her base on her back and waved the girls over.

Just as they were almost to her, Shay noticed a weird looking dude in old timey clothes walking down the path. He had a top hat on and was dressed in a way people hadn't in a really long time. Somehow though he didn't seem out of place. As he came up to her she very briefly considered asking him where he got his finger-less gloves. "Are you the same person who was playing here a few hours ago?" he asked.

"I've only been in this spot for about an hour."

"Whatever." he said waving it away like the amount of time wasn't important. "I'd like you to have this." He handed her two, one hundred dollar bills.

Shay went slack jawed. She took them from the man and looked at him like he might be fucking with her. "Are you serious? This is too much."

The man seemed genuinely confused. "Is it? Well no matter, I say just keep it. " Shay couldn't place his accent but it sounded vaguely British.

She couldn't help herself, she rushed forward and hugged him. "Thank you sir."

As she came away the man smiled. "You are most welcome." He turned to go and saw Nya and the red head standing there. "Hello Nya." he said. "I enjoyed your last letter, tell Nan I said hello."

Nya looked a bit shocked, but when she was over it she nodded., "I will. I And it's good to see you too Flink."

The two of them hugged and then he hugged the red head. She looked like she had just been assaulted and wasn't sure what to do. "Oh, sorry, you're not a hugger are you?"

"No sir." She said.

"I am terribly sorry. I am always forgetting that the custom is to ask first. Terribly sorry indeed."

"It's okay."

"Thank you." He started to walk away and then turned back, tipping his hat. "I must be going. I will see you soon I hope."

Shay and the red head girl stood watching with equally shocked looks on their faces. Nya, on the other hand, was smiling and waving. "What?" She asked upon seeing their faces. "He's a friend of mine."

They both, despite not knowing each other, seemed to come to a silent agreement not to ask. They moved right on with the introductions.

"Shay," Nya began. "This is my friend Amber. She is starting a band, and I thought of you for the basest. Amber, this is Shay, the single most gorgeous base player on the planet. She can play just about any song's base part."

"I also play Piano and Violin."

Amber extended her hand. "It's nice to meet you."

Shay shook her hand. "Likewise, what kind of sound is the band looking for?"

"Anything we want. We can go from a rock song to a country song to a punk song or whatever. I write all genres."

Shay nodded with respect. Amber seemed timid, but she also seemed a lot like Shay, laid back and not forth coming at first, but hell on high heels when you got to know her. All she needed to do was get out of her own way. Shay had had ideas about what she was going to do, but she decided right then that she wanted to take this band as far as it went. She turned to Nya. "So let me get this straight Nya, I don't see you in person for five months, and when I do you come with an offer to form a band?"

Nya smiled. "Pretty much."

"I am fuckin' in." Shay said with a laugh. "What else are we needing? I know Nya plays piano, I'm guessing you're on guitar Amber, am I right?"

"Yes ma'am."

"So what's that leave? A drummer?"

"Yep." Nya said.

"You know Wade's working at O'malley's downtown."

"Wade Dobsin?" Amber asked.,

"You know him?"

"She had a big crush on him in high school."

Amber blushed. "Can you blame me?"

"Hell no, dude's smokin' hot. Shay told her and Amber smiled.

"True." Nya said matter of factly. Shay and Amber both raised an eyebrow at her and she shrugged, "I'm gay, not blind."

Amber wrote down her address and they set up a time and date to meet. As they were walking away Shay, having locked up her base and headed to get something to eat, called out, "What about a singer? Is one of you doing it? Because I can't carry a tune."

"That would be Amber," Nya called back. "She's going to be our singer."

The look of shock on Amber's face was almost palpable from this distance. Even from where she was, several yards away, Shay could see her face get red. She said okay and went on her way, she couldn't wait to get started.

"I am?" Amber asked. They had not discussed this.

"Yes, you are." Nya said. She waved to Shay and Shay yelled goodbye.

"I am not singing."

"Yes, you area" Nya said. She turned around without another word and started back towards Bert.

Amber wasn't sure they were even allowed to be in the bar. But Nya acted like it was no big deal as they walked into O'malley's. Amber started to walk over to the bar, but back when she noticed that Nya wasn't following her. "I want you to do this one yourself." Nya said without her having to ask.

"Why?"

"Because you're the fuckin' boss."

Amber nodded. Without another word she turned around and began to walk to the bar, hoping to god that she didn't get tongue tied around Wade. He was still just as gorgeous as he had been when she had last seen him, two years ago. He had blonde hair that went to just past his shoulder and gave him a sexy viking look. He was just in jeans and a grey T-shirt and he was serving some guy his drink. The bar was mostly populated by alcoholics this time of day, and the bikers in the corner who were currently playing darts with Nya.

"Can I get you something?" Amber came back to reality and turned back to the bar to see Wade looking at her.

"Uh, no I'm fine. I actually came here to see you."

Wade smirked. "Is that so?"

"I don't know if you remember me but we actually went to the same high school."

"I know who you are Amber."

Amber could feel her face getting red. She moved a strand of hair behind her ear like she did when she was nervous. "Really?"

"Yeah, you were the cute sophomore that was always in the music room or had her head in a notebook writing."

"Yeah, that was me." Amber said smiling.

Wade put the bar rag over his shoulder and put his hands on the bar. "So what did you need?"

"I'm starting a band and I heard you're a pretty good drummer."

"I'm okay." Wade said in that way that people speak that is bragging and not bragging at the same time.

"Well would you be interested in joining a band?"

"What kind of band?"

"Still up for debate, but I'm thinking all genres because I write songs in almost every genre."

"Who all is in it?"

"Me, Nya, and a girl named Shay. She's our base player."

Wade sighed and ran his hand through his hair. Amber was worried that they weren't going to get a drummer, but she was also distracted yet again by how hot Wade was. Then she thought of her dream and got really confused. She got so caught up in what she was thinking about that she almost didn't hear Wade when he spoke. "Okay, I'm in."

"Really?" Amber asked, excited.

"Play drums in a band with a pretty girls? Hell yeah." Amber gave him her number, he said he knew where her house was, and told him when they were going to meet for their first practice. She walked back to the door and saw Nya, still playing darts. She saw Amber standing there, said something to one of the bikers, and came back over to the door.

She turned and waved at them saying, "Bye boys!" She turned to Amber, "Do we have a drummer?"

"We have a drummer."

Nya started to jump up and down, clapping. "This is going to be awesome!"

They walked out to the car and Amber handed Nya the keys. As she walked around to get in the passenger seat she asked, "Did you really make friends with those bikers?"

"Yeah, they're great. I'm going to Jimmy's wedding next Saturday." Amber stared at her incredulously until Nya said, "What?"

"How in the hell do you make friends so fast?"

CHAPTER FIVE

Nya had asked Wade to pick up Shay and bring her to Amber's. He also brought his drums. When the pickup pulled up both Amber and Nya got up from the couch and hurried over. Amber seemed to realize that she wasn't as familiar with them, because she stopped just short of the truck. Nya on the other hand, plowed right into the both of them. "Hello! Welcome to the garage. This is where we will be practicing and where Amber operates out of as Batman."

"Wouldn't I be Bat-woman, or Bat-girl?" Amber asked.

"No you would not, because Bat-woman sucks, and Bat-girl ends up paralyzed."

Shay and Wade started to walk around the garage, looking at the piano in the corner and the few guitars hanging from the ceiling and on the wall there were the more classical instruments like the violins and the saxophones. "Are you rich?" Shay asked.

Amber got that shy look of hers but Nya stopped herself. She had been doing it for so long that it was almost instinct to speak for her when she got shy. But she didn't want to do that now. Amber needed to learn how to speak up. "No," Amber said. "They collect instruments that need repair and they fix them up. Then they find a kid or student who needs one and they either give it or sell it for less than a new one. Depending on the kid's financial status."

"That's awesome." Wade said.

"Yeah, Dad also teaches piano and guitar here sometimes. Mom teaches some of the others."

"Your parents sound really cool."

"They are."Amber showed Shay her song that they were going to play while Nya helped Wade get his drum kit out of the truck" When it was set up they all got ready to play.

And they were terrible.

Shay and Nya were playing different parts, no one was in sync really. When Amber called out for them to stop she looked like she was going to cry. Nya doubted that Shay or Wade could tell, but she saw her best friend gathering her courage. She moved a strand of hair behind her right ear and took a deep breath. "Okay, let's try that again."

Ronda stood at the kitchen sink, staring at nothing, but listening to Amber's band in the garage. She looked over at Mark with a smile on her face. "They're terrible."

He laughed. "Remind you of anyone?"

"My first band."

"Mine too."

They gathered their things to head to work. When they got to the car they tried not to look at the kids out of fear that they would laugh. Ronda gave them a general thumbs up and said, "Sounds good."

When they got into the car and were backing down the drive way Mark said, "They'll get better."

The band practiced all the time. When they weren't at the garage working on something, or when one of Amber's parents needed it, they went to Nya's or Shay's. Her Dad was a musician and had a full set up.

They were all at Nya s one night, Wade watching TV while the girls were sitting at the table working on songs. "Don't you want to weigh in?" Shay yelled to Wade.

"I can weigh in from here. I'm not much of a writer."

Shay waved him away. Amber was going over her notebook and some papers from the rest of them while Nya was working at a really old typewriter that she kept on the table… or wherever she was working really.

Shay was a bit bored so she mostly stared at the other two while they worked. Over the last few weeks she had grown to like Amber quite a lot. She was much more reserved than the rest of them, which was good. Amber also had, in Shay's opinion, the most deep soul. They were all artists, but Amber had a look about her, like when most people were just thinking about random shit, she was thinking about deep stuff, like what it meant to be human, or other existential things that gave Shay a headache.

They had a good group going. Nya was the crazy chick, she would frequently do something weird just for the sake of being weird. Sometimes she would do it just to break the ice and put everyone at ease. A few days ago, when they were all struggling over a hard song that they had spent all night trying to get they had gotten pissed. Wade looked like he wanted to put a foot through his drums, Amber looked like she was going to cry, and Shay fell somewhere in between. Nya had simply lifted her top and bra and showed everyone her boobs asking, "Does this mole look funny?"

That had put them at ease quickly. Not long after they had got the song down. She was always doing stuff like that. She simply cared more for the group's well being and happiness than she did about her own self, that and Nya couldn't really be embarrassed. Shay knew some stuff about Nya s home life, or back when she'd had one, so it was no wonder that she joked and played around to keep everyone happy...she was trying to beat back the sadness and make sure that no one felt as bad as she did.

Wade was the guy. He acted like a slouch and a weirdo. He frequently made comments about stupid shit that he expected to get a rise. But Shay got the sense that he was hiding something too. Like he was playing the slouch because he didn't want them to see something in him. She had talked to the girls and they all saw it. He was a good guy despite his insistence on commenting on subjects like the way women dressed and other things that normally got a guy labeled sexist or pig.

Those comments had come to a stop when Nya whipped around and told him that while she didn't mind when a girl dressed like a slut, she preferred a girl who was more into a sun dress or something that left things to her imagination. After that Wade had settled into being one of the group and no longer trying to get a rise from them. It was also how he'd found out Nya was gay.

Shay fell somewhere in between all of them. She wasn't the happy go lucky drummer guy that Wade had turned into since he stopped being such an ass, but she also wasn't as reserved or as crazy as the other two. She was just somewhere in the middle"I want a typewriter now." she said, not realizing it was out loud.

Amber looked up from her papers, "I know right!"

The line came to an end with a bell and Nya looked up from her machine. "What?" The other two girls broke out in laughter as Nya took the paper out of the machine and handed it to Amber. While she read Nya turned to Shay. "Did you say you want a typewriter?"

"Yeah, that thing is awesome."

"Well why don't we buy one for the both of you tomorrow? I mean, you both go shopping and get one, not like one for you to share."

"Where did you buy yours?"

"Downstairs, Nan has a whole section of them in the far left corner of the store."

"Wow, we can go tomorrow?"

"Absolutely."

"Holy shit." Amber said. They both looked over at her and she looked up at Shay. "You have to read this." She handed Shay the paper. She got lost for a minute in the typed words. Shay saw the impression it made from biting into the paper, she ran her hand over it and wanted one even more. Finally she read the song.

It was the best song they had. It was like Nya had opened up an emotional vain and let it leak onto the page. Shay almost cried as she read the lyrics. It was the story of a girl who told someone a secret, but that person, who she thought she could trust, that she thought loved her, they betrayed her. As Shay read the song she started to choke up. She turned around and called, "Wade, come read this." He walked over, still paying more attention to the TV than to anything else, but he picked up the paper. Wade looked down at the paper, she could see his eyes rolling over the page. After a while he looked up and said, "Holy shit."

Nya looked briefly embarrassed, which was not an emotion one associated with Nya. "Well I'm glad you like it."

"We absolutely have to learn this song." Wade said.

"As band leader I declare we are going to learn this kick ass song." Amber said. Wade leaned over the table and presented a large hand to Amber. They high-fived and Wade went back to the TV.

The following Friday, after eating a lot of pizza with everyone's parents, the band was playing for their first audience. Amber couldn't tell, since she was by no means an impartial observer, but she thought that they sounded pretty damned good. Nya's parents were the only ones not present. Even Wade's parents had come, though they admitted that they were not very into music.

As the song ended, Nya's song, the parents were all clapping and hollering about how great they sounded. Amber's Dad had his arms around her Mom's waist and Amber could not remember the last time she had seen him look this proud. "You kids are pretty good." Shay's Dad said.

Nya did a very theatrical bow and said, "Thank you."

Amber's Dad checked his watch and the two of them got up. "Ronda and I have to get going, but you kids should really consider signing up for the battle of the bands that we are having at the club at the end of next month."

"You really think we're good enough?" Amber asked.

"I think so." Ronda said. This was followed by echoes from the other parents. Amber looked at her band mates and they came to a silent agreement, something they had gotten a lot better at over the last few weeks.

"We'll think about it." Amber said."In the meantime, practice is over and I am going to go with you guys."

"How come?" Her Dad asked.

"You could use the help, and I could use the tips."

Nya stepped behind Amber, putting her arm around her. "We'll be right behind you."

Mark smiled, "Okay then."

Her parents went to their car and drove off towards the club. Amber and Nya started to get their stuff ready so they could follow after them, when Shay looked at her parents. "I'll see you guys later. I'm going with them."

"Me too." Wade said. Though it was less important because he didn't live with his parents. He told them he would be there for dinner on Sunday and they went home.

"You guys really don't have to come help." Amber said.

Wade waved that away. "What are band mates for?"

Amber couldn't help but smile as they all piled into Bert and headed off to the club.

Nya brought her fifth tray back to the bar and told Wade the drink orders. While he set to making them she took a small break. They were only three hours in, yet the club was packed. Amber's parents were onstage because the band had shown up down two players, so they had ended up needing everyone.

"So why are they up there?" Wade asked.

"They fill in whenever a band is down a player or two. Hasn't anyone told you that?"

"I've been trying to ask for three hours but everyone has been too busy. This is like the fourteenth rum and coke I've made in the last five minutes. Can this building even fit this many people?"

"How the hell should I know." Nya shrugged.

"They should clear out a bit in a while. After three it's normally just the chill people."

So they worked the rest of the night and into the morning. Drunk people tipped very well. Nya made fifty three dollars. She tried to give it up but Mark and Ronda insisted that every one keep whatever tips they got.

Around five O'clock in the morning everyone was sitting around the now empty club. Nya was laying on the floor and Amber was at a table with her head in her arms. "So...tired..." Nya groaned.

"I haven't worked that hard for that long in...ever." Amber said.

Mark and Ronda were at the bar doing the books with a drink in front of both of them. They laughed. "Amber used to be an old pro but she hasn't been around in a while." Mark said.

Amber groaned without lifting her head, so when she spoke it was a bit muffled. "Feet Hurt."

Her parents laughed again and Mark said, "It's almost five thirty and I need some sleep. Let's go everybody."

They slowly made their way to the door. Just as they were leaving Shay turned back and yelled, "WADE!"

He popped up from behind the bar, looking exhausted."C omin'."

CHAPTER SIX

The four of them were standing in an alley, waiting for the guy to tell them it was time to go on. They had all decided that they needed to preform in front of someone, a real crowd, away from home. So before committing to battle of the bands, they had driven three hours to a town in Alabama that no one could remember the name of.

They had scoured a three show spot for a guy who was opening a club similar to Amber's parents' place, though not nearly as classy. Shay, Wade, and Amber were all pacing and looking like they were going to vomit, and there was already enough vomit in the alley. The door to the club opened and a guy wearing a black T-shirt said, "Five minutes guys." He gave the others a look and looked at Nya."Are they going to be okay?"

"They're fine."

The guy shook his head like he wasn't sure. He went back inside and Nya looked at her nervous band mates. "I hope."

The performance went horrible in every sense of the word. Nya was so focused on the others that she knocked over her keyboard, which got a big laugh and almost got her landing on some drunk guy. But she decided not to beat the hell out of him. Amber got scared and ended up sounding like one of the chipettes had a head cold. Wade lost control of his sticks and threw them into the crowd, where they hit the drunk guy who'd yelled at Nya. And Shay...she seemed to forget where she was. She went catatonic until Nya finally got her to play. Then she played the wrong song from the rest of them...it was just awful. They drove home in silence. All to sick to eat. They just didn't talk.

The second gig only went slightly better. The owner didn't even want them to come back for the last one, but Nya told him that she would sue for breach of contract if he didn't give them the third shot...and she offered to pay back his three hundred bucks if they sucked the next time.

They crashed at Nya's after the second performance because they ended up getting home pretty late and didn't want to wake up all of their families. As they walked into the apartment Nya said, "Well that went horrible."

"Yeah," Wade said sitting down at the kitchen table and rubbing his face with both hands. "Two gigs in two weeks, and we fucked them both."

"We are so good in rehearsal.," Shay said. 'I don't get why we can't get our shit together in front of a crowd."

They all looked over at Amber, who was slumped down on the floor in the corner of the kitchen. She was crying as they all looked over at her. She raised her head out of her hands and just looked into space, crying even harder. "What's wrong?" Nya asked.

"I can't play in front of people. I've screwed up this band before we even really did anything. I'm done. I'm sorry you guys."

Shay and Wade leaned back, they seemed resigned to their fates, but Nya did what she did best. She got good and pissed off. "Okay." She said looking at Amber."I don't know if you've noticed sweet heart, but none of us have done good playing in front of people. Wade assaulted a member of the damn audience and Shay went catatonic." She looked at all of them. "How can you guys be ready to quit?"

"Maybe she's right Nya. Maybe we just can't play together."
"Yeah." Wade said.

"Yeah? Great response." Nya started to pace, thinking. She paced for a couple of minutes, the rest of them watching her while she did. Finally she stopped and looked at them."Just play the final gig. If it doesn't go well then we will not even sign up for the battle of the bands, and we will stop trying to make the band a thing. I won't even complain."

"And if I refuse?" Amber sobbed out.

"We've been friends since the first grade, I think you know how annoying I can be when I want too"

Amber sniffed and smiled. "Okay, I'm in."

Nya turned to the others. "Well, what say you?"

"I'm in." They said in unison.

Nya slumped down into a kitchen chair. She sighed and looked at everyone, "We need to practice."

The next Friday they were all backstage waiting for the performance that would determine the future of their band o Amber felt nervous, like she might throw up. Nya came over to calm her down. Behind her, Amber could see Shay and Wade jumping up and down, getting pumped.

"It's okay, you're going to do great." Nya said.

"How do you handle it? You haven't broken at a single gig. And you only knocked over your keyboard once."

"It's easy. I just find a beautiful girl in the audience and I pretend that I'm playing for her."

"Huh?"

"Not important." She said shaking her head. "Just pretend you're singing in the garage, no one around. If you have to, close your eyes. People will just think you're emotional or really into the music. They eat that crap up."

A stage hand came over to them and said, "Two minutes. Take the stage."

Amber stood there, unable to move, until she felt a hand on her back and a shove onstage. The crowd started laughing, seeing them come onstage for the third time. Someone yelled, "You suck! Get a life."

Amber heard Nya's voice come over the microphone. "You come to the same club every Friday, get a girlfriend."

The room filled with laughter, Amber scanned the crowd and she caught sight of a girl that looked a lot like the one from her dream. She instantly clamped her eyes shut and as the others started to play, she struck her guitar and started to sing.

And they didn't suck. They played their whole set perfectly. They got the crowd to like them to the point that when they were going off someone yelled, asking their name and Amber realized that they had never actually chosen one. So she yelled out, "Thank you! We are Nashville Panic!"

They filed off the stage and they erupted into cheers as they made their way back to the car. As they were packing their stuff into Bert's trunk, Amber said, "We did it!"

"So..." Nya began, "Battle of the bands?"

Wade and Shay nodded. Amber looked at Nya and said, "Battle of the bands."

CHAPTER SEVEN

The night of the battle of the bands they were amazing. It was the best performance they had given yet. They played three songs, the last of which was Nya's. The three judges, each from one of the organizations or businesses that had agreed to sponsor and donate the prizes, were sitting at the front of the stage. And one of them had tears in her eyes at the end of the band's set.

They filed off the stage while the last band set up. They all held hands, intensely worried about what was going to come. They had made the agreement to not be upset or go into it worried, to just let what happened happen. None of them, however, was sticking to that agreement. Wade looked ready to pass out, his face was as white as a ghost.

At the end of the other band's set, they came back stage. Their band had one more member than Nashville Panic did, and they were a lot better. "You guys did so good." Shay said to them.

"Thanks. I hope we win," said their lead singer, a nice looking guy with brown hair. "But if we don't, you guys are so good that I wouldn't mind losing to you."

Shay smiled. She started to say something, but everyone turned to the stage, where Ronda was at the mic ready to announce the verdict. She thanked the sponsors, and then she said, "The winner of first prize is.....Twenty Wolves!' The other band rushed out onto the stage and started to thank everyone. When they filed off, Ronda continued. "Winner of second prize and ten thousand dollars is...Nashville Panic!"

They were stunned. Neither Amber nor Wade looked like they heard anything. Like always, Nya was the first person to react. She pushed everyone onstage and they graciously accepted the award. Then they filed off stage and went to sit near the bar .. Wade missed his chair and ended up on the floor, where he just sat. Behind the band, Ronda was still announcing the third and fourth place winners, but the band just sat there, stunned.

They all stayed there for the next three hours with very little conversing taking place. The club emptied out mostly after the competition was over, but the regulars were still there until closing time. Mark brought over a tray of drinks for the band while Ronda brought some for everyone's parents.

"The club is closed," Mark said. "So technically I am not serving minors. However, if anyone tells I will deny it." Everyone laughed. They did a cheers and toasted the group's victory. Amber coughed at the taste of scotch, it was never something she liked.

"I would have thought you'd be a better drinker with your parents." Wade said.

"We've never been big on drinking." Ronda said. "We didn't hit her for it, hell Mark let her try beer when she was like ten, but we never encouraged it."

"That's a cool attitude." Shay's Mom said.

"Yeah," Mark said. "we didn't want Amber to grow up not knowing anything about alcohol, that's when kids go crazy. They don't anything and then they don't drink responsibly. So we just acted like it was no big deal and let her figure out what she liked and didn't."

"That's what we did with Shay." Her Dad said. "She can have a beer or something, and she knows how to do it responsibly."

"Well I hate scotch." Amber said. "It's vile."

Ronda coughed in that way that signals that the conversation is going nowhere and that she is going to start talking about something else. She said, "So what are you kids going to do with your money?"

The band looked at each other, realizing that they probably should have been discussing that in the three hours that they sat there in shock. "What do you guys think?" Shay asked.

"My band won something like this, though not as much money, but we used ours to tour." Shay's Dad said.

"But we didn't win," Nya said. "Do you really think we' re good enough to tour?"

Mark laughed. "I've toured and made a decent living but none of my bands ever won a single battle or contest in first place. " He looked at Shay' s dad. "How about you?"

"Nope."

"Not a one." Ronda said. "But I've ended up with a pretty damn good life. Something I might not have had otherwise."

Shay's Dad nodded. "Me too." he said taking a sip of his drink. "My buddy was in a band that won first in every contest they entered. He ended up OD-ING."

Shay looked at the others. "Maybe we should tour for a while."

"I'm in." Wade said. He looked at his parents and they said they thought it was a great idea.

Amber and Nya looked at each other and, in unison, said "Hell yes, let's do it!"

Shay's Dad still had the RV that his old band toured in, a nineteen sixty something or other. There was a nice bathroom that had a large shower and a sink and toilet, it was only a little bit smaller than the one in Nya's apartment.

There was a bedroom in the back that Amber's mom fitted with fresh sheets and it had enough storage compartments that everyone could fit three weeks of clothes in it. That left the closet across from the bathroom for instruments and jackets and hanging up things, most of which were Nya's.

There was a fully functioning kitchen in the RV. They stocked it full of food and things they would need. There was a kitchen table with booth seats and Shay's Dad and his band had taken out a row of cabinets and put in a couch just behind the driver's seat.

The band came up with a few rules for living in the RV with each other.

1.No pooping in the RV. Let someone know they would pull over. They had to empty their own toilet and no one wanted to deal with that.

2.No sex in the bed. They were going to be taking turns sleeping in the bed and if anyone got a groupie or met someone, take them somewhere else.

3.If you eat Nya's cocoa puffs, she will knife you.

4.Respect everyone's possessions. Don't take someone else's shit without asking.

Shay's Dad checked the engine for the twentieth time as they were preparing to leave. Amber said goodbye to her parents, promising to call often. "Be careful." her Dad said.

"I will be."

"We are proud of you kiddo." Ronda said as she wrapped both Amber and Mark in a hug.

Over at the engine, Shay touched her Dad's arm as he was bent over the engine. "It's good Dad. If you check it anymore I think the motor is going to give out just so you will have some thing to do."

He stood up and hugged her. "I love you Mija. I just want you to be safe."

"I will be." Shay told him. "I promise." She hugged her Mom and Dad again and she got into the RV before it got too hard to leave.

Ronda and Mark walked over to Wade and Nya. Wade's parents couldn't come to say goodbye, so he didn't have anyone. Ronda and Mark hugged Nya asking her to be careful. "If you don't be careful I will-"

"Yeah yeah," Nya said with a smile, finishing her sentence. "The thing with my rectum."

"You're just as much our girl as Amber," Mark told her. "So be safe and we love you."

Nya wiped a tear from her eye and spoke softly as she turned to get into the RV. "I love you guys too."

They turned to Wade, who looked concerned. "Is she okay?"

"Nya hasn't had the easiest life, she's not real used to people showing their love for her." Mark said. He stuck his hand out to Wade. "You be careful too, and watch out for them."

"I will." Wade said. He was caught off guard by Ronda's hug.

"And make sure they watch out for you." She said, kissing him on the cheek.

"Yes ma'am." Wade said and he got into the RV. He was to drive first so he could see all of them waving in the rear view mirror as they pulled away.

CHAPTER EIGHT

The band had been on the road for almost three months. They did all kinds of gigs. Sometimes they would just pull into a parking lot and talk to the manager of whatever business it was, and they would put on a concert a few hours later, splitting admission with the manager. They always sent in Nya. She got more yeses than nos.

Ronda would call them often and tell them she had a gig for them in whatever state, and they would have to be there by a certain time. The record was Florida to Washington in thirty hours. They only stopped for gas and they made that quick. When Wade, who had started the trip, got tired, they didn't even stop the RV to switch drivers. They slowed down just a little and Shay went under him and slipped into place as he slipped out and went back to the bed.

Sometimes they would park at a camp ground for a while. The longest was a whole week. They would just chill. They had a tiny TV, the kind that had a VCR built in, and they would stop at a Goodwill or something and just buy a bunch of movies. They set it up on the picnic table and they would just relax. Go hiking, roast hot dogs, whatever they wanted.

And they wrote.

They were constantly writing new songs. Nya had brought along her typewriter, as had the other girls, but they were all portables so they tended to move along with the road. Nya had a close call with a pot hole and her machine had almost went off the table. So Shay, who had done four years of wood shop along with numerous projects with her Dad, stopped at a home depot and bought the supplies, and she put a stand between the couch and the counter that was bolted into the motor home. Then they stopped at a store that still sold typewriters, which they had to be dragged out of by Wade, and they bought a Royal KMM machine. Shay used some extra long screws so that they hooked the feet into the machine and the machine was bolted into the RV, so when the home was moving there would be one person composing at the typewriter, and one or two at the table or on the couch writing into a notebook. By the end of their second month, they had a binder of nearly one hundred songs.

Nya had asked them, as they went into the third month on the road, if they liked the transient lifestyle they had. She loved it, living basically on the fringes of society, only going back in to play music, but she was worried about her friends.

"I enjoy it. " Amber had said. "You know I don't like a lot of people so spending all of my time around the ones I do is great with me."

"Same here." Wade told her. "I pretty much lived like this before, the only difference was I lived in one place. Now I get to travel."

They all looked to Shay, who had her feet up on a picnic table looking calm and collected. "I'm good."

They were playing a gig in a tiny town outside of Vegas. They had kicked ass in the show. They had played almost exclusively new songs, something the crowd didn't notice but that caused them a great deal of stress. Pulling it off made them feel elated. As they exited the club Nya shouted into the cold night air. "That was fucking awesome!"

"Hell yeah?" Wade said and the two of them high-fived.

Shay and Amber high-fived and Amber started to count their money as they walked to the RV. As they approached the RV they saw a guy in a suit standing near the door looking down at his phone. He looked up as they approached and they assumed their positions. Nya and Wade parted to let Amber greet the man and Shay came around the side to make it look like Amber had a lot of protection, which she appreciated. "Can I help you?" she asked the man.

The man reached into his pocket and brought out a business card. He handed it to Amber. "My name is James and I represent Swaim records. I have been monitoring your band over the last year that you have been on tour, and I want to sign you."

Amber's eyes went back and forth between the card and James. "Holy shit...holy shit. Sorry I just...holy shit."

James smiled. "That's okay. I take it you're interested?"

"Um, I have to..." She turned around and saw the others, all looking just as shocked as she was.

"We're interested." They said in unison.

James nodded and handed them all business cards, as if it wasn't okay for just one of them to know who he was. They all had to know. "I've got to get some things together," he said. "but do you think you can be in LA in say...two weeks?"

"Yes sir. We have a gig in Portland and then we will be there." Amber said. James shook everyone's hand and walked away. They waited until he walked around the corner to erupt in squeals of delight.

Days later, after their gig in Portland, they were parked at a rest area. Nya was sleeping on the bed, and since she was a kicker, Shay was on the couch and Wade was laying on a pallet on the floor.

Amber couldn't sleep so she left the RV and went over to a picnic table and she called her mom. She explained everything and her mom said, "It sounds amazing."

"I know right." she said flatly.

"Then why do you sound upset?"

Amber ran her hand over her face and then through her hair. She had a bad feeling but she couldn't place why. "I don't know." She told her mother.

"What does the band think?"

"They're excited."

There was a long pause before Ronda spoke on the other end of the phone. "It sounds like you're a bit scared sweetie. I know I would be."

"So you're saying I should just get over it."

"I think you need to do what your heart tells you."

Amber sighed. "I hate when you say that."

"I know." Ronda said and Amber could hear the smirk she was making over the phone.

"Love you Mom."

"Love you too."

Amber hung up the phone and sighed.

CHAPTER NINE

Nya and Shay were locked in the bedroom with Amber sitting on the bed. They weren't so much locked in as their clothes were everywhere and they couldn't get out easily.

They were trying to decide what to wear to the studio meeting. Nya put on a black shirt with puffed sleeves and a frilly bit on the chest. She turned to the others and asked, "What do you think?"

"I think it would look better on me." Shay said. "You don't really have the chest for it."

Nya looked down at her breasts. She sighed. "Yeah, you're right."

She took off the shirt and handed it to Shay, who unbuttoned her shirt and tried on the top. After a moment she took it off. "No, it feels weird." She took it off and threw it on the ever growing pile of clothes they didn't want to wear

Amber, who was some sort of freak of nature in Nya's opinion, had found what she wanted to wear in the first few minutes, and was now sitting on the bed looking over some papers and only half paying attention to the other two.

She and Shay were standing there, in their bras, looking for something to wear, when Amber looked up for the first time in several minutes. Her eyes went wide and she started to get up. "Where are you going?" Nya asked.

"Wade needs help." She said without looking at her.

She threw the door open, almost breaking it off as she pushed it against the pile of clothes. Nya looked at Shay and back at the door. Could Amber...no, she wasn't...Nya put that out of her head. "I am so jealous of you." Nya said.

"Why?"

"Look at your boobs." She said motioning to them with both hands."You're super hot. I look like a twelve year old."

Shay cocked her head sideways, examining Nya. "Nah, you're good."

"Please, B stands for barely there."

"And D stands for Damn I wish my back would stop hurting."

Nya thought about that for a moment. "Fair enough." she said.

They eventually settled on clothes that still made them look like musicians, but didn't reveal the fact that they hadn't been to a laundry matte in several weeks.

As they stood outside of the tall sky scraper looking up at the sunlit windows, they all looked scared. Nya didn't know for sure, but she knew she felt scared. And she hoped they did too. "Should we go in?" she asked.

"I think we should stare at it a while longer." Wade suggested.

"I'm scared." Amber said.

"Me too." echoed Shay.

Nya and Wade spoke in unison. "Me too."

Never taking her eyes off the building, Amber said, "Together."

"Together." They echoed. They joined hands and walked inside.

As they walked into the lobby they saw a woman in a pants suit walking up to meet them. She had her hair tied in a nice bun and she looked like there was a fair chance that they would be taken into a room and murdered by her. She shifted her portfolio to the other arm and extended a hand to greet them. Amber stepped forward and shook her hand. "Hi, I'm-."

"Yes, yes I know who you all are. I have been instructed to take you to conference room B."

Without another word she turned and walked away towards a bank of elevators. Amber turned around to say something but was cut off again, this time by Nya. "I think she's going to leave us." They hurried after her, catching up just in time to make it inside the elevator.

The woman in the pants suit was utterly unmoved by the records on the wall and the posters from famous musicians. But the band were all staring at them as they walked down the wood paneled hallway. The woman was several yards away, waiting at a door. "Come on guys." She said.

They quickly overcame their awe and walked down the hall and into the room. There was a long table running down the middle of the room, an impossibly long table. At the other end sat James, the man from the alley, and on either side of him sat another woman in a pants suit, and a guy in a suit identical to James'.

They all took seats a little ways down from the group. That way they weren't too close, but they could still hear. "Glad you could join us." The alley dude, James, said. "This is woman is Laurie, our attorney. The gentleman to my right is Mark. He manages the acts that we sign. He'll be booking venues, covering the tours, basically anything you need."

Amber waved. "Hello everyone."

"Hi." Shay said.

"Hello." Echoed Wade.

Nya held up a peace sign. "Sup."

"This meeting is a straight forward contract signing. Laurie will get them for you, Laurie."

She picked up a large stack of paper and handed a huge bundle to each of them. Wade had his mouth hanging open while the girls were looking at them. They knew it was not a good idea to sign before going over each and every word, but after looking at a few pages their heads were swimming and they all signed the contracts."Wonderful. Now Alesha will get you to your apartment and make sure you are taken care of." James said.

They all shook hands with everyone and the executives left the room. The band was left alone in the giant room. Nya looked around at her friends and asked, "What the fuck just happened?" None of them had an answer. The first woman, who they now knew was Alesha, came in and ushered them all to the lobby and told them to follow her in a black car that had parked in front of the RV.

They followed the car, not really used to LA traffic they almost got lost a bunch of times, but they eventually pulled up in front of an apartment building. They got out holding all the bags and gear they could carry. Alesha motioned towards the RV with a dismissive hand. "Give Johnny your keys and he will take care of that...thing."

Shay handed over the keys, "Careful it's not ours."

"Oh he's only going to park it in our garage. It will be there when you want it."

Alesha turned and walked into the building. As they moved to follow her Shay asked, "How the hell does she move so fast in heels?"

Nya laughed. "I don't know but that bitch needs to slow down before I throw my bag at her."

The apartment was very large, the living room and kitchen area was the same basic open floor plan as Nya' s apartment back home. The only difference being that the one they were standing in was three times the size of Nya's entire place. That did not include the other rooms they hadn't seen yet.

There was a large TV and a big leather sofa and a love seat that was still big enough to fit all four of them on the other side, blocking in the TV and living area in it's own square of space. Across from the door was an entire band set up. New instruments for everyone. The band stood by the door, no one really knowing what to do. Alesha set a bunch of keys on the counter and said, "Here are all of your keys. There is a pool on the roof, a gym on the third floor, and...I guess that's it. Bye." She scurried out of the room, shutting the door behind her.

"Bye..." Amber said.

Amber stayed by the door, not quite sure what to make of this place. Wade and Shay walked around gingerly while Nya threw her bag down and went over the side of the couch, leaving only her feet visible. She kicked off her shoes and spoke. "Apparently this is our apartment now." She said. "So why don't you all stop acting like we're burglars and go explore. Find out where everyone is sleeping, raid the fridge, on second thought," She flipped over the couch and walked around, headed for the kitchen. "I'll raid the fridge."

Amber saw Wade and Shay disappear into separate parts of the apartment and she became a bit more comfortable. They had been on the road a long time, it might be nice to have a regular home. Though she still felt unsure.

From the fridge Nya yelled to the house, "There's nothing in here but pizza and beer...who the hell puts hot pizza in the fridge? I mean come the hell on people!"

Wade and Shay came back from opposite ends of the apartment."Two bedrooms and a bathroom on this side." Shay said.

"Same over here."

Nya came from the kitchen, sitting on the counter with a slice of pizza in her mouth. "Then Amber and I will take that side." She took another bite and spoke while chewing. "And you and Wade can take those." She pointed in the direction Wade came from.

"And why do you get to decide?" Wade asked.

"Because," Nya said hopping down and standing in front of Wade. The two of them looking like prisoners about to have a yard fight. "I have spent a year smelling the two of you fart in your sleep and shout about different things. Now that we have a bit more privacy, you two can share the gassy end of the apartment."

Shay walked over and got a piece of pizza. "Do I really fart in my sleep?"

"And you say your sex dreams out loud...like really loud. " Amber said walking over for some pizza.

Shay shrugged. "I knew that one."

CHAPTER TEN

Shay thought that she might barf. She was looking at the crowd, and they were…well there was just so many of them. The amount of people packed into the Arena was equal to the last seventy five shows they had played on the road.

That night they were set to open for some big artist they had never heard of, one of those tweenie-bopping chicks that bounced around the stage a lot while a generic band that she probably didn't even know the names of played the actual music and she sang pop songs that were identical to every single other pop song.

They were set to go out in a few minutes and it terrified her. She had grown used to playing in front of crowds, but this was the size of a town. There were literal towns in America who's populations would fit inside this arena several times.

There was some weight lifted though, they were new. These people were here for the poppy girl and that meant that even if they sucked, they weren't the main event.

The manager guy had them opening for this chick several times over the next few weeks. He said that piggy backing off of her was a great way to get a fan base of their own.'Two minutes." A stage guy told them.

The band gathered together, they all looked nervous. Shay was thankful for that...she wasn't alone. "First major show." Amber said.

"Ten thousand people." Nya said.

"I think I peed a little just now." Shay told them.

"Me too." Wade said.

They played a kick ass show. They did five songs. They were only supposed to do three but they got the signal to keep going because the teeny bopper was running a bit late. "Thank you! We are Nashville Panic!" Amber called out as they filed off the stage. The singer they were opening for met them as they came off.

"Great job guys, you rocked out there."

"Thank you." Nya said. The rest of them echoed their thanks. The singer, Shay really needed to learn her name, went out on stage and they heard her say that they were great and she had. the audience give them another round of applause. That was nice, getting some praise for another act from her audience.

The crowd cheered and Shay's heart felt warm. She wasn't sure if she'd ever heard anything so beautiful as a crowd cheering for her and her band. They opened for that same singer, and a few others, over the next several weeks. And not just in LA, though that is where most of them were. They flew them out to Chicago, New York, and Atlanta for some strange reason.

The group had grown up in small towns their entire lives. They marveled at the big cities they went to, but they didn't understand it. These people could afford all kinds of things, their apartment building had a pool bigger than the one in their home town open to the public, but they hadn't the time to use them. It was like everyone in these cities was so obsessed with making money, and showing off what money they did have that they didn't stop to enjoy what they had worked for. And that was not something any of the members of Nashville Panic were used to. They liked to work for something and then enjoy that something. They loved hard work, but the people they were around now, they only seemed to like hard work if it meant someone else working hard and them running around acting like it.

They were back stage one night after a show, what was supposed to be their last opening show for someone else, when Nya, laying on the greenroom couch, asked Amber, "Is it just me or is this going out and meeting famous people at parties thing getting really fucking old?"

"Yeah, it's like no one ever stops. They're like sharks." The two of them were silent for a while before Amber asked, "Where is Shay? And Wade for that matter""

"Wade," Nya answered, "is with some scantily clad bimbo in one of the other dressing rooms. Shay went...somewhere."

Before anyone could say anything else one of the guys from the record label came into the room without knocking. "Dude, I could have been naked!." Nya said.

"Why would you have been naked?"

"I dunno." She shrugged and motioned for him to continue.

"Anyway,' he said eyeing Nya, "You guys are going on tour again."

"But you said that we needed to cultivate a fan base first." Amber said.

"Yes, but we did not expect you to blow up like you have online. You have millions of hits on every videos, and we set up several social media accounts for you that all have millions, or at least a few hundred thousand, followers. We have decided it would be good for you to go on tour again."

Wade walked into the room and Nya gave an overly dramatic sigh" "Does no one knock?"

The man explained to Wade that they would be going back on tour and he looked excited. But the real excitement came when the man said that they would be on a much larger buss and that Wade would not have to drive, and that there would be groupies. "That's awesome man." Wade said. "Has anyone told Shay?"

Shay was in the bathroom of the stadium. The backstage one reserved for talent. She had a bag of the stuff that one of the main act's drummers had given her, but she wasn't sure if she wanted to try it. The guy said that it was a fun time, and that it was a sure fire way to stay up late. Shay needed to stay up. These people had her up until three or four in the morning playing shows, and back up at five or six for a radio interview or rehearsals, or some sort of stupid ass meeting.

She hadn't had a proper rest in weeks. The last time she had talked to her father, he warned her once again about his brother, her Uncle. He had died of an overdose when he was twenty three. There was a history of addiction in their family. That was part of the reason her parents had stressed teaching her that drinking was no big deal, so she wouldn't drink in secret and end up like so many of her family members.

Shay sat on the closed toilet and she actually felt herself falling asleep. She jerked awake and she emptied the bag onto the toilet paper dispenser. She packed the grass like substance into one of the little papers that was in the baggy. She licked the edge and rolled it up, some of it fell out but it looked okay. She took the match book and lit the joint.

She breathed in the smoke and her lungs felt like they were on fire. She coughed loudly. When the burning subsided a bit she felt light headed. Then, after smoking a bit more, she felt electricity moving through her fingers. She felt like she could run a marathon.

She smoked in the bathroom stall until her fingers started to get singed. Then she dropped it in the toilet and ran towards the bathroom door. "I can't let them know I'm high." She thought to herself and started to walk very slow. She noticed that the walls of the stadium looked enormous. She felt like she was a fish that was born in a bowl but was suddenly swimming in the ocean. She saw the band corning towards her, and she stopped, her eyes wide.

"Are you okay?" Wade asked, his eyebrows raised.

"Good. I am good. How are you?" He looked at her like she had three heads and he shared a look with Nya.

Nya stepped forward and touched her arm. "Why don't we go get you something to it eat? I suspect that you'll be needing it fairly soon."

Shay nodded and started to jump up and down in excitement. She let Nya lead her in the direction they had came, towards the green room where there was pizza.

Amber looked at Wade. "What the hell is wrong with her?"

"She's high." Wade said.

Amber looked towards where they had went, shocked. He guessed that she had never been around drugs. "Seriously? Why?"

Wade shrugged. "How the hell should I know, I don't even know where she would have gotten it. But yeah, she was high dude."

The two of them started to walk back to the green room at a slower pace so that Nya would have time to get Shay some food and get her in a car headed home. "Have you really never seen someone high?" Wade asked.

"No," Amber told him shaking her head. "My parents told me stories of people they knew who had let drugs ruin their lives and how they didn't want that to happen to themselves or me. My Dad told me he tried pot once and he hated it. Mom said she did it a few times before deciding she hated who she was on it. After that I never had any interest in even trying it."

Wade nodded. He respected that. He had gotten high in high school before coming to a similar conclusion as Amber's parents.

"Wade," Amber said, shocking him out of his memories. "Can I tell you something?"

"Yeah."

"I don't like what this is doing to us."

Wade looked at her and saw the sadness in her eyes, the fear that this deal would tear them all apart. She wasn't the only one afraid. "Me neither Amber." he said. "Me neither."

CHAPTER ELEVEN

The tour only made things worse. They went everywhere from Alaska to Hawaii. The managers were talking about an international tour in a year or two, but Amber didn't know if the band would be around then.

Wade had become i quite the ladies man and a regular jackass. It wasn't like when they had all first gotten together and he had tried to be a joker. Those jokes hadn't been funny, but they had also been harmless and no one was upset. They told Wade to stop being an ass and he just did, quickly becoming a part of the group and finding his place.

But over the last six months that they had went on tour and came back to LA, Amber was the only one who hadn't lost her mind. Now Wade thought his shit didn't stink, there was an almost constant stream of girls, each one skankier and more poxen looking that the last, coming to and from the apartment, He regularly missed rehearsals and was over all just a pain to live with.

Nya was being slammed by anti gay people, and had been ever since she'd let it slip that she was gay in a radio interview in Chicago. She hadn't been hiding it but she also wasn't advertising. There were thousands of social media posts about it and an endless stream of articles from various sites pretending to be news. Nya had become obsessed with the people that hated her. It didn't matter how many of them loved her, she was just concerned with the people picketing outside signings and concerts. The signs that said things like, 'God hates fags' and calling her a carpet muncher.

Shay...well no one really knew what the hell Shay was doing. She was there for rehearsals and concerts, and she would be at home sometimes, but when she was she was stand offish and she rejected any conversation above the surface level

Amber walked through the apartment one morning, she saw Nya on the couch with a computer and it was as if she'd seen a dog using a remote. Nya closed it when she saw Amber. "You need to stop reading that garbage." Amber told her.

"I wasn't I was emailing someone."

"Since when do you know how to use email?"

"Okay, but I promise not to read anymore."

Amber sighed. She wished that she believed that. "Where are the others?"

"I have no idea."

"I'm going to the store, do you need anything?"

"Pizza rolls."

"Got it."

The store they shopped at, because they insisted on doing this one normal people thing, was in a neighborhood where they were not likely to be recognized, and the people here who did recognize them, weren't likely to care.

As Amber pushed the cart up the aisle she met a group of teens that wanted an autograph. Since this only happened about once every three shopping trips she was totally fine doing it. She thanked them for being fans, all the normal stuff. When she turned around to go to the freezer section she noticed a guy standing at the end of the aisle. He looked like he was just passing by, but he had stopped to stare at Amber.

He was a stocky man. He had a receding hair line and he looked like he could have played a child molester on a procedural cop drama. Amber turned around, trying her hardest not to act afraid. Maybe the man wasn't looking at her. That was it, he probably needed something and was looking down the aisle for it. She rounded the corner and headed for the freezer section. She looked around, when she didn't see him she breathed a sigh of relief.

As she was rounding the corner to make her way to the checkout, she saw him coming around the other side. She moved a little faster. She got into line and threw her things on the belt while she looked around for the man. The cashier, a large black woman who looked like she wasn't about to take shit from anyone, saw the man three or four carts down the line. "He bothering you honey?"

"Not really. I think he's just nervous. He probably wants an autograph."

"You famous?"

"Not very. I'm the lead singer for Nashville Panic. We're kind of new."

The woman's eyes lit up and she smiled. "My daughter and I went to your last concert. Could I get an autograph? I don't mean to hold you up, but she would love it so."

The woman handed her a piece of paper and Amber asked, "Who do I make it out to?"

"Angela thank you so much."

She handed her the paper. 'Happy to do it"

The cashier looked down the line and Amber saw that the man was nowhere to be seen. She turned around. and saw that he was half heartedly looking at produce. She pulled a phone off the hook and Amber heard a ding as the PA turned on. "Trevor, come to the front. Code blue." Amber started to push her cart away, thinking that was about something else, when the woman held up a hand to stop her. "Hold on honey."

It didn't take long for the tall muscular white guy, who she assumed was Trevor, to come running up to the front. He just stood there by the cart as the cashier spoke to Amber. "He's gonna help you to the car."

Amber felt like a weight was lifted off her, she looked at the woman. "Thank you so much." she said.

"You have a good day baby. And keep making that music."

When she got home she didn't tell anyone about what happened. She'd wrestled with the decision all the way home but finally decided, literally at the front door, that since nothing happened she didn't need to worry anyone.

"Did you get the stuff?" Nya asked immediately as she entered.

"They're pizza rolls Nya, not crack." She threw her the bag.

Nya caught it and said, "I beg to differ."

The band was rehearsing at the studio. The same songs they could play in their sleep, but it didn't hurt to stay good, said the label. They finished a song and Wade stood up. "I'm out for today."

Nya couldn't believe this. "What the hell dude? We've only been rehearsing for two hours."

"Sorry, got a date."

He walked out of the studio and Shay said, "What an ass."

They had a concert that night, which Wade was almost late for. He came in at five minutes until stage time, two girls wrapped around him and more on either side of the first two.

When the show was over Wade was out the door. Nya wanted to talk about how bad they had done. She wasn't sure the crowd could tell but she sure could. They had been off and their songs were growing old.

She didn't realize it until that show, but they hadn't written anything since they got their record deal. Hell, they didn't even switch songs any more. They used to sub out songs on different shows, picking new ones from the binder every so often to prevent any one song from getting too old, lifeless. But they didn't do that anymore.

She saw Shay head off to the bathroom. "Hey, where are you going?"

"I've gotta pee." She said without turning around.

Even Amber was looking different. She was looking around at the stage hands and people coming and going like they might have a knife. Nya walked over and put her hand on Amber's shoulder. "Are you okay?"

"Huh? yeah, I'm good."

But she didn't look good. She looked scared. Like she didn't even realize Nya had spoke she was so deep in fear like an animal that could hear a predator coming, but didn't know from where so they couldn't find out which way to run.

They left the arena and walked out to the limo. Nya had always thought it would be cool to ride around in a limo when she was a kid, but to be perfectly honest...all she wanted right now was that old RV. They walked past the usual crowd of people holding their signs. Nya had to admit some of them were creative. Like the one that said 'Finger the keys, not our women.'

Nya didn't like to let on, but they bothered her. Her parents had made her ashamed of who she was, and now it was like someone had magnified that. Added a few million to the two people who originally hurt her. She felt Amber's hand on the small of her back, leading her to the car. She got in, sucking in breath and trying not to cry.

CHAPTER TWELVE

Amber got up and headed to the kitchen for some breakfast after she peed. She was still half asleep, but she glanced out the window and she saw the man from the grocery store. She dropped down so fast she was sure to have a bruise on her boobs, and a pain shot through her arms as her palms hit the floor. Her wrists hurt and the wind was knocked out of her. "Isn't it a bit early for impromptu combat exercises?" Came Nya's voice from somewhere behind her. Amber scrambled to her knees and she moved into a sitting position with her back to the window, but that felt too vulnerable, so she moved where she was facing the brick wall under the window, her back to the love seat.

Nya was still standing there. "Amber, what's wrong?" There was none of the usual kidding in her voice. She was all seriousness.

"Get down." Amber said and she could hear the fear in her own voice. Nya dropped down instantly like the true friend she was.

"What's going on?" She asked again, a little more forcefully.

"The man outside by the car, he's been following me. I think he might be stalking me."

"Are you sure?"

"No, but he was at the store the other day and I've seen him a handful of other times. Now he has a camera and I don't know what he could be taking pictures of besides me." Nya reached for the phone on the table beside the couch. "What are you doing?"

"Calling the cops."

"I don't have any proof."

Nya looked at her and it was the most serious that Amber had ever seen her friend look. "Fuck proof."

Ronda sat in the living room, enjoying a morning alone. She didn't often, but Mark was asleep and she was rested so she took the time to enjoy a bit of peace and quiet. She turned on the news mostly as back ground noise while she ate breakfast.

…'And the stalker of Amber Bronson"…

Ronda spit her cereal out. She rushed over to the TV and watched the story. She was so close to the set that she thought she might hit her head.

The news caster said that Amber, her daughter, her baby girl, had been being stalked for months by some creep. He'd been to every stop on their tour, even the one in Atlanta where she and Mark had driven down to see her and the band. The cops investigated his home and found evidence that the man was planning to kidnap Amber. "Mark!" She screamed at the top of her lungs.

He came running in and she ran the news story back. He watched it, ordering her to go call Amber after three seconds. She had to try twice before she got her. Shay answered the phone and Ronda was a bit rude when she said, "Go get my daughter."

"Hi Momma."

"Don't you hi momma me girl, why the hell am I learning about your stalker from the god damned news and not you?"

"It just happened yesterday, the man wasn't fully arrested until this morning. I've been at the police station."

Ronda sighed, relieved the man was behind bars. "Are you okay?"

"I'm a bit shaken up, but I'm okay."

Before Ronda could say anything else she felt the phone being yanked out of her hand. She saw Mark put it to his ear and heard him start being a father. He asked if she needed him to come there, what kind of security they bad on her, all the Dad stuff. She knew it must be killing him not to be there to protect her. It was killing Ronda and she was just the mom. She didn't have the family protector instinct in her DNA.

Finally he hung up the phone, telling Amber that he and her mother loved her. He looked at Ronda and asked, "Are you okay?"

"Yeah, I'm okay babe." She wasn't fully okay, but she knew one of them needed to be strong and rational right now, and his Dad/caveman instincts were going crazy.

"Okay, I think I'm gonna go to the club, clean some shit, play louder than the neighbors like...will you be okay?"

"I'll be fine baby."

"Okay, I love you." With that he grabbed his keys and went out the door. She wondered if she should tell him he was in a T-shirt and underwear but she decided that he could just use the spare clothes they kept in the office. The garage was sound proof. Mark didn't need to go to the club to play, but Ronda knew him. He'd done the same for her more than once, staying around while she had to go. Sometimes you just needed to be alone.

CHAPTER THIRTEEN

The band was to have their picture taken for their album cover. They went to the studio's photography division and met the woman who would be taking the pictures. She was a petite girl with dark blonde hair. She wore jeans and a tank top with a flannel wrapped around her waist. All in all she looked like a pretty rad chick.

"I'm Ivy." she said, shaking each of their hands in turn.

"I love your tattoos." Nya said. Ivy had a bird on her right inner wrist and a dandelion blowing in the wind on the left side of her collar bone.

"Thank you." Ivy said. "I like your boots." Nya looked down and saw that they were both wearing combat boots. Nya's heart fluttered and she took a sharp breath in.

"Easy dude, she's engaged." Wade said.

They all laughed and Ivy held up her ring, which Nya just now noticed. "He's overseas right now but yes, I am engaged."

"Army?"

Ivy nodded and Amber said, "Thank him for his service."

The band echoed their thanks.

"I appreciate that." Ivy said. "Let's get started."

Ivy took them over to a background set up and loaded some fresh film into her camera, which Nya admired. They took several pictures in various configurations in front of different backgrounds. They even went around the city and took some.

When it was over and Ivy had released them and said her goodbyes, as everyone was leaving she asked Shay to stay. "What's up?"

"I just wanted to give you my card. I'm not in LA very often but I almost always have access to a phone. If I can't be reached there, a message can be sent to me."

"Awesome...why are you giving it to me?"

"I'm seven years sober and I can recognize someone else who you know...isn't."

"I'm not, I-"

Ivy put her hands up in defense. "No judgement. If you aren't ready that's fine. But if you need help, or just general support, call me."

Shay took the card gingerly as if it might explode. Ivy patted her on the shoulder as she slung her camera bag over her shoulder. "Well I hope you will call. And I'm gonna go call my sponsor." Shay nodded, said a final goodbye, and went to meet the others at the car.

The phone rang and Nya picked it up. "Hello?"

"Hello? Is this Nya Reynolds, the keyboardist for Nashville Panic?"

"Yes, is this the devil?"

"Um...no ma'am."

"Then why in the name of god would you call me at five in the morning?"

"My name is Diana Ranburn and I am in charge of booking for channel nineteen. I am calling to ask if you would like to come on a new talk show we are premiering."

"When are you premiering it?"

"Well we already have the show, but we are trying to take it in a new direction. We would tape the show on Thursday and it would air on Friday."

"So you want the whole band?"

"No ma'am, just you."

"Why?"

"You're the controversial one."

Nya was disappointed this meeting wasn't face to face. She was making one of her best disgusted faces and it was wasted on this woman. "I don't want to go on your show because I'm gay." she said flatly.

"No, no, we want to because you're the...forgive me for saying this, but you're the weird one. You dress goth and,-"

Nya interrupted her. "I am not goth. I have been telling people that since high school."

"Goth adjacent then," The woman continued. Nya had already forgotten her name. "You are also the most outspoken of the band, and yes there is the gay thing and all the hate, but I promise that won't be the only thing discussed."

Nya sighed. "Okay."

The woman gave the name and address of where she was supposed to go and when. She hung up the phone and looked around, she felt like she had just gone through some sort of ambush. "What the hell just happened?"

Shay had decided not to go with the others to the TV show taping. They really wanted her too, but she told them she was going to see a family member. She'd told them a cousin or something like that had moved to LA last year to be an actor.

In truth, she was in a hotel downtown. She had been there a few times and she always loved it. It was the kind of hotel where some rich kid always had a party going on. She just had to let the guy at the desk see her face and he would give her a key.

She could hear the party as she got off the elevator. There was loud music coming and the smell of weed was so powerful she thought she might be high before she made it to the door. Shay opened the door and saw the party in full swing. There was a couple making out that barreled past her and into a bedroom. The hallway was so full of people drinking that Shay almost had to hit someone to get i past. The person was so high that she just gave Shay her beer.

In the living room area, Snip was on the couch, bent over the table snorting a line. When he finished he raised up and looked at Shay. "Shay baby, how are you?"

Shay took the last drink of the woman's beer, fortifying herself for what she didn't want, but had, to do. "I'm out." She told him.

Snip smiled. The diamond earrings he wore made him look like Eminem's gay cousin. He smiled and Shay felt a shiver go down her spine. She hated Snip. He was a guy whiter than sour cream who like to act like he was ghetto, and he enjoyed taking advantage of people. Unfortunately, he was the only dealer she knew. "How much do you need?" he asked.

"Just a little bit more than last time." Shay said.

He smiled again. "That's what I love to hear. " He walked over to a bag by the couch and he started putting things into a small tin. When he was done he handed it to Shay and said, "Five grand and it's yours."

She reached into her jacket pocket and threw him a bundle of cash. He handed her the tin and she opened it to make sure she was getting what she'd paid for. There was a bit of heroin and a needle, she didn't like heroin that much, and there was coke, and several kinds of pills that she had forgotten the names of.

She walked back down the hall and opened the door to a bedroom. Inside the couple from earlier was fully naked and having sex in a way that did not strike her as comfortable or fun. Shay closed the door and went to another bedroom. She shut and locked the door.

Nya watched the TV people setting up for the show from backstage. She was nervous, she'd never been on TV, and Amber wasn't helping.

Nya couldn't blame her, after what she had been through. But Amber was constantly looking around at everyone that passed them like she was looking for a new stalker. She had started biting her nails when she got nervous, which was all the time now, and her being nervous was making Nya nervous. Just as she was going to ask Amber if she was okay, a woman came over and told her it was time to go on. "You'll do great." Amber said.

The host, Peter Daily, was talking to the audience as Nya waited for her cue. "My next guest is the keyboard and piano player for the new band Nashville Panic. Give it up for Nya Reynolds!"

Nya was dressed nice. She had on a black dress, her. signature combat boots, she even had her nice silver dangley earnings on. But she felt naked as she walked out and sat in the red leather chair across from a grown man in skinny jeans. "It's nice to have you here Nya."

"Thank you for having me, it's nice to be here." Nya said with a smile.

"So tell me about yourself, are you from Nashville?"

"Actually I'm from a tiny town no one has heard of. I was born in Memphis and my family moved when I was very little."

"When did you first get into music?"

"In kindergarten when I met Amber."

"She's the lead singer correct?"

"That's right. We'd been friends for a few weeks before I went to her house and met her parents, who are both musicians. They showed me all of their instruments and stuff and I was just hooked."

"Why the piano?"

"It just spoke to me. Amber's Dad told us that the piano was a great first instrument, but that we were allowed to learn any of them and he would teach us for free. So I walked along the garage, where they keep everything, I remember it like it was last night, I saw all these other instruments, but I knew I wanted to learn the piano the first time I saw it, right as I walked in the door."

Peter Daily turned to the audience. "I think we're going to take a few questions before the break, is that alright with you Nya?"

"Yeah, absolutely." She said, starting to have some fun.

Nya saw a few hands go up but the lights were so bright that she didn't see much. Peter said, "Yes ma'am, what's your question?"

"Yes, I was wondering when you made the decision to be a homosexual?"

"I don't understand." Nya said. She looked at the host but he looked equally lost.

"I believe she is asking when you discovered that you're gay." he suggested.

"No sir," said the woman. "I was asking when she made the disgusting choice to be a homosexual."

"Um...I didn't decide to be gay ma'am."

Peter seemed to sense her discomfort and he looked to another person, "Maybe another question."

A man's voice came through the microphone, though she couldn't see him. "Are you afraid you will go to hell?"

Nya could feel the tears welling up in her eyes. She tried to hide them but she wasn't doing a very good job. She could barely hear her own voice. She asked, "Did you bring me on this show just to talk about me being gay?"

Peter looked shocked. "Honestly no. I was going to ask you about the media and all that they are saying about you but I guess the audience did that for me in their own, very rude, way."

Nya felt ashamed when she started crying. She hated letting these people see that they had gotten the best of her. "I think that the things being said about me are very mean and without cause. I've never hurt anyone."

The people in the audience started to yell things at her. They also started throwing things. A tomato landed near Nya and she saw Peter Daily stand up to shield her, holding his jacket open for extra cover. She started to walk off stage and he went with her, protecting her.

She came off the stage and a well placed tomato, rotten to add insult to injury, hit her in the back of the head just as Peter moved. The sudden impact shocked her and she fell to her knees, bawling. She felt Amber wrap her arms around her as they knelt backstage. "I've never hurt anyone." She repeated, crying. "I've never hurt anyone."

CHAPTER FOURTEEN

S hay didn't know where she was. She could feel that she was on the ground, but that was about it. She looked down at herself, her shirt was partly unbuttoned, her bra visible, though she couldn't remember why and she was covered in vomit. She didn't know if it was her own, or someone else's, but it was all over her. She started to heave at that, but her throat burned too much. She moved against some trash that was leaning against her. She saw where she was then, sitting in between two dumpsters, surrounded by trash. She pushed against the trash bag that was leaning on her. It was heavy. The bag fell against her and its hand fell into her lap.

Shay freaked out. She jumped up and fought the urge to barf when the puke slid down her body. She saw that the thing she had thought was trash was actually a body.

She didn't know what to do, so she ran.

"So have you heard from the kids?" Ronda asked Shay's mother. She thought her name was Estelle, but for some reason Ronda had always had a hard time remembering names.

"Tomas got a call from Shay before she went into Rehab."

Ronda was shocked. She and Mark hadn't heard from Amber in a while, and the rest of the band didn't really call them. Even Nya would usually just piggy back a call from Amber instead of calling herself.

Ronda and Mark had befriended Shay's parents when the band had first been getting together and they liked to get together every once in a while and have a few beers and talk about when they had toured like the kids.

"She said that she got involved with drugs out there and that she realized she needed help." Tomas said walking over to the patio table with a fresh beer for everyone.

"She also said that they broke up." Estelle continued. "She said that she doesn't even know where everyone is. Amber got on a bus and went somewhere and she had no idea about Nya or Wade."

Ronda was truly shocked. Something big must have happened if Nya and Amber didn't even go the same way.

Nya walked onto the used car lot, having been dropped off. She looked over the line of used cars until she saw a yellow Sixty three ford galaxy. An older, heavy set man walked out of an office and made his way over to Nya. "Well," He asked. "What do you think of her?"

"Three grand is a bit much, especially with those tires."

"What would you say to twenty five hundred?"

Nya paused for a brief moment. The car was shabby and it needed a coat of paint. She wasn't sure how far she could get on those tires, but she needed the hell out of town. "Done."

She followed the man into his office, laying her bag and case down on the floor beside the desk. "So what made you buy the car? Hobby project? Most kids your age want new fancy stuff."

"I like old cars." Nya said. "But mostly, I don't own a car and I've had enough of LA."

The man handed her the keys. He saw the bandages on her wrists and he put a hand over hers. "I get what you mean." he said. "This city can be too much at times. I hope you find what you're looking for."

"Thank you."

They shook hands and Nya left the office. She got in the car and was pleasantly surprised when it started up without trouble. She drove to the edge of the parking lot, as she stopped to adjust her mirror she saw the band's old home being driven onto the lot. She sighed, glad she had gotten her things out. She drove to the freeway and kept driving.

CHAPTER FIFTEEN

...ONE YEAR LATER...

The music playing was loud. Loud enough to drown out and and all troubles. That was how Trent liked it. When someone took their hard earned money and spent it on a ticket to his show, he didn't want them even capable of thinking about whatever troubles they had come in with. The final song ended and he spoke into the mic, "That's all for tonight y'all. Thanks for coming out."

The band filed off stage and Trent walked after them. He saw his base player hand Amber the base and walk away. He liked Amber, she was a hard worker. She'd been with them about a year. Trent could tell that something had happened with Amber before she'd joined up with them, but she never talked about it. She didn't really talk with anyone more than just business. She did her work, was polite and respectful with everyone, and then she took her bunk in one of the buses every night.

"Where's Amy going?" he asked as he walked over.

"The bathroom." Amber said.

Trent leaned against a large amp and looked at Amber. He had figured out where he knew her from. He didn't know her story, but he knew who she was. He had decided that now was the right time to confront her about it. "I know who you are." He said.

"What?"

"Nashville Panic, I loved your music."

"How long have you known?"

"Only about a week. I've been trying to decide whether or not to say anything." Amber looked like she was going to bolt out the door. "How come you've never played me anything?"

"I don't really play any more." Amber said.

Amy walked back over. Trent loved his wife. She was five seven with brown hair that had just a titch of red in it, and she was hell on hell on high heels when she wanted to be. "What's going on?" she asked.

"Nothing much, just waitin' on you." He wrapped his wife in his arms.

"No one ever waits on a woman. They are fortunate enough to be there early for her arrival. Isn't that right Amber?"

Amber smiled. "Yes ma'am."

Amy broke away from Trent and said, "I'm going back to the bus to take a shower. We're gonna get supper started, I'll have it for the two of you when you're done...you eat with us Amber, you don't eat enough to keep a bird alive."

Amber blushed. Amy kissed Trent and walked away to get dinner ready with the other guys' wives. Trent jumped up and sat on the amp with Amber. "So why don't you play anymore?"

"I don't like to talk about it."

"Come on, remember I'm your boss and I can fire you."

They both laughed. Amber knew he was kidding, but it had the desired effect and she sighed, at ease. "Things didn't end well with my band. After we got a little famous we kinda lost our minds. The drummer turned into a complete asshole. My best friend, our keyboard player, went through some really hard stuff that I wasn't really there for because I got some serious PTSD after my stocker was arrested.

"And our base player, she's in rehab in LA and I didn't even realize she had a drug problem. We saw her high once and I guess we got so caught up in our own shit that we didn't even notice when shit got worse."

Amber started to cry and some of the band members looked over. Trent held up a hand, letting them know it was okay. He got off the amp and he wrapped his arms around her to comfort her. "So you don't play music because you don't want to remember them?"

"Yeah."

"But you're still writing:?"

She broke the hug and looked at him with curiosity, "How did you know that?"

"I've seen you on the bus, and when we stop, and I am a musician too Amber. I know what it feels like to have stuff going on inside and needing to get it out on paper." She nodded like she understood what he was saying. "So where is it? Can I have it?" he asked.

"What?"

"Your notebook. Is it okay if I read it?"

Amber nodded. She walked over to the wall next to the amp and got a really beat up composition notebook out of the bag she carried. She walked back over and handed it to Trent. "Thank you. I promise I will give it back."

Amber nodded again. It was like she was afraid to speak because she might start to cry again. "Now get back to work." Trent said in his mock serious tone.

Amber smiled and saluted. "Yes sir."

Hours later, after dinner was done and the dishes clean, the band had put their kids to sleep and Amy and Trent had retired for the evening. Amy was in the bathroom as Trent lay shirtless on the bed, reading. Amy came out and got on her side of the bed. She took the notebook from Trent. "I was reading that."

"You've been reading this for hours." Amy read silently for a few minutes, flipping from one page to another and back again. "This kid should not be a roadie."

"I know."

"You know what you have to do right?"

"I know."

CHAPTER SIXTEEN

Amber sat at the picnic table while the people who could cook did so. The band she was with was more like a gypsy circus. Amy and Trent had started it with just them and the other band members, but after a while when other people got married and had kids, it had grown into three buses, which were now parked in a semi circle.

Bus one was for the crew, Trent and Amy. Bus two was for the other band members and their kids. Bus three was for any one else who didn't fit somewhere, or wanted to be alone, and the equipment.

They had set up awnings for the cooks to cook under, and the members who couldn't cook, or who were watching the young kids, sat at tables that were stowed on bus three. Some of the older kids ran around playing, so for now Amber had a table to herself.

Trent walked over and sat down. He was a good boss and Amber liked to work for him. "You're fired." he said.

"Is this about what happened? Cause Donnie broke that amp, not me."

Trent looked over his shoulder at one of the men working the grill. "Donnie what?...never mind, you shouldn't be here, not anywhere, as a roadie. You need to be playing this stuff." He tapped her notebook for effect.

"Find your band," he said. "or get a new one, I don't care. But you need to be playing music. The world deserves to hear this stuff." Amber thought for several long moments of something to persuade him to let her keep her job, to keep hiding. But she knew Trent was right.

She nodded and he smiled. "Good."

Without another word he got up and went over to the grill tent where. Amy was barking orders at everyone. Amber could see him tell her what they had talked about and Amy looked over, smiling.

A few hours later at a truck stop, Trent was talking to a guy while Amy handed Amber a small cooler. "I put enough snacks to last a while, and there's some cash in there for when that runs out."

"Thank you." Amber was more grateful to them then she knew how to show. "You really didn't have to do this."

Amy smiled. "Honey if I hadn't had someone to help me, I wouldn't be where I am today. I really hope you can work things out."

Amber started to speak, but was interrupted by Trent coming over. "This guy is headed to New Orleans," He told them. "He says he'll take you."

"Is he safe?" Amber asked.

"Oh yeah, he's a good ole boy. He'll make sure you get where you need to."

"Well I'd better be getting back to the bus. " Amy said, "Amber, be safe and keep in touch."

"Yes ma'am and thank you again." The two of them hugged and Amy walked away.

"Are you sure your friend is in New Orleans?" Trent asked.

"I read this fan blog that said someone saw her playing piano in a bar there. It's the closest lead I have." Trent nodded his understanding. Amber moved to walk away but she turned back and asked, "Can I ask you something?"

"Sure."

"How come you never tried to get famous? I mean, your band is really good. You could have made it."

Trent laughed. "I like to think we have." He laughed a bit more to himself and continued. "We tried, Amy and I, separately though. Once we got together we decided that all we wanted was to have friends and family, and to play music for the rest of our lives."

"Really?" Amy asked. "You never wanted to be all rich and famous and stuff?"

"We're happy traveling with our group, making enough money to feed everyone and keep the bus running." Trent had a habit of thinking of their entire caravan as one bus, Amber liked that. Trent continued. "Too much money has a tendency to get in the way of happiness."

"That's for damn sure."

Trent gave Amber a big hug and said, "Well, you'd better get going Darlin'. But you keep in touch, I mean that."

"Yes sir, I will. I promise."

CHAPTER SEVENTEEN

Nya didn't smoke, she didn't like that anyone did.

More than that though, she didn't think it was smart for someone who's money and passion relied on their lungs, to smoke. Still, she would be lying if she said that the smoky smell of the bar didn't bring her a little bit of comfort. This was one of only a few bars that still let you smoke, so it was filled with a lot of clientele that smoked. From the old timers who had been smoking so long they probably couldn't breath without it, to the people who just came here for a 'Drink' so that their spouses didn't know they smoked.

This place had been her home for quite a while. Sure she slept elsewhere, but she worked a lot here. She tended bar when her voice hurt, and she would just sit for hours singing and playing when it didn't. She was singing a jazz song about a guy who's woman left him for dead at a train depot. Playing was mostly therapy. She collected tips and she technically 'worked' there, but for most of the day she would just watch her hands roll over the keys, pressing the right one for the right sound, playing was just about the only instinct she had, and she would just forget. She would forget about all her problems, forget about the best friend she hadn't seen in a year, forget about the disaster that had been her life. Playing let her forget everything.

The song ended and she felt her back cramping up. She rose from her seat and announced, "Back in a bit guys." There were several moans coming from the old guys who liked her playing, and the rough and rowdy 'Day drinkers' as they liked to call themselves, they were really just alcoholics in denial. "Come on guys, do you want my fingers to fall off?" she asked playfully.

"Maybe!" Yelled a familiar voice from the back of the bar

"Can someone get a ride home for Carl?" Nya called out. She turned around to go get a drink, and maybe something to eat, when she saw Amber sitting at a table. "What the fuck are you doing here?"

"Can we talk?"

Nya sat down. She could feel the anger coming off her in waves. She had no idea why she was this mad at Amber. Wasn't it Nya herself who had left LA without warning or telling anyone? "I want to get the band back together."Amber said.

"What makes you think I would want to get back together?" Nya saw her move a strand of fire engine red hair behind her ear. She could tell that Amber was nervous, but for the first time in her life, she didn't care.

Amber was almost crying as she spoke, "I've been working for a traveling band this past year. I was a roadie. I stayed near music, but I haven't picked up a guitar."

"Must have made a shitty roadie."

Amber snorted a laugh as Nickki came over to the table. Nya gave her a kiss and she extended her hand to Amber. "Hi, I'm Nickki."

"Amber."

Nya put her hand on the small of Nickki's back. She had told her enough about the band for her to know who Amber was, and what had went down. "Can you give us a minute? Maybe get me a beer?"

"Yeah, sure." Nickki walked away. She wasn't dressed in anything special, just jean shorts and a tank top, but she looked amazing to Nya. She was all light colors and a positive attitude. She had blonde hair down to her shoulders and Nya's favorite thing to do was twirl it in her fingers as they went to sleep at night.

"She seems nice." Amber said.

"And so very unlike me?"

"Yeah."

Nya smiled. "That's why I love her. She found me in a bad place and she rescued me."

"What do you mean?"

Nya hesitated a moment before holding up her wrists, the deep gashes she'd made left scars, but she thought of them more as reminders now than something to be ashamed of. "I did the first one in LA and more while I was on the road. When I found her in Kansas, also leaving, she forced me to stop. She taught me how to get over my hurt. She's the one who got my shit together, not me."

"I'm happy for you. She's cute too."

Nya raised an eyebrow at her friend. Momentarily they were just that, friends again. "What?"

Amber said. "I'm straight, not blind." They both laughed for a little while. When they stopped Amber grew serious. "I'm sorry I wasn't there for you Ny."

Nya didn't say anything, she just stared into space for a minute before she said, "You really want to do this? Get them back?"

"I do. I miss our family."

Nickki was up for anything. She was just as much a gypsy as Nya, another reason she loved her. She still had the car she'd bought in LA, though she'd made some improvements on it since then, namely decent tires. Those tired carried them all the way to where Wade's Momma said he'd been living.

On the car ride Amber and Nya rekindled their relationship. It didn't take long for them to get over what a had happened in LA. Nickki had pulled Nya into a truck stop bathroom and told her, "You need to forgive her."

"Why should I?"

"Because I can see that you love her, and that you miss your friend. The only way to heal is to let go of the past babe."

Nya had kissed her again. "You know I love you."

"So I've been told."

Amber and Nickki were fast friends. They bonded over stories of how weird Nya was. Nickki told her all of the embarrassing stuff Nya did at night, like repeatedly ending up on top of

Nickki and waking up not having realized she'd been thrown in the floor. Amber would respond to every story Nickki had with one from childhood. Like the time Nya had liberated a biology lab pig.

All in all, by the time they pulled into the dirt parking lot, they were all getting along. They got out of the car and Nya looked up and saw the sign on the building. They'd been given an address, but she hadn't realized it was this place. "Son of a bitch." she said a little to loudly.

Amber looked up from her phone. "Shit."

"What's going on?" Nickki asked.

"We played here three years ago." Nya explained.

"He came back to somewhere the times were good." Amber finished Nya walked towards the bar, flanked by the other two. She heard Amber ask Nickki, "Can I ask, how come you are so cool with all of this. I mean, you guys left your lives really fast."

Nickki responded in a way that made Nya love her even more, though she wasn't entirely sure that was possible. "I'm an artist, I can work from anywhere. All I have to do is send the paintings to the right people. I love Nya and she and I have already spent some time on the road together, so if this is where she is meant to be, then I am perfectly happy with being here, or anywhere."

Wade was tending bar when they walked in. He was talking to a customer and when he was done an other came up, so the girls found a table and they sat. They sat there for hours. Nickki took a small pad out of her bag and started to draw. She could do that anywhere, Nya had seen her do that in the middle of a grocery store.

When closing time hit, Wade walked the last patron out, sent the staff home, and went to the register to count the till. "You have to talk to us sometime dumb ass."

Wade spoke without looking up from his money. "It's been a year, why are you guys here?"

Nya stood up, she looked back at the table and saw Amber getting up to follow. Nickki had her head bent over the table, asleep. Nya wondered when that had happened. they walked over and Nya said, "We're getting the band back together."

Wade finally looked at them. "What?" he said incredulously. "I can't guys."

"You heard her Wade."

Wade sighed. He ran a hand through his hair, that looked like it hadn't been cut in some time, and he looked at them. It was the kindest he had looked since before LA, the most vulnerable. "I can't guys."

Nya rolled her eyes, he was starting to piss her off. "Why the fuck not?"

"Because LA messed me up."

Amber took a much more sensitive approach. "LA messed us all up Wade, that's why we're not going back."

"What do you mean?"'

Nya smiled at him. "Playing, touring, being a family. Like it was before..."

Wade was silent for several seconds. He turned around and grabbed a bottle off the top shelf. He grabbed three glasses and poured them each a shot. "Who's the girl?"

"Nya's girlfriend."

"Actually," Nya reached into the pocket of her dress and got out a simple silver ring, she put it on her left ring finger. "She's my wife."

Amber made a very strange cooing sound and gave Nya a big hug. Wade fist bumped her and they picked up their shots. "Let's get our family back." Wade said, and they drank.

CHAPTER EIGHTEEN

"Guys, there she is." The ride to Los Angeles had been a bit rougher with four people in the car, but they made it early enough to be outside the hospital for Shay to be released.

They all looked over at the building and saw Shay coming out. She looked better, healthier. She walked out of the building carrying a bag, wearing a gray T-shirt and jeans. Shay stopped several yards away from them all, they moved forward but stayed far enough away that they had to shout. "What do you want?" Shay shouted.

Amber, as soft as her voice was. had to cup her hands over her mouth. "We're getting the band back together."

"Will you do it?" Nya asked.

"Yeah Shay, will you come back?" Wade chimed in.

The look on Shay's face told them she was thinking. They hoped she was thinking of all the good times they had had, but after a minute her face darkened. "No." She said.

The band didn't know what to do. So they went home. They were all sitting in Amber's parents back yard one night, after explaining their missing year, around a campfire when Ronda walked up. "Guys, there's some one here for you."

They all looked up as Ronda moved aside and Shay stepped forward. They couldn't find the words to speak. Finally Ronda looked over at Nickki. "Nickki, why don't you and I let the band have it out amongst themselves? I'll tell you all the embarrassing stories I know about Nya when she was a kid."

Nickki stood and walked over, Ronda put her arm around her and they started to walk towards the house. "Don't worry sweetie, there'll be plenty of time for you to be involved in the fights, trust me. I've spent many an evening drinking and talking with friends while Mark fought with the band, but I've spent just as many fighting with them too."

Back at the fire, Shay was still standing there, the rest of the band still unsure of whether or not to move. "What the hell do you people what?" Shay asked. "I got a message saying that if you've ever meant anything to me then I should come see you one last time."

Nya smiled. "God I love Nickki."

Amber stood. "Shay please sit down."

Shay sat but she made sure to maintain her distance from the rest of them. Amber was still standing as she looked at all of them. "We are going to have a fight, and we are going to take care of all our serious shit that needs dealt with. I want it all on the table. Shay do you want to go first?"

"No."

"I'll go." Wade said. He stood up and Amber sat. Wade shifted uncomfortably and sighed. "I am sorry that I turned into such a cocky douche. I let the fame thing get to me, more so than the rest of you. I let myself believe I was some big bad mother fucker. I slept with so many girls that I don't know the number, I didn't even bother to learn most of their names. I might have bastard off spring out there, I don't know I...I even tried to do a gig without you guys, I thought I was the most important member and that I could just fill the other spots with anybody...I fell on my face and I was snapped back into reality.

"I didn't apologize then because I was ashamed. I was ashamed that I'd failed you guys. I didn't want to see you look at me like you are now, and to know what a piece of shit I am."

They all fell silent before Nya finally spoke, "I started to do what I'd never done before and, well long story short, " She rolled up her sleeves and showed off her scars. Everyone instantly gasped at what had happened, save for Amber who already knew.

Amber started to open her mouth but Shay spoke. "You can all go fuck yourselves." They looked at her, shocked, but they didn't say anything in their own defense. They all knew, individually, that they didn't have a defense. "Some guy gave me weed in our first, I'd say month, in LA. He said it would help me stay up. It did, and on those days when we would be up for like, fifteen hours and then have to operate on very little sleep, I would take more. Then I took more, and more. Then I got into harder stuff, I took cocaine, heroin, pills of so many different varieties that I had more drugs in me than a Rite Aid when I checked myself into Rehab. I woke up in an alley one night next to a dead body. I ran for miles, afraid that the cops would be after me. The next day I checked into rehab and I stayed there the entire year."

"Shay," Nya said "I understand that you' re hurt, but you got addicted. That's not on us, that's on you."

Shay held up her hand like Nya had made a good point. "No," she said. "it is not on you that I got addicted, that is all on me. It is your fault though, that you didn't fucking notice! You people were my entire life for over a year. You were more than my actual family, and where were you when I needed you? Nowhere! Yes, I got into drugs, and that's on me, but you didn't notice when someone you supposedly loved was killing herself and that is fucking on you!

Silence hung in the air until Nya said, "You're right." Shay looked mildly shocked by this, Nya walked over and Shay allowed herself to be hugged. When they broke Nya looked at everyone. "Wade failed us. Amber and I failed each other. And Shay...we all failed you. We failed each other. We would like to make it up to you if you'd let us."

Shay gave a teary nod and Nya hugged her again. Amber and Wade joined in and soon they were all in one big, tear stained hug.

THE TRAGIC TALE OF ELIZABETH BLANEY

A young girl survives a brutal frontier massacre only to be raised by the very people her world fears, forging a life that is torn apart again and again by violence, love, and survival. As Elizabeth Blaney grows into a woman shaped by loss and resilience, her journey becomes a haunting search for belonging in an unforgiving world.

PROLOGUE

They were loading up the carriage with a trunk full of books when Elizabeth was led out of the house by a servant. Her mother and father were standing nearby looking impatient while Elizabeth hugged the servant woman, Martha, crying. "Don't cry now child. Your Father's business will take off in California and then you'll be surrounded by books in your new home"

"But I want you to come." Elizabeth said wiping her tears on the sleeve of her dress.

"I cannot. Now go before I start to cry too." Martha handed her the bag she had packed for her. It had all of Elizabeth's favorite books in it. She just loved to read. Her Father had wanted a son, but when he got

her he made sure that she was educated enough to make him look good. Elizabeth knew that other girls her age didn't get to learn like she did, and she was grateful.

She walked to the carriage and lifted her skirts as her father helped her up. It was just the three of them, so she got an entire seat to herself in the beautiful carriage. She looked out the window and waved at Martha until they were out of sight. Then she settled in for the long journey to California.

Elizabeth read for hours and hours until it got dark and her Father told her to go to sleep. And that is how it went for two days. On the third day, Elizabeth's mother pulled her violin out of the storage area under the seat and Elizabeth played for her parents like she did for their society friends at parties.

Every few days they stopped at an inn or a town and they got new horses Elizabeth always said goodbye to the other horses and hello to the new ones, which her Mother said was 'Childish.'

"I'm nine," she said in response. "I'm supposed to be childish."

Her mother was infuriated, but her Father said, "She has a point there Mary."

Her parents thought it was a hard and grueling journey, but Elizabeth didn't mind it. She read about adventure all the time and not she was getting to have one of her own. Sometimes they would make camp for the night and she would pretend to be asleep, and when she knew that her parents were asleep she would take a stick and make a torch and go exploring. She even went for a night time swim, though she was caught the next morning and given a spanking for putting herself in danger.

"Father, I have to use the privy." Elizabeth said one day when they were going across a plain in the Colorado territory.

"I suppose I could do with a stretch of the legs." He said. He banged on the door and signaled for the driver to stop.

When the carriage stopped Elizabeth jumped down and went over into the tall grass. She squatted down after lifting her skirts and started to pee. The grass was over her head standing, so squatting down felt like she was in a forest that threatened to block out the sun.

She stood up and walked to the edge of the grass. Just as she was walking out, she could see her parents and the driver near the carriage stretching and walking around, she heard thunder. Before she could find out what the sound was she saw the driver die. One second he was okay, the next an arrow was coming out of his chest.

Elizabeth screamed, and her parents looked towards her as arrows sunk into both of them. She took off running towards them and then she was on the ground.

Her head hurt, her vision was blurry, and she could see two figures silhouetted by the sun. She knew English, Latin Italian, and French, but they were speaking something else. One of them seemed to be angry and the other one seemed to be telling him what to do. As she raised her head they turned to look down at her and she said softly, "Please don't hurt me. "

"We won't." Said one of them. She saw his foot coming towards her face and then everything went dark.

CHAPTER ONE

...Five years later...

Avasa finished tanning the hide and went to work making arrows. They let her do as she liked, learning everything. She had gotten their language down in the first year and had spent the rest of the time learning.

She learned how to skin an animal and make everything from clothing to rope with its body. She also learned how to fight and hunt with the braves. "Come inside with me."

She looked up and saw Asha standing near the tipi. Asha was beautiful. She had hair as black as night and looked like as close to an angel as you could find on earth. But the reason that Avasa loved her was her heart. She had been her best friend when they brought her to the tribe, and her mother had taken her in and taught her how to be a woman and a member of the tribe as she came of age.

As they had gotten older and seen the other kids beginning to get together they both talked about how they hadn't been interested in any of the boys. "Avasa?"

The sound of her Indian name brought her out of her memories. "Yes, my dear?"

"It is late, come inside with me."

She let Asha take her hand and lead her into their home. She liked living so simplistically. They could have their home down and ready to travel in a matter of hours. Inside Asha laid her down on the bedding and laid on top of her. She kissed her and said, "You look tired."

"I'm okay."

Asha smiled and kissed her lower on her neck. Avasa shivered. Asha kissed lower and lower until she got where she was going. Later on that night, Avasa returned the favor.

They should have been asleep. They would have to go about their chores in just a few hours, but they were awake. They had finished their fun and were laying in each other's arms and talking. "Tell me about New York."

Avasa laughed. "I've told you all I remember."

"I know, but I love to hear about all the people and the places inside one small space. Did you really have just one whole store for women's clothes?"

"More than one, but I only went to a couple when my parents would have a new dress made for me and I would have to go to a fitting. I really didn't leave our house much."

"Your very big house yes?"

"Yes." She said with a giggle. She kissed her and tickled her on her sides, where she knew that she was ticklish.

"Why does the white man live in one place for so long?" Asha asked. "Don't they know that to live well you must see many places, and move around so that you don't use up too much of the land at one time?"

Avasa knew what she was saying, and she agreed with her, but she also remembered what it was like to be white, though that faded more every day. "They don't care about the land. They just want money and to be powerful and to look good in front of others."

Asha turned to look at her, their faces inches from each other. "I am glad you are with me."

Avasa kissed her on the nose and said, "I am too." They fell asleep in each other's arms. She knew that her parents had died to bring her here, but she was happy that she was here. She was happy.

Avasa was cooking breakfast when she saw the soldiers coming down the hill. There were so many of them that heir horses sounded like thunder coming in, louder than the horses had sounded when she'd come to the tribe. "Everyone stay calm, I will handle this." The chief said as he walked to the front of the camp. Avasa stayed where she was as the riders came into the camp.

A man in a very large hat got down from his horse and rested his hand on his sword as he walked up to the chief. "This," he said presenting the chief with a piece of paper he knew the chief could not read, "Is a document from the government of the united states giving me authority over the members of this tribe."

The chief looked around at the members of the tribe until his eyes came to her. "Come to me." he said.

She came closer and he asked her to translate the paper. When she had finished the soldier said, "My my, is this a white girl living among the savages? Are you okay darlin'? Have they hurt you?"

English felt strange in her mouth as she spoke. "These people are my family, they saved me."

"Well you are rescued now my dear. We will take you to civilization where you will be reunited with your own kind."

She shook her head backing away, "Please, no."

"I am afraid I must insist." She started to back away and he soldier said, "Sergeant Pierce, please retrieve her."

A younger man with less hair and a smaller hat started to come towards Avasa. Her mind was fluttering with whether or not to run. Finally, she pulled a knife from her belt and she ran at the man. She jumped on him and brought him to the ground the way Asha's brothers had shown her and she plunged the knife into his neck. Soon there were several holes in his neck and blood was spurting everywhere.

Avasa felt hands grip her arms and she was suddenly being dragged away from the camp. She was thrown into a metal cage. Three men were ordered to take her away and she struggled against the bars. Asha ran towards her and soldiers put hands on her. Tears streamed down both of their faces as she called out, "Asha don't! Don't fight, they'll hurt you!"

"I love you!"

Avasa sobbed. "I love you too!"

CHAPTER TWO

E lizabeth was taken to a city called Saint Louis and aban-
doned by the Army. It was decided that she could not be
punished for behaving like a 'Savage' when she had no civilized
life to compare it to. They said that the Indians had corrupted
her and that she should be absolved of her 'Sins' because of it.

For the past year she had been wandering the city and eating
whatever she could find. She had almost perpetual wounds on
her from fighting with other people for what little food could
be found in the bins outside the businesses. She spent her nights
hiding from police and dreaming of her tribe.

White folks didn't like knowing that she could speak an Indian language. She had been beaten by a group of boys because
of it and only narrowly escaped being raped. She'd stabbed one
of them with his own knife.

As she walked down an alley way, Elizabeth noticed that
a large bin was unlocked. She walked over to it and looked
around, seeing no people, she opened it and started eating,

shoving the occasional bit of foods inside her rags for later. "You know there are easier ways to get food." Elizabeth jerked around in shock and fell into the garbage. When she came up she saw a girl standing before the dumpster.

She was pretty, long brownish blonde hair and a welcoming face that made Elizabeth instantly at ease, somehow round and sharp at the same time. Her eyes said that she could make you her whole world or burn your world down around you. She had breasts that weren't too big, nor too small, and were certainly enough to distract Elizabeth for a moment.

She was clearly a street rat like Elizabeth though. It showed on her clothes and in her hair. Her dress was older, dirty and a bit ripped in a few places. And it was clearly a size or two smaller than she needed given the way her breasts and stomach strained against it. Her hair was clean but looked tangled from a lack of a comb. Elizabeth guessed that she washed in the river but ran her fingers through it in place of a brush. "Is this your place?" she asked.

"No silly, I was walking by and I didn't know if you knew that there are easier ways to get food." She walked closer and extended her hand. "I'm Alexis, and you are?"

"Elizabeth." She said shaking her hand.

Alexis helped her out of the dumpster. "Come with me."

Elizabeth let herself be led onto the street and several streets down, almost to the other side of the city it seemed. Alexis led her down an alley where there were several pallets stacked up along with a bunch of other garbage cans and scraps of wood against a wooden fence.

"Come inside." Alexis said mischievously She got down on her hands and knees and crawled into the little pile. Elizabeth followed.

It was a nice little shelter. There was a pallet that looked much more comfortable than the hard ground that Elizabeth had been sleeping on for the past year. More blankets were nailed along the makeshift walls, making the shack quite warm. "You lay down and I will go get you something to eat." Alexis said. She crawled out of the shack and Elizabeth laid her head down on the pallet. She hadn't realized how exhausted she was, but as soon as her head hit the cloth she was asleep.

When she woke it was dark and Alexis was next to her on the pallet. She jerked awake and noticed that she was not wearing any clothes. She yelped a bit, waking Alexis up. "What's wrong?"

"Why do I not have any clothes on?"

"Yours were rags and when I got back you were freezing. So, I stripped us both down and let my body heat warm you up. I would have asked but I couldn't manage to wake you."

Elizabeth calmed down, she was warmer now. Alexis was apparently not shy about her body as she let the blankets fall and she crawled over to a sack in the corner, fishing out a dress and handing it to Elizabeth, who had to shake her head to bring herself out of her distraction "I got this for you." Alexis said.

Elizabeth took the dress, grateful. "Thank you." she said.

"Let's get dressed and I will show you how to get food and drinks for free."

The two of them got dressed and crawled out of the shelter. Elizabeth stopped and pulled on her dress in the back side, this was much more restrictive than her old clothing. "What's wrong?"

"I haven't worn a dress like this in quite some time." she said. Alexis gave her a curious look but didn't ask any more questions.

Alexis led her down the street to a saloon. Elizabeth usually tried to avoid the crowds that hung out inside and outside saloons, but Alexis walked right up like she owned the place. At the door she turned back to Elizabeth and, "Don't be alarmed if they grope you a bit. I know it feels wrong, but it's easier if you let them think they have the right to touch you."

Elizabeth nodded, and they walked into the saloon. The entire room was filled with smoke and smelled like unwashed men. There was a long bar that went down the end of one side, a staircase going up to the rooms, and the rest of the room was filled with green tables where men were drinking, smoking, and playing cards.

She followed Alexis over to a table where men were playing cards. As she walked over behind them, Alexis mouthed for Elizabeth to follow her lead. Alexis rubbed the neck of one man, who turned around and pulled her into his lap. "How are ya Dwight?" she asked.

"I'm good darlin'. How're you?"

"I got an awful problem see, my friend here ain't got enough money for supper and I could use a drink."

Dwight cupped his no card hand around Alexis' breast and smiled. "I think if I win this hand then the three of us could sit down to a meal."

Elizabeth sat uninvited on the lap of the man across from Dwight, seeing what Alexis' plan was. The man looked at her breasts and she realized why there was so much open space in her dress. "How're you doing?" she asked.

"Lot better now than I was." The man said as he planted a kiss on her breast. She had to fight the urge to vomit when his disgusting, sore covered, mouth touched her skin.

"I win, pay up you sons of bitches." Dwight said.

The man jerked his eyes away from Elizabeth and realized what was going on. "You bastard, I'm not paying."

"The hell you ain't," Dwight said. "You put your cards down in a fold and I played the better hand. Pay up. now."

The man stood up, knocking Elizabeth into the floor. He drew a gun, but Dwight was faster. There was a loud ringing in her ears and soon the man had landed on top of Elizabeth, dead.

She couldn't move, he was heavy. Dwight walked over and pulled him off her, helping her up "Sorry you had to see that sweetheart."

"That's okay, it's not my first dead man."

Dwight looked like he was trying to figure out if she was telling the truth. He must have decided yes because he turned away from her without asking any more questions. Fishing out a few bills from the pile and handing them to Alexis he said, "I'll have to eat with you another time, I'd best be heading out of town."

Alexis kissed him, and he headed out the door. She turned to Elizabeth and said, "Usually no one dies, I swear."

They went to the other end of the room and got a table where they used half the money that Dwight had given them to fill their bellies. Alexis said that they needed to save a bit for later because you could only pull things like this every little bit. The owner usually had their own girls in here to entertain the men. It was the first time in about a year that Elizabeth had had a hot meal. It was the greatest thing she had ever tasted.

CHAPTER THREE

Elizabeth never forgot about Asha or the tribe, but over the next two years she was able to find some sort of happiness with Alexis. They made five different shelters around the city and they would roam from one to the other, occasionally just sleeping underneath the stars.

They had been sitting on a blanket in the grass one day when Elizabeth and Alexis talked about their lives. Elizabeth told her about her childhood and living with Indians, and Asha, she even told her about the soldier she'd killed.

Alexis told her about growing up on a farm in Virginia and always wanting more When her Father had died, and her mother moved in with Alexis' aunt, she had taken the opportunity to leave. She had scammed, stolen, and occasionally whored her way all around the country, only stopping in Saint Louis on her way west, only staying for Liz, her nickname for Elizabeth.

That was also their first kiss. Alexis kissed her and told her that she had thought her beautiful since she first saw her in the trash bin. Elizabeth did like her, but she always thought of Asha when the subject of love came up. She had no way of finding her love, and no money or resources to even get out of Saint Louis if she could find her.

She had no experience in the kind of relationship that she and Alexis had. They were great friends and lovers...it brought to her mind a book she'd snuck out of her mother's things when she was younger, and the word she'd read there, paramour. When she asked Alexis if that fit them she said, "Yes, I think it does."

Elizabeth was walking down the street to meet Alexis, her pockets full of stolen goods from stalls and shops. Alexis had gone to see if she could get anything from the people who were in town to see the circus. She thought that two pickpockets being in the crowd might attract too much attention.

She got to their meeting place under the bridge and saw Alexis looking very happy. "Did you get a lot?" she asked.

"Yeah, and a job offer."

"A what?"

"The man who owns the circus caught me and asked me if I wanted to come work for him. I would be doing the occasional act when someone needed me too, but mostly I would be working the crowd and stealing things. He offered me a fifty-fifty split of what I steal."

"That's great." Liz said smiling.

"I can't take it though. He won't let you come."

Liz felt her face fall. "That is bad."

"Yeah," Alexis said. "I just sort of liked that someone thought I was good enough to hire, and not for my quim."

They were both silent for a long time. Finally, Liz said, "You have to take that job."

"What?"

"You should go and take the job. You have to. I know what seeing the country and the world means to you."

Alexis had tears in her eyes. "Liz-,"

She waved that thought away. "I'll be fine. I promise. You want to go, and you know you do."

"Yes, I do. But I also don't want to lose you."

"We will find a way to keep in touch, I'm sure that I will be around here for a while. You could write."

"You really want me to go?"

Liz nodded. When she spoke, she did in the tribe's language, which she had taught to Alexis. "I do."

Alexis rushed forward and wrapped her in a hug. The hug lasted for a long time because neither of them

knew if they would ever hug again. When they finally broke, they kissed, and Alexis said, "Goodbye."

"Goodbye." They left on opposite sides of the bridge, and Liz hoped that Alexis was crying like she was.

...Six Months Later...

Elizabeth walked down the street in the part of the city that was for the poor. She vastly preferred this part of the city because people didn't judge her quite as harshly as the rich folks did. She stood across the street from the supply depot, waiting to see if there was someone from whom she could liberate a few bits, when she saw him.

He was by far the most beautiful man she had ever seen, the only one who had ever even turned her head. He had bushy brown hair and thick, strong arms. His face reminded her of a painting that had hung in her mother's drawing room, though she couldn't remember the Italian name. Despite trying to practice with the immigrants around the city, a few of her languages had gotten a bit lousy. She could picture the name, but she couldn't remember how to say it.

He was loading supplies into a wagon, he picked up an entire barrel by himself, his thick ropes of muscle tensing. Though she was trying to make out more of his face, she couldn't help but notice the way his backside looked in his trousers. She walked across the street, putting on the front that Alexis had taught her so well.

She'd gotten a letter from Alexis a few months back, said she was in San Francisco. The significance of that city was not lost on Alexis, who knew all about Liz's parents.

She waited by the wagon until he turned around. He was a bit startled by Elizabeth but soon regained his composure enough to say, "Hello ma'am."

Her entire lie melted away at the look of his deep green eyes. She was suddenly so tongue tied that all she managed to say was, "You are beautiful."

He smiled and said, "Why thank you. You are quite beautiful yourself."

They stood there for a few moments in award silence before she asked, "Where are you headed? This is clearly not the supply wagon of someone who lives in the city."

"Well I've purchased a homestead in Oklahoma and I am getting ready for the journey there."

"Aren't you a bit young to have that kind of money?"

"Well I don't have it any more. I saved everything I've made working since I was twelve and I had enough for about half. My Grandfather made a bit of money and when he died I got the other half."

"How old are you?"

"Eighteen."

"I'm seventeen...don't most young men homestead with a wife?"

"Well if you're offering I'd take you up on it." he said.

They both laughed, when their laughter died down she looked up at him and sad, "Okay."

She would remember the shock on his face until the day she died.

Two hours later they were standing in front of a church with a preacher. They'd told him that they wanted to get married fast, but he didn't want to do the ceremony. Liz's couple extra dollars made that particular hesitation disappear. As they were walking out of the church to the wagon that would take her to her new life Elizabeth asked, "What is your name?"

"Morgan Blaney."

She dipped her head in a small bow. "Elizabeth Blaney."

He smiled and helped her into the wagon. He cracked the reins and she left the city behind.

CHAPTER FOUR

They talked. There was nothing to do all day, every day, so they talked. Morgan told her about his family and the docks he 'd grown up on. He'd taken a ship to England when he was very young, and he remembered two things about London, there were too many people, and by the time they got off his father's ship his mother had been pregnant with his sister.

All his life he'd wanted a farm. The incoming and outgoing of the merchant business wasn't what he wanted. Morgan wanted a home where he could live, working the land and finally getting to eat what he'd grown. Not what he'd bought from an incoming ship.

And she told him her story. All of it. She told him about being taken by Indians and Asha. She told him about Alexis and their friendship. She also told him about Alexis being her paramour. He looked at her and said, "So the two of you-,"

"We did."

He nodded. "Okay then."

"You're not upset?"

"That the stranger I've just married has shared bed with someone else?"

"No, that I was with a woman."

Morgan shrugged. "Not really. Though it does beg the question of why you chose to marry me."

"You were the first boy I had ever thought was beautiful. It was like I was called to you by God or something."

He didn't say anything, but she could tell on his face that he liked hearing that. "It's a might strange that we've only knew each other for a few days."

"Not really. I've read about a lot of different places and sometimes people only meet at the church."

"Well," he said. "I suppose we have a bit of time on those people. We had two hours before the church."

Elizabeth laughed, and they continued to talk about anything and everything they could think of. When they ran out of subjects Elizabeth climbed into the back of the wagon where Morgan had told her his books were, and she read to him.

They laid together for the first time four days into the trip. They'd slept next to each other for warmth, but this was the first time they both agreed to share their bed in more than a literal sense. It was nothing like she had ever experienced before. Both Asha and Alexis had been special to her in different ways, though despite subtle differences sharing their beds was much the same.

This was different. This was a feeling that she had never had before. She'd married Morgan because he was beautiful, and he could take her out of the city, give her companionship. But more and more every day she loved him for who he was as a person, and what she saw in his soul.

It took almost three weeks, but they eventually made it to their land. They stood on a hill looking at their land and Elizabeth saw the look on Morgan's face. It told her that he was home. She looked at the land below them, a flat valley with a small group of trees towards the far side of it, and she felt the same way.

She couldn't help but think about Asha. She thought of what she had said about using the land right. and giving back as much as you took. Elizabeth had been through a lot of hardship, but looking down at all of what was before her she felt like maybe she would be able to move on from all of that and find some peace.

The next six months were hard work. They cut down enough trees to build a house, and while Morgan shaped the logs into what they needed, Elizabeth shed them of their branches and she went back to the forest and planted the seeds. "Why did you do that?" Morgan had asked her.

"Don't you want trees for our children? If we take care of the land it will take care of us."

Morgan had gone away for two weeks once. He came back with a wagon full of supplies and a few chickens and pigs. He was also pulling a team of Oxen that would plow their field.

They got up with the sun and didn't stop working until it got dark. It was hard work, but they loved every minute of it. It was the closest Elizabeth had come to living in the tribe since she was fourteen. They would build a fire in a pit outside the house and spend hours reading to each other or just sitting and listening to the sounds of their home.

One morning, when she woke Elizabeth noticed that Morgan was already gone. Normally he woke her up if she wasn't already awake, but the sun was already shining through the west window. As she rushed up and moved to put her clothes on she noticed that she'd put on a bit of weight. There was a bump just like she'd seen...oh dear. Just like she'd seen on the women in the tribe when they had babies. She was pregnant!

She left off her underclothes. The bump in her belly wouldn't allow them. She felt a bit strange at the breeze going up her dress as she walked out to find her wondrous husband plowing the field. She walked up and took her boots off. She loved walking barefoot on freshly plowed soil.

"There you are sleepy head," Morgan said as he walked over. "When you didn't stir on the third shake I decided to let you sleep. You think you're sick?"

She shook her head, a smile crawling across her face. "I'm pregnant"

She didn't think she'd ever seen anyone's eyes wider than Morgan's. "Are you serious?"

"I don't know for certain, but this is the same bump that the women always had when they were with child. Except for one girl who ended up having a sickness that killed her."

"I'll go fetch the doctor"

"Do you have a doctor I don't know about hidden in the woods? Because the nearest doctor lives two weeks south west of here."

"I don't care. I'm going right now. I'll bring him back here by gun point if I have too"

"Something tells me the musket hanging over the door isn't going to threaten the Doc."

"Why?"

"It hasn't been fired since the eighties. The last ball that went through that thing killed a red coat."

"Fine. I'll ask the doctor politely. And I'm going to buy a better gun so I can protect you."

Elizabeth laughed. "If you insist, you should fetch the doctor. But I think we can wait on the gun. My bow works just fine."

Morgan unhitched the Oxen and hitched the horses to the wagon. They only had one set of tack. She packed supplies for him and he was off to fetch her a doctor. He gave her strict instructions not to do anything too strenuous.

The second he was out of sight she got to work making a rope harness and plowed the rest of the field. The Indians worked up until the moment they gave birth, and then the day after. It was a bit frightening every time Morgan was gone. She'd slept alone more than she'd slept with someone, but she missed him sharing her bed. Her most favorite way to sleep was curled up in his arms.

That month went by agonizingly slow. She would get up and do all the chores then she would work on whatever project inevitably popped up, and then she would read.

On a trip to town Morgan had been able to trade with a book seller so that the next time he came through he brought Elizabeth books in Italian, French, and Latin. It had cost her beloved dearly she knew, but he wouldn't tell her what he had paid.

Then the day came that Morgan's wagon, loaded with the supplies they wouldn't need for months, came over the hill. He was followed by a black coach she assumed belonged to the doctor.

Doctor Harris was a large man. He was a few inches taller than Morgan and had muscles twice his size. His face was full of wrinkles and looked too beat in for his eyes to be very good. His hands looked much too large to be able to wield medical instruments with any certainty or precision.

His examination consisted of Elizabeth taking off her clothes and being inspected, poked and prodded, to see if she was physically prepared for birth. She hadn't attended medical school, but she knew for certain that her breasts had gotten exponentially larger and had started to hurt. She had not yet started to make milk, but she knew that would come soon.

The most uncomfortable part of the examination was when the doctor told her to lay on the bed and put her knees up. He then proceeded to stick his gigantic hands inside of her until it felt like he was tickling her throat. When he extracted his massive dadles from her less than accommodating quim, he said, "Everything looks healthy I suspect that you will deliver in two or three months. I'll be back around that time."

The doctor left to the east, so he could check in on a few people in the area. Morgan looked over the planting and plowing that she had done and, after pretending to be upset, thanked her for getting so much done.

They made love that night and afterwards they laid in bed, Morgan's hand never leaving her belly. "Oh," he said, "In all the commotion I almost forgot." He got up from the bed and she thought once again that she was lucky. Her husband was not only a wonderful man, he was also very attractive both with and without his clothes. She laughed to herself as he came back to bed with a letter. "What's funny?"

"Nothing, what have you got?"

"It's a letter from Alexis." Elizabeth smiled, and she took it from him, opening it at once.

Dear Liz,

I am so happy to hear that you've settled. I'm sorry it has taken so long to reply but we've been in in Mexico for a while and I didn't get my letters until recently. I hope to come see you soon.

I have so many stories to tell you Liz. So many that I'm afraid I don't have enough paper for all of them. I have taken a paramour. It's not like what you and I had. It's mostly physical. But she's nice Her name is Bridgette and I she s got blonde hair and a bosom that would make you weep if you saw it.

Are you ready for the scandalous bit? She and I have been making love after shows and when we make camp, nothing anyone in this place cares about, but sometimes she and I ride in the wagon completely naked! We are occasionally found but the looks on the men's faces are truly hilarious.

One even asked me how I'd managed it. When I asked

what he meant he said, fucking such a beautiful thing?
Oh, I wish you were with me Liz, perhaps we could
share Bridgette, though from your last letter it sounds
like your heart and loins are taken...perhaps I need to
find a man like Morgan.
With Love,
Alexis

Elizabeth smiled to herself. "So, it's good then?" Morgan asked. She nodded, smiling. She got up and walked over to put the letter in the wooden box where she kept all of them. She would write her friend tomorrow. She mentally scolded herself for not sending her other letters with Morgan when he'd went to town. She had several stacked up for his next trip.

There was nothing to be done about that now. In a few months they would need supplies and she could send all the letters if they got enough money selling the crops. She walked back over to the bed and laid her head on Morgan's chest.

CHAPTER FIVE

The next three months went by slowly. She could feel the baby move more and more every day. She'd been in the fields the first time when it kicked. It hurt a bit, but it was a joyous pain. She'd smiled the rest of the day. It took nearly an hour to convince Morgan she was okay, and he didn't need to fetch the doctor.

The doctor arrived early one morning. He started to address Morgan about the baby when she said, "Don't you think the best person to discuss the baby with would be she who is having it?"

The doctor's mouth turned up in a smile. "Quite right."

Morgan went to tend to the doctor's horses while she and the doctor went to the chairs near the house to sit. Her belly was big and she didn't walk well. She sighed loudly when she sat. "How are you feeling?" The doctor asked.

"My feet swell up, my belly makes it hard to work, and quite frankly my breasts feel heavy enough that I fear they may fall off."

"I have to say you are rather eloquent for a farmer's wife."

"I was not raised one," she said. "Now, about my health?"

He laughed again. "Well the feet swelling is normal. The engorged breasts are good, more milk for the baby, and I'd say that you are doing more than enough work growing a child. You'd better take a break from field work."

"Well when I lived with my tribe the women with babies always had them and went back to work right away. hey also worked right up until they gave birth."

The doctor raised an eyebrow. "Indians?"

"My life has been a complicated series of events doctor." '

"Aren't they all, but I suppose it isn't polite to pry."

The doctor was there with them for another two weeks before she went into labor. Walking into the house she felt something give, her feet were wet, and a sudden pain hit her stomach. The doctor helped her to the bed and she began labor. It hurt so much. It took hours. She was sweating and screaming well into the night, only occasionally getting a moment of rest.

Just before daybreak the Doctor checked on her again. He looked up at her with a smile and said, "I believe this baby wanted to come into the world on a brand-new day. It'll be here in only a few moments" He sent Morgan to get a washtub and fill it with water. "Okay now Elizabeth, I want you to push."

She didn't feel like she could, but she gritted her teeth and pushed. After only a few pushes she felt instant relief and heard crying. She lay back against the pillow and waited for the baby.

The Doctor came up with the baby wrapped in his arms. "You are now the mother of a beautiful baby girl."

Elizabeth, as dirty and exhausted as she was, looked down at this thing, this creature who had grown inside her all this time, and she had never loved anything or anyone more. She looked for Morgan and found him standing on her other side. "What do you think of the name Josephine?"

"I love it."

She looked down at the baby. "Hello Josephine Blaney. welcome home."

She was up later that day. The doctor tried to tell her that she needed rest, but she knew enough to know

that she was okay. The doctor headed back to town and after he was out of sight Morgan said, "I've got something to show you."

He led her into the barn where he went behind some hay and brought out a beautiful wooden bassinet. It was marvelous. He'd polished it and even made the cushions to fit inside. "How'd you do this without me knowing?"

He smiled. "I took advantage of you not being able to walk much."

They both laughed, and Elizabeth put Josie down into the crib. She giggled. "You like it?" She looked up at Morgan. "She likes it." Morgan came forward and gave her a kiss.

When they broke she picked up the baby and he carried the bassinet to the edge of the field. He'd built it with a half roof so that she would be covered and it helped to keep the sun out of her eyes as she napped. With the baby safe and sound, they went back to work.

CHAPTER SIX

"M organ, riders."

He turned to look and saw the three figures riding up. They'd been harvesting crops all month and hadn't seen anyone since the doctor left. She almost thought she was mistaken until Morgan said, "Take Josie in the house and bring me my gun.

His tone brokered no argument. Elizabeth scooped up the baby and headed towards the house. She pulled up the door to the cellar and sat Josie down in the corner behind a sack, nestled in her blankets. "Please be silent honey." she said. As she went back up She went to the bed side table and took Morgan's pistol out. She made sure it was loaded.

Leaving the house, she grabbed a knife and put it in the back of her dress. Elizabeth put the gun behind her back. She walked towards Morgan and was still a ways off when the riders got to him. They dismounted, and she could hear some words exchanged, though she couldn't make them out.

Then one of them shot Morgan in the chest.

She was so shocked that she stopped walking and screamed. All three riders turned to her and she whipped the gun around, firing blindly. She dove to the side as they shot back and she looked over at them. One of them was slumped to the ground and the big one was tending to him. The rider walking towards her wasn't particularly tough looking. He wore a green jacket, faded red shirt, and plain brown trousers. She closed her eyes and tried to act as if she'd been hit. He bent down and called out to his friends. "I don't see nothin' but she ain't breathing."

"Well shoot her just to be sure." Came a voice. Her eyes snapped open and in one motion, she lunged at the man and pulled the knife from behind her back. She went rolling, the man's neck in her arms and came up on top of him. She plunged the knife into his neck and blood sprayed all over her for the second time in her life. She wiped her eyes and took the dead man's gun, letting him slump to the ground.

As the biggest man looked over at her she started firing as she walked closer. She hit him once and he laid there immobile as she walked up. She knelt down and opened the man's throat.

The last man was still alive. He was choking on his own blood. She knelt down next to him and asked, "Why? Why did you have to kill my husband?"

"Because..." he choked out. "He said we couldn't stay...so we just decided to take the place."

She couldn't believe what she was hearing. They had killed a man just because he told them to leave his land? She could have cut the man with the gaze she gave him. "I hope it was worth it."

She didn't see the knife. With one last bit of energy he thrust the knife into her belly. He let go and she fell backward. After a moment she struggled up and she put her own knife through his eye, twisting it and enjoying the cry he gave out. Before he died she said, "If you leave my baby motherless I will follow you to hell and the devil will cringe at what I'll do to you."

She put the knife back in her blood-soaked dress and struggled to get up. Morgan was dead when she got to him. She cried as she cut off his shirt and suspenders. She cried out even more as she made herself a bandage and cinched it tight.

Somehow, she managed to get a bridle into a horse's mouth. She couldn't stop thinking of how happy she had been only a small while ago, and how those men took it from her. She retrieved the crying Josie from the cellar, put some provisions into a bag, and used a sheet to tie Josie to her chest. She left her breast out for Josie and as she got onto the horse she felt her daughter begin her midday meal. She'd long since gotten used to the feeling, but she started to cry yet again.

Her daughter had no father. It was up to her to protect them both now.

She rode the horse to the point of near exhaustion. Letting him rest she built a fire and did the best she could to clean her wounds with water from a nearby stream and a bowl she'd brought for her to drink from. She bit down on a stick as she poured the boiling water on her naked belly. Josie got upset when she cried out, the pain was so great that Elizabeth soon passed out. She thanked God that Josie didn't know how to walk.

She was in the same place when she woke the next morning. Elizabeth put her tattered dress back on, cleaned the baby, and they rode.

When she got to town she realized that she didn't know where to go. She hadn't been here since they'd come in nearly a year ago. So she just started screaming. A crowd soon gathered and she saw no one she knew until the doctor walked out, presumably to find where the screaming was coming from. "Doctor Harris! It's me, Elizabeth!"

He came closer. "What happened child?"

"Morgan was killed by riders. The sheriff will find all four bodies laying out. I am in need of someone to look after Josie, and your assistance."

"My assistance? With what?"

She shifted Josie to the side and showed him her stomach "I've been stabbed." The world went sideways and the next thing she knew she was falling. She felt the doctor's arms around her and then everything went black.

CHAPTER SEVEN

Elizabeth's mouth was dry. She licked several times, but her mouth still felt like the time the tribe had been unable to find water for several days. She looked around, trying to remember what happened.

Then it all came back. Morgan, the riders, everything. Her thoughts immediately turned to her daughter.

"Josie!" she cried out. "Josie!"

"Here she is." said a girl coming through the door with the baby in her arms. She gently gave Josie to Elizabeth.

"Who are you?"

The girl was young. She couldn't have been more than fifteen. She had honey blonde hair that came down around her shoulder, She was beautiful, deep blue eyes and a round, welcoming face. Add her ample bosom and Elizabeth knew she'd have no trouble finding a husband. She probably had loads of suitors already. "My name is Bethany," she said. "I help Doc look after things."

'You are his daughter?"

Bethany nodded. "Yes ma'am."

Before she could ask any more questions, the doctor walked in the room. He knocked but didn't wait for a reply. "Thank goodness I was starting to think you'd not wake up."

"How long have I been asleep?"

"Five days. You were near exhausted. And I do not mean simply tired, much longer and you would have died." Elizabeth sat up in bed, cringing at the pain. She was wrapped in bandages from just under her breasts down to her waist. "I don't know how you're alive." The doctor said. "You nicked more than one thing that should have bled you out."

"I boiled water and poured it into the wound."

Doctor Harris looked genuinely impressed. "That saved your life. I don't know many men who could have done that. Cauterizing that wound must have been immensely painful."

"It was."

"Oh," He said as if remembering. "I was sent to see if you were awake, the sheriff needs to speak with you."

Elizabeth handed Josie to Bethany and struggled out of the bed. Bethany went over to a hook and brought her a dress. "I'm a bit wider than you, so it might be loose."

She pulled the dress on and it was just right. Bethany was a stocky girl, but Elizabeth had apparently put on a bit of weight. "You must be skinnier than you think because it fits remarkably well." Bethany blushed and agreed to watch Josie.

She walked down the stairs and out to the boardwalk. The man she deduced was the sheriff, due to the badge, was standing with and older man in a duster. He had the beginnings of grey hair and a squinted stare like he was looking at the sheriff, but also assessing his surroundings. Both men turned to look at her as she approached. The sheriff extended his hand and said, "My name is Sheriff Edwards and I need you to tell me about what happened on your farm."

"Right into it then," The other man said.

The sheriff didn't look at him. Elizabeth sighed, which hurt, and launched into her story. "We were bringing in the harvest when the riders came up. My hus...my husband sent me inside to hide the baby and get his gun. When I came back I saw one of them shoot him in the chest."

She took a painfully shaky breath and continued. "I fired at the men and hit one. The second saw to his friend while I played dead and killed the third. I took the third's gun and shot the second, and then I finished both the first and second men with my knife. I didn't see the other man's knife before he stabbed me."

"I would hope not." said the other man. "It would've been awful foolish to let him stab you."

"Tomorrow I plan to set out for your place. I'd appreciate it if you'd come." The Sheriff said.

"Yes sir."

The sheriff walked away, and the other man stayed. "Name's Bartholomew Did you really kill them men?"

"Yes sir."

He made a face. "Huh, I'm coming with you and the sheriff and if I like what I see you and I might have some talkin' to do."

Elizabeth looked at him confused. "I don't understand."

Bartholomew smiled. "Might be that's best for now. Too much understandin' ain't good for folks."

Elizabeth raised an eyebrow at him. Her Father used to say something a bit like that, though he'd used better English. She tried to remember her Latin and said, "You are a strange man."

He smiled and replied, also in Latin, "You have no idea."

The next day Elizabeth readied her horse and Josie. Bethany had offered to watch her, but she declined. She couldn't stand to have her away. She nestled the baby down in her wrap and they followed the sheriff and Bartholomew out of town.

They rode hard. They didn't stop for nearly a day. When they did, the sheriff dished out some food and

Bartholomew built a fire while Elizabeth tended to Josephine. When the baby was sleeping, Elizabeth

walked over and retrieved a letter from her saddle bags. She was reading by the fire when Bartholomew asked, "From a friend?"

"Yes. She was with the circus but now she has taken over a boarding house. "

"Where at?"

"San Marcos Texas."

Bartholomew nodded like he was privy to a secret. "I know that town. I hope she took over Jake's boarding house. That place was shit."

Everything got quiet. The sheriff was asleep and Bartholomew was keeping the first watch. When she

had finished the letter he said, "You should get some sleep, that baby'll be up with the sun."

Elizabeth nodded. She laid her head against her bundle and nestled Josie in her arms, drifting off to sleep.

CHAPTER EIGHT

"Damn." Was all either of the men could say at seeing the bodies. Buzzards and other creatures had been on them, and they smelled. But you could still see the marks and wounds she had inflicted.

Bartholomew knelt by each of the bodies in turn. Raising up he looked at the sheriff. "These are the men I was after."

As she stood there holding the baby she couldn't help but feel a bit proud of the looks on the men's faces. These two were clearly fighters, and they had been through things like this before. Yet they were still impressed with her.

"You killed these men?" The sheriff asked again.

"Well who else could have done it?" said Bartholomew.

The sheriff sighed. "I'll get to burying them."

The two men went to bury the bodies. Elizabeth stood far away from Morgan. She squeezed her baby harder, as if someone would try to take her away. Bartholomew must have seen her looking at Morgan because he called out to the sheriff. "This one first." And they got Morgan, taking him behind the barn.

Josie's bassinet was still next to the field. She walked over and sat the baby down inside it. She wept when she ran her hand over Morgan's work. "Are you okay?" Bartholomew asked.

"Yes, I just...my husband made this for her."

He looked at the bassinet, running his hand over the dark wood, "I made something similar for my daughter. though he did much better work than I did."

Elizabeth wiped her eyes and turned around just as the sheriff came up, wiping his hands on his legs. "Where do you plan on going?" he asked. "You can't work this place by yourself."

She ran a hand through her hair. She hadn't thought about any of that. She could work this place alone, but she didn't know if she could stand living in the house without Morgan, working the same field he died next to.

She could go to Alexis, but she didn't have enough money to get there. "I'll take you." Bartholomew said. "I could teach you bounty hunting."

"What is that?"

"I hunt bad men and bring them in dead or alive. Then I get paid for it."

"And you would teach me how to do that?"

He nodded. "Yes ma'am, looks like you'd be very good at it."

"What about Josie?"

He looked apprehensive, not wanting to tell her what she knew he would have to say. Finally, he said, "This is no life for a child."

Elizabeth looked over at her child. She needed away to provide for her, and to protect her at the same time. This would be hard, but she knew it was the best way. "Okay," she said. "But we have to drop her off in Texas with my friend."

Bartholomew nodded. "Done. Gather your things and we'll take off now."

"Excuse me," The sheriff interrupted. "But what would you like done with this place?"

She thought for a moment. "You can have the animals. Close up the house and, if you wouldn't mind, keep anyone from moving in. I may have need of this place someday."

"You don't want to let someone else use it?"

"If I had a neighbor I'd have them look after it, maybe farm the fields, but no one is around. So, if you'll take the animals as payment, I would appreciate you looking after the place from time to time. Let the forest take back the land while I'm gone."

The sheriff looked like he didn't like the idea, but it must have hit him how much he could sell the animals for because he said, "Okay. I have to come through this way every few months, Doc too, so we'll keep an eye out. Anything else?"

She thought. "Yes, I'll be taking the wagon and the horses, but I'll sell you all the equipment that's left for your gun belt."

"You want my gun?" he said, incredulous.

"No sir, just the belt."

He handed her the belt and she walked over and picked Morgan's revolver up off the ground. She put it in the belt and strapped the belt on.

Elizabeth packed the wagon with only what she needed. They would have a big trip ahead, so she took all the food, a bit of bedding, and her box of letters. She looked around, wondering if there was anything else. The two of them hadn't had much in the way of earthly possessions. They'd lived here with nothing besides each other. She left the house and found Morgan's hat lying on the ground. It was even more weathered from the last month on the ground. Bartholomew and the sheriff helped her get the basinet in the wagon just behind the seat.

Everyone mounted up. The sheriff was heading back to town to get some help moving animals, and they were headed to Texas. She shook hands with the sheriff and thanked him again before heading out.

San Marcos was a tiny town. One street really. They had a store, a boarding house, a saloon, and a depot for stages and mail, a stable was at the end of the street. They pulled up and Bart, as he had told her to call him, watched the wagon and Josie while she went in to find Alexis.

There was a staircase going up to the rooms directly across from the door. To the right was a little sitting parlor with a desk that had a secretary behind it. Little boxes for mail and things, each one had a key hanging on it. There were couches in front of the windows directly to the right.

To the left was a dining room with a large table that ran the length of the room. The back door to the kitchen swung, but she didn't see who had gone in. "I'll be with you in just a minute!" Called Alexis' voice from upstairs.

"No trouble, I can wait." she called back.

She heard thundering footsteps and a moment later Alexis was looking over the banister at her. "Liz?"

"Hello."

Alexis ran around the banister and took the steps three at a time. She hadn't changed much. She'd filled out a bit more in all the right places, but for the most part she was exactly like she remembered her, young and beautiful. She launched herself at Liz and was soon winging in her arms. She kissed her, and Liz sat her down. "It's so nice to see you! Is Morgan with you?"

Liz took in a shaky breath. "He uh…"

Alexis' face fell. "Oh, I'm so sorry."

"Thank you, would you like to meet my daughter?"

Her eyes went wide, "You have a daughter? Oh my goodness!"

Alexis ran out the door and started looking around. Liz pointed her to the wagon and she ran over, hopping up and looking down at, the crib. "She's beautiful."

"Yes, she is. Thankfully she looks more like her Poppa."

Alexis looked at Josie and spoke without looking away. "I'd say she's got a bit of you in there too darling."

Bart, who had been watching all of this from atop his horse, said, "I'm going to the saloon. I'd like a room if you have one."

Alexis looked at him, "Yes sir."

"Thank ya, I'll be back tonight."

He rode off and Alexis looked at her, "Who's the dude?"

"Let's go inside and I'll explain."

They went inside and sat at the dining room table. Alexis held Josie and the baby slept. She seemed to like Alexis very much. "Do you have many customers?" Liz asked.

"Yes, not many people stay in town but a lot pass through."

"Is it just you here?"

"Me and the girls."

"Girls?"

"Did I not mention in my letter that this is a boarding house and a whore house?"

Liz balked at that a bit, "Um, no you didn't mention it."

"Sorry about that. They all share the two rooms in the back. They're sleeping now, though I think Rosie might be reading."

"Do you-"

Alexis shook her head, laughing a little to herself. "No, I don't share my bed for money. I haven't shared my bed with anyone in a while."

"I'm sorry Bridgette didn't leave with you."

"I'm not, thank you, but she had a very nice offer to apprentice with the knife thrower Philippe. I would have taken the same offer in her position."

The two of them got to talking, bringing up the things that had happened in between letters. Liz went back to the wagon and got the box of letters that she hadn't been able to send. And then they got into what she had really come for.

Liz told her about Bart's offer and she asked her if she would take care of Josie. She could tell that Alexis was not in love with the idea. "I'd send most of my money to you," Liz added. "To help take care of her, and you."

"That's wonderful, but that's not what I'm worried about. Do you really want her to be away from you? You'll miss a lot. Even with frequent visits like you say, you're gonna miss quite a lot of her life."

Liz wanted to be angry. She felt like she should be. But, she knew that her friend was right. "I don't have a lot of choices."

she said. "You have a life here, I know you make money, but can you really afford to have the both of us here indefinitely?"

"No" she said reluctantly.

"I have to make money, and I won't, whore. I don't look down on them, but I can't do it Alexis."

"I understand, that's the reason I don't. I just wanted to make sure you had considered that. I'm being your friend."

Liz put her elbows on the table and her head in her hands. "I know. You're the best friend I've got." She wasn't looking at her, but she knew the look on Alexis' face. It was the same one she'd seen time and again when her friend would get her out of trouble. It was the look that told her she was one of only a very small number of people that Alexis cared about. "I would be more than happy to take her in while you play bounty hunter. She'll be here when you need her."

"Thank you."

They were silent for a while, then Alexis asked, "Is she still on the tit?"

"Yes."

Alexis thought for a moment. Liz could practically see the wheels turning. After a couple of minutes, she asked, "Have you any objections to me feeding her?"

"But you've never had a baby."

Alexis laughed. "You don't have to. We had cows that had babies and the calves would suckle on any tit they could find. Some of the heifers fed babies when they didn't have any of their own."

Liz looked at her confused. "You would do that for me? Taking her in is one thing, but acting as her wet nurse?"

"What's that?"

"Royalty, like princesses and Queens, they had someone else to feed the young royals."

"Huh…I guess I'll do that then. I'll be her wet nurse."

They laughed. "There has to be another reason." Liz said.

"Not really. You're my friend and I know that if the shoe was on the other foot you'd do it for me."

Liz looked at her. She was touched, but she also knew Alexis very well. Finally, Alexis said, "Okay, I've known women who feed kids like that and they always have huge tits. I figure the big tits will help the customers tip better."

Liz slapped the table. They both immediately looked at Josie, but she was still fast asleep. "I knew it." Liz said laughing.

Alexis shrugged. "When men are distracted they over pay."

Liz was tired. Alexis needed sleep before everything got going that night. They took Josie upstairs to her room and Alexis put someone else in charge of minding the front. Liz got the crib out of the wagon and, after feeding her and letting her suckle at Alexis' breast for a bit, she said it would get her milk started, they went to bed.

Alexis woke her in the dark with a hand on her quim. She looked at her and Alexis asked, "For old time's sake?"

Liz couldn't help but think of Morgan. She knew he would want her to be happy, even if that happiness was just to dull the pain of her loss. She nodded, and Alexis' head disappeared under the blankets. Moments later she felt a pleasant shiver go up her body. For the first time in a month she forgot her pain. She just reveled in Alexis' love.

CHAPTER NINE

The last man's body git the ground. Bart threw him over the back of his horse and, as he mounted up his own, said, "After we deliver these boys I say we've earned a break. What'd you say to Colorado? We're fairly close."

"We're also close to San Marcos" she said. I'd like to see her soon."

"I know Liz."

They started their ride to Albuquerque where they would collect the bounty for their men. They had been a group that attacked a town, burning three businesses down and killing and raping a group of young women. They'd declined the offer to come in alive and started shooting.

The two of them rode in silence. Neither of them was keen on talking right after killing. The next day they would be fine, chatting in any of the languages they knew, she'd taught him hers and he'd taught her Spanish. It came in handy being able to talk covertly no matter who was around, but today they wouldn't talk much.

She was eager to go to Texas. It had been six, almost seven months since she'd been there. "I missed her birthday." she said out loud.

"I remember. I'm sorry that we missed it."

"We had to work," She said. "That town needed their revenge."

"Yes." They rode on. She thought about Josie. She was five years old now. It seemed like she'd grew a foot between every time she saw her. It broke her heart the last time she'd visited. Josie had not done her chores, feeding the pigs they kept out back or some such, and Alexis had put her foot down. She told Josie she would get a spanking and loose her dessert if she didn't hop to it.

She'd started to object, but it wasn't her place. Liz was her mother, but she wasn't the one raising her.

They made it to Albuquerque in just a couple of days. As they rode into town Bart said, "It's my turn." She nodded and turned her horse towards the hotel. They took turns collecting the bounty so that when the other was done they already had a room and could get some sleep. Divide and conquer.

She booked them two rooms and went to the bar for a drink. She'd taken a liking to whiskey over the last few years. It helped her numb some pain. She'd killed men over the last five years, enough that she didn't bother keeping count. It didn't bother her, the killing. But sometimes she thought of Morgan, or Asha, or even her parents, though they came up less often.

It was the people she'd loved and lost that haunted her.

Bart came through the door and she signaled for the bartender to get two, more. "I've got an idea." Bart said walking up. He handed her a small bag of coins and without looking she put it in the inside pocket of her duster.

"What's that?"

"I'll go to Colorado and you head to Texas. I think we've earned maybe two weeks off. What say we meet up then in...well here I reckon."

"That's quite a ride for both of us. Might take most of our time off... "

Bart thought for a second before he said, "Fuck it then, let's take two months. Two weeks there, a month in town, and two weeks back."

"You sure you can go that long without working?"

"Hell yes. We've done three jobs back to back in the last six months. I'm going to spend all my time with whores and playing poker."

Liz laughed. "You'll be broke coming back."

"And you won't? You're gonna pamper that little girl of yours and you know it."

"Fair enough." She said, and they laughed again. They played a round of poker with some men, adding quite a bit to their respective purses.

Liz barely slept that night. She was eager to see Josie, so eager that she almost left a dozen times. She and Bart parted ways the next morning and she started the long journey to see her daughter, her saddlebags stuffed with presents for Josephine and Alexis.

She rode as long as the horse could take it. Roco had never done her wrong. She'd kept him even when Bart had switched horses. She slept in the saddle until he needed a break and then she made camp.

She got to San Marcos in the middle of the night. Lamps were burning in the boarding house and she dismounted, walking up the steps and looking into the open front door. Alexis was walking into the dining room and hadn't seen her. Josie was coming down the stairs.

Her eyes went wide and she yelled, "Momma!" She ran down the stairs and jumped into Liz's arms.

She spun her around and gave her a big kiss. "I missed you darling."

"I missed you too Momma. Guess what?"

"What?"

"Alexis gave me a job."

"Really?" Liz spied Alexis walking in from the dining room. She stood in the doorway, watching them.

"Uh hu, she gave me a very important job. I am in charge of getting the baths together for the girls when they're done with a man, and I clean the room."

Liz was a bit shocked to hear that her daughter was around things like that. But then again what had she

expected, sending her to live in a whore house? Alexis came forward and said quietly in her ear, "She's never anywhere near them while they're working."

Alexis kissed her. She sat Josie down and took her hand as they walked towards the dining room. There came three quick knocks from upstairs as a man was coming out of the first room. Josie broke away saying, Be right back. I've gotta work. "

Liz smiled after her. She looked so grown up. She was almost chest high now. She came up to just below her belly button. "She's gotten so big." she said to Alexis.

"I know, she's so smart too. She takes care of the hogs and chickens almost entirely by herself, and she does wonderfully with her numbers. She's helped me do the books more than once."

"How's her reading?"

"I can't get her to stop." The sole reason I gave her a job instead of chores was so she could buy books. Mr. Hanson, the store owner, he orders books in just for her."

Liz's heart swelled with pride. She followed Alexis the rest of the way into the dining room, where she went and got Liz a plate. Josephine came in a few minutes later and sat on her lap. "Where is Bartholomew?"

Liz laughed at her insistence on calling him by his full first name. "He went to Colorado."

"Did he not want to see me?"

"No no sweetie, he just had some friend she wanted to visit."

"Whores?"

"Among others yes."

"Well we have whores here. And ours are real clean." Liz wasn't sure how to respond to that. Thankfully Josie lost her attention when another knock came from upstairs. "I'll be right back."

Liz stayed in Alexis' room. Her bed was nice, probably the nicest in the place, four posters and a canopy. Josie had a bed in the corner along with a small desk and a shelf crammed with books. Across that wall was a taller desk and another shelf with books and ledgers on it. A table on the side wall had a pitcher and basin. There was a tub in the middle of the room and a stove on the far-right wall near enough to both beds for everyone to be warm.

She sat down at the taller desk and did what she always did before bed. Her saddle bags had been brought up so she took out her rifle, revolver, and her belly gun and she set to cleaning them. When she was on her last weapon, the revolver, she heard the door open behind her.

Josephine ran in and stood by the desk. "What're you doing?"

"I'm cleaning my weapons."

"Can I help?"

"Unfortunately, I'm just finishing. But how about tomorrow I teach you how to do it?"

"Okay." She picked up the derringer "I like this one."

Liz grabbed the gun from her, "That's loaded. You must never point a gun at something unless you want to kill it. Always treat a weapon as if it is loaded."

Josie gave a solemn nod. "Yes ma'am."

The tiny girl walked over and started to undress. She went to a hook by the bookshelf and took down a night gown, pulling it on. She climbed into bed, adjusting her pillows and pulling the blankets overtop herself. "Do you always put yourself to bed?" Liz asked. She didn't remember this from the last time she'd been here.

"No," Josie said "I only put myself to bed a few times a week. The nights when Alexis watches the desk."

Liz nodded her understanding. It was strange to hear her say night when it was really the beginning of the day, but there had been a few times when she herself had followed that schedule. She walked over and knelt next to Josie's bed, "Can I ask you something?"

"Yes ma'am."

"Do you think I'm a bad Momma?"

Josephine looked utterly shocked by the idea. "No. I think you're the best Momma. You take bad men to jail and you always bring me nice presents from your adventures so that I feel like I have been there too."

She smiled down at her daughter. "I'm sorry I'm not around more baby. Have you been getting some of the money I send?"

Josephine nodded. "Alexis used to give me some when it came. But I asked for a job so I think that's what she pays me with."

"It wasn't Alexis' idea? You asked for a job?"

"Uh hu. I wanted to work for money just like you."

Liz laughed. "You remind me of your father."

"Can you tell me about him?"

So, she did. She told Josie about how she'd met Morgan and how quickly they had been married. She told her about the farm and finding out she was pregnant. Josie laughed at how Morgan had reacted, immediately heading for town. She didn't leave anything out. She wanted her daughter to know exactly how great a man her father had been.

CHAPTER TEN

She woke up next to Alexis. For the briefest of moments, she was back in St Louis, the two of them holding on to each other not only in love, but in order to keep from freezing as well. "Good morning sleepy head." Alexis said waking. She kissed her and Liz heard giggling.

They both looked to the foot of the bed. Josephine was standing on the trunk looking at them. "Can we go for a picnic? If You're done kissing."

Both women laughed. "Did you get your work done?" Alexis asked.

"No." Josie said looking down at her feet.

"Well hop to it, tell Claire to make us up a basket. When you've got your things done we can go."

A smile spread across the five-year old's face. She jumped down from the trunk and hit the floor running. Alexis laughed and looked back at Liz. "I hope that's okay, I knowhow much she's been wanting to go on a picnic with you."

"It sounds like fun." Liz said. "I'd like to spend the next month doing as much with her as possible, without messing up what you have going. I know you're the one who's actually in charge around here. Not me."

Alexis looked sad for a beat, then she leaned forward and gave Liz another kiss. They broke apart only slightly, their mouths less than an inch apart, their noses touching. "You know, it takes her about an hour to do her chores." Liz smiled and locked their hips, rolling on top of her as they both giggled.

There was a nice spot in the outskirts of town. They climbed up a hill looking over the edge, Liz saw the most serene spot she'd ever seen. There was one lone tree by a small river and a lush field of grass. There was a handful of other trees down the field, as if someone had cut this spot just for the perfect picnic area.

They laid out the blanket and sat down. Alexis sat the basket down and Josephine asked, "Can we go swimming?"

It hurt to see her ask Alexis that. She shook off the desire to be the one in charge. She was here to enjoy time with her daughter. "If it's okay with your Momma." Alexis said.

She looked at Alexis and mouthed, "Thank you." Turning back to Josie she said, "I would love to swim. You run and make sure the water isn't too cold, I'm very sensitive."

Josie giggled. "No you're not."

"Oh okay, I'm not." Josie ran off smiling and they walked after her. Getting to the river Liz saw Josie hang her dress on a branch. "How's the water?"

"It's good" She said walking towards the edge.

"Throw her in." Alexis whispered in her ear as she undressed.

Liz walked forward, turning Josie around. "Do you know how to swim?"

Josie nodded. Liz picked her up and threw her out. She hit the water and went down, coming up with a smile on her face. Liz turned around to find a naked Alexis looking at her, hands on her hips. "Have I ever told you how amazing you look naked?" she asked.

Alexis smiled. "Yes, yes you have." Liz started to get undressed. She hung her coat on the tree and Alexis looked at her, "You brought your gun on a picnic?" she said incredulously.

"I bring my gun everywhere." she said taking it off.

Alexis rolled her eyes and waited for her to finish undressing. They got in the water and Josie swam up to them. "Isn't this fun?"

"Yes." She said. "This is the most fun I've had in a long time."

They swam until they got pruney and cold. Gathering their clothes, they walked back to the blanket and dried off in the sun. They ate their lunch and dressed, it was one of the happiest days of her life.

Josie was running around in the grass while the adults laid out on the blanket. Josie came running up and asked, "Will you teach me how to shoot?"

Liz was laying long ways on Alexis' belly. She looked up and said, "I don't know if you're old enough yet."

"I am, I promise."

"You can keep her safe," Alexis said. "Let's do it."

Defeated, Liz stood up and retrieved her gun from where it laid on the blanket. She stood up and started to walk away towards another tree. "Follow me," she said.

They stood a few yards away from a tree. Liz raised her gun and shot three holes near each other in the tree. Then she handed it to Josie, kneeling down to help her steady it. The gun was plain, seven and a half inches of blue steeled barrel with a dark wood grip. Josie held it and looked at the MB carved into the handle. "I did that." she told her. "Your Poppa bought it to protect us. I carved that cause I wanted him to have his name on his gun. Turn it over."

Josie turned the gun over and saw the LB on the other side. "I put that so he'd remember me when he was away from the house. Now adays it's the other way around."

Josephine looked up at her like she might cry. "Do you think of him a lot?"

"Every single day." She wiped her eyes and looked forward, pointing the gun at the tree. Liz put her hand on her back. "Okay, close your left eye, see that little notch at the end? Line that up with the tree and squeeze the trigger."

The shot sent the small girl back into her hand. The gun fell to the ground and Josie looked at her, a smile on her face. "That was fun."

Liz smiled, she retrieved the gun as Alexis stepped forward. "Can I try?"

Liz handed over the gun. Alexis shot the rest of the rounds in the chamber in quick succession, all of them hitting the tree. "Wow." Was all Liz could say.

Josie was jumping up and down, clapping. "I want to learn how to shoot like that. Can you two teach me?"

They shared a look. "I tell you what," Alexis said. "I'll head home and grab the rifle and my shotgun while you two stay here and keep shooting."

"Yes ma'am." Josie said with a smile. Alexis winked at Liz and started back towards the boarding house. Liz moved a bit closer and she let Josie fire round after round until her belt was empty. When Alexis brought back the shotgun and Liz's rifle Josie picked up her Momma's rifle. She shot the Winchester Carbine and flew a few feet backwards. The gun was lying in the grass as they went to Josie. She was on her back in the grass, crying.

"What's hurt baby?" Alexis asked kneeling down.

"My shoulder. "

They gently helped her up and took the right arm of her dress down. A bruise was forming on her shoulder. Alexis wiped her eyes and gave her a kiss on the cheek. "You'll be fine. But I think we should be done for today."

Josie shook her head. "I wanna shoot the big one."

Alexis stood up, thinking. Liz could see her considering whether or not she would let her continue. "No I think we'd better get going before it gets late. And you wouldn't want a bigger bruise would you?"

"I don't care. I want to shoot the big one."

"And I said no."

Josie looked at Liz. "You are my mama"

She didn't look , but she could feel Alexis' gaze boring into her. "Alexis is right." she said.

Josephine stomped her foot and turned around, walking off towards town. Alexis looked at her, thankfulness written on her face. "I appreciate you backing me up."

"Any time."

The rest of her vacation went by too fast. Josie didn't stay mad for long when she found out she would be getting presents. Liz had brought her some books and a few toys. Alexis got a beautiful necklace she'd found in a shop in the east. It had a leather cord with a small pearl colored pendant with black trim.

They went fishing, just her and Josie. They had more than one picnic, though they didn't shoot anymore. They just spent as much time together as they could. When she had to go, she gave Alexis a deep kiss and

hugged Josie so tight she thought she might break her.

She got on her horse and rode away, waving as she sat backwards and calling out her love until Alexis took Josie inside. Turning around to ride right she patted Roco on the neck. "Were you taken care of baby?" She laughed. She could have sworn he nodded, raising his head up and then back down. She'd went to see him a few times, even taking Josie. for a ride or two. But Roco had spent the majority of the time in San Marcos running in the paddock, breeding with mares, and being fed good grain.

She thought of her daughter the entire ride to Albuquerque. Camping her first night she took out her knife and carved a J into the butt of the gun. The entire family now rode with her.

CHAPTER ELEVEN

Liz had been in Albuquerque for almost a week before she thought something had happened. She thought Bart had just gotten drunk or held up with some woman and he would be there soon. But when it started going into his second week being late she decided to set off for Colorado, wishing desperately that she knew where in Colorado Bartholomew had been headed.

The first town she came across was much like San Marcos, small and more of a stop along the way rather than a destination. The locals hadn't seen Bart, so she supplied and went on. She hit every town in the two week radius.

Finally, after three weeks of looking she found it, La Junta. She rode into town and stopped off at the sheriff's office. As she walked in she saw a man stand up. He was large, a good foot taller than Liz and twice as broad. He had a thick gray mustache and a dirty white hat that looked like it had seen almost as much use as her own. "Can I helpyou ma'am?"

"I'm looking for a man by the name of Bartholomew."

"Bounty hunter?

"Yes sir."

The sheriff sighed. "I recall the man." He walked over to another desk on the right side of the room. From a shelf behind the desk he took Bart's gun belt, hat, and his other effects, a journal and an old saddle bag.

Liz put her hand to her mouth. Bart was dead. She didn't need the sheriff to confirm it. "How did it happen?"

"The Burlap brothers shot him coming out of the saloon. Shot him in the back and stood over him, all seven putting bullet after bullet into him."

"Did you get them?"

The sheriff shook his head. "My deputies came after them, but they shot them too before they left town." Liz was fuming with anger. She clenched her fists together as the sheriff said, "I'm sorry if he meant something to you young lady."

"Sheriff," she said ignoring his sympathetic, if not slightly patronizing comment, "What do you know about these men?" The sheriff sat down at the desk and ruffled through some papers. He came up with a set of wanted posters.

"The Burlap brothers. There was eight of 'em, but one got killed a few years ago. Since then the other seven have only gotten worse. They're wanted for everything from horse theft to bank robbery. But it's mostly been murder, rape, and just causing general terror wherever they go." He handed her the posters and she went over them, Jona, Mason, Ruben, Graham, Bill, Jackson, and Augustus.

They had crimes listed longer than any of the men that she and Bart had ever gone after. They had a ten thousand dollar bounty on each of them, save for Jackson, the youngest. His bounty was five thousand. "Sheriff," she said. "I am going to kill these men."

"They took off in different directions, or so I'm told."

"Well then point me in one of the directions and I will work from there."

An hour later, after feeding and watering Roco and getting something for herself, she headed West where one of them was supposed to have gone. She had Bart's things in his saddle bag, she'd put the wanted posters in there too.

She didn't know how long it was going to take to hunt these men down. They had over a month's head start.

CHAPTER TWELVE

S he rode up on the party. Ruben and Graham Burlap were leading slaves for sale. Liz rode up fast, her rifle on them at a high gallop. She shot two of the Burlap's men before anyone had time to react. The third was dead before Ruben fired a shot. "Drop your guns!" she said pulling up. She had her rifle on Ruben and her revolver on Graham.

They both dropped their guns and put their hands up. "Who the hell 're you?"

"You remember killing a man in La Junta Colorado?"

"Shit, that was eight years ago. You still mad about that old bastard?" Ruben asked.

"Mad enough that I've killed three of your brothers."

Their eyes went wide. "That was you? You killed Jackson?"

"Put a bullet through each eye." Graham kicked his horse into a ride and she shot him dead before he got close. Ruben tried to get away but she rode him down, slicing his throat as she rode by.

When his body went rolling she grabbed the reins of his horse and led it back to the slave party "We thank you for saving us miss." said a woman.

"Honestly I don't give a shit. I needed those men dead. Your freedom just came as an extra benefit to you." She rode around shooting their chains off. Holstering her gun, she pointed to a direction. "That's north. Take their horses and make for the border as fast as you can. But try not to arouse suspicion." Without another word she rode away.

She made her way to the town where she had a room. When she got in the man running the front desk told her that she had a letter. She slid into a hot bath and opened it.

Dear Liz,

I hope you're doing well. I want you to come by. I know you've had this quest, but Josie would really like to see her Momma. I know I'm wasting my ink. You're not going to come to see her, or me. But the men you're looking for came through town about a week ago. Josie convinced me to wait this long to write. Jona and Mason Burlap. You can check their names in my book. I bet you come running now Right?

Love,

Alexis.

P.S. I love you. I always will. But if you have any desire to see your daughter, I'd come before she realizes you don't care.

Liz let the letter fall to the floor as she soaked in the warm water. She started to cry. She and Josie had written for a long time, but it had been nearly a year since either of them had written. Liz kept up with Alexis, but still not as much as she should have.

She got out of the bath, not bothering to dry off. It was warm and she didn't even get under the covers. She just let the warm night air coming through the open window dry her.

The next day she set out for San Marcos. The entire week she traveled she thought about what she would say to her daughter and her best friend. What she might say to make up for the fact that she never went back. She knew that Josie hated her, rightfully so. But the letter currently in her breast pocket told her that Alexis had turned too.

She had a young boy named Pedro watch Roco for her, promising him a fair amount of money for his time. She took her things up the street and she sat on a bench outside the boarding house. It looked like Alexis had taken over the building next door and added a gambling establishment.

She sat on the bench fighting tears, she knew that she was about to have her heart utterly shattered, and that she would deserve every single bit. She wiped her eyes as she heard footsteps approaching.

The girl was walking up the wooden porch with an arm full of fire wood. She was a pretty girl. She had brown hair pulled back in a bun behind her head with a loose strand falling on the left side, she was constantly blowing it out of her face. She had a round face with features that were symmetrical and perfectly proportioned. Her beauty made it hard to discern how old she was.

"You alright miss?" she asked in a Texas accent.

"Fine, I'm just about to see my daughter. I've not been a very good mother and I was preparing myself."

"Preparing for what?"

"For all the hurt that I'm going to get and deserve."

"What did you do?"

"A friend of mine was killed. I went off to get revenge and I haven't been around in the last eight years."

"That's a mighty long time."

"Yeah. We wrote for several years but then she stopped and I'm ashamed to say so did I."

"I'm sure she still loves you."

"I wouldn't blame her if she didn't. I'm awful."

She cried some more, and the girl looked down on her, "I would get angry. She has a right to be angry with you."

Before Liz could say anything, Alexis spoke from her left. "Josie, take that wood inside, I need to talk to your mother."

Liz jerked her head up to look at the girl. Josie wore a scornful look on her face now. "You couldn't even recognize me." She walked past Alexis and into the boarding house.

Liz leaned back on the bench, crushed. Her daughter was beautiful. She had grown up to be such a beautiful young woman. Alexis walked over and sat next to her. "I knew that letter would get you here."

Liz started to speak and then held her mouth closed. Alexis looked at her, "Why haven't you been around? I know that you've been hunting the Burlaps, but you couldn't come by for a day or two?"

"Alex-,"

"No, I'm speaking." she said. "You don't even know your own daughter. You didn't even know what she looked like until a moment ago. You don't know what she's been through. You weren't here when she became a woman, and you didn't meet her Beau. You barely even thought of me."

"May I speak now?"

"Yes."

"I am sorry. I became obsessed with killing them when Bart died. I still am. I didn't even stop to think how I was hurting you or Josie until it was too late. I will never be able to make it up to you," She took a shaky breath in. "Or Josie."

They were both silent for several seconds. Finally Alexis said, "Put your stuff in my room, Then go talk to your daughter. Actually, I'll have someone deal with your things. Go talk to Josie."

Liz stood up and walked down the porch and into the boarding house. The right wall had a doorway in it now that led to the gambling area. She saw Josie walking out from the back and she went up to her. "Can I talk to you for a minute?"

"Just a second. " she said, and walked to the gambling area. Liz followed and watched as she walked through the room. She made the rounds. She went behind the bar and poured a patron a drink and exited on the other side, speaking with the person dealing blackjack, and walked through the room talking with patrons, knowing them by name. She whispered some things to the girls who were sitting on the laps of men and stopping at the large fire place that was on the left wall, put some logs on it, and walked back to Liz., "Come with me."

She led her back into the boarding house and into the back, out the door and outside where they had their pigs and chickens. She walked over to the pigs and started to feed them from the bucket of slop she'd picked up on her way out. "Why are you here Momma?" she asked as she worked. "To see us, or to get your information so you can kill those men?"

"I came to see you."

Josie stopped, setting the bucket down and looking at Liz. "I almost wish that was true." She walked over to the barn and came back a moment later with a bucket of grain. She spoke as she threw handfuls to the chickens. "You can be honest. I know that she wrote you. I convinced her to wait just to spite you. You came here for the information just so that you can leave again."

"Can we not do this right now? I know you hate me. I know I deserve it. But I would rather hear about your life. Alexis told me that you have a Beau."

"Had. He left town over a year ago."

"What was his name?"

"James."

"Was he nice?"

"Quite. He was terrific lover."

Liz betrayed her shock. She knew it was what Josie wanted, but she couldn't have helped it if she'd wanted to."

"What's the matter?" Josie asked. "Alexis says you two were together at fifteen, and that you and Asha were together when you were younger than me."

"You just shocked me is all. I didn't know you were old enough to be interested in having relations."

"Can I ask you a question?"

"Of course."

"Why can't you talk normal with me? You've been a bounty hunter for thirteen years, and your best friend runs a whore house. Yet when you're around me you act like you're still among New York society at some fancy party."

"Okay, I didn't know you were old enough to want to fuck, happy?"

"That's better. At least that's how you actually talk." Liz started to say something, but Josie interrupted her. "As to you not knowing I was old enough, I will give you five dollars right now if you can tell me how old I am."

"Thirteen."

"No, I turned fourteen last month." Josie finished her work and walked past her saying, "Why don't you just leave us to our lives?"

She walked past but Liz grabbed her by the shoulder and spun her around. Liz dropped to her knees and brought her gun out, handing it up to her daughter. "If you hate me enough that we can never repair the damage I have done, then kill me. Put me out of my misery because I do not want to be alive if my daughter hates me."

It broke her heart when Josie took the gun. She looked at it with a mix of shock and something that could only be described as consideration. She cocked the hammer back and tears streamed down both their faces, something seemed to catch her eye and she raised the gun up, looking at the butt.

She dropped to her knees crying. "I'm sorry Momma," she bawled. "I'm just so angry."

Liz wrapped her arms around her. "You have every right to be angry. I've been a rotten mother."

She wasn't sure how long they stayed like that. At some point Alexis was standing near the door, "So you've made up then?"

They broke apart and they stood. Josie wiped her eyes and she said, "I don't know about completely, but I don't think it's right to hate her. I stopped writing first."

Alexis came forward with her arms out. "I am so proud of you." They hugged, and Liz cried some more as they broke apart and looked at her. Josie went inside and Alexis walked over to Liz. "I forgive you for staying away."

"Just like that? I don't deserve it."

Alexis put her arm around Liz and started to lead her back to the house. "It's mostly for me. I love you and I don't want to spend the rest of our lives angry." Liz smiled. Alexis kissed her and they went inside to bed.

The next morning Liz came down to find Josie and Alexis at breakfast. They didn't see her approaching and Josie said, "I want to tell her now." before Alexis noticed Liz and hushed her.

"Morning sunshine, I'll get you a plate." She eyed Josie.

"You keep your mouth shut missy."

Josie shoved some food in her mouth and refused to look her mother in the eye. Alexis was only gone a few minutes and when she came back she said, "Okay, Josie and I have something to tell you.'

"What is it?" Liz asked.

"We're coming with you." Josie blurted out

"Where? After the Burlaps? No." she said ,shaking her head.

"Then say goodbye to the information you need." Alexis said.

They were all silent. The two of them looked at Liz and she knew she was beat. "Okay." she

said. "But I want to see you shoot. Because you won't be saved from shooting someone if you go "

Josie stood up, slapping her hands on the table. "Let's go."

She walked out and Alexis looked at Liz, "I'd scarf that down if I were you." Liz did as she was bid and they followed Josie outside. They walked down to the picnic area, and the tree where Josie had shot for the first time. As she walked Josie put on a gun belt and Liz looked at Alexis, "Where did she get that?"

"She bought it with her own money a few towns over when I sent her on some business, paid double so they would sell to a woman."

Josie held a sheriff's model peace maker and fired Six shots in quick succession, most of them hitting the same hole, the rest getting close. She looked at Liz, "How was that?"

"Good. But can you kill a man?"

"Yes," she said without hesitation.

Liz turned to Alexis., "You still good with a gun?" Alexis held her hand out and Liz gave her her gun. She shot at the tree and hit Josie's shot, an excellent grouping around the hole. Liz sighed and looked at them both.

"Okay, you can come. But we're gonna be riding hard. We'll need to get you both some trousers."

They went to the store and Josie and Alexis went behind a divider. They put their dresses over top the divider and she waited as they pulled on men's trousers and put on shirts. As they came out Alexis said, "No corset is very freeing. I love having my breasts free."

"Me too." Josie said tucking in the too big shirt. It was the first time Liz had even noticed that her daughter had grown breasts. Breasts only slightly smaller than her own.

Liz went up to the store owner and paid for the things the girls needed. "Two Winchester rifles and saddle holsters, and that revolver there, with a belt."

"I don't sell guns to women." the man said.

Liz brushed her coat to aside, laying a hand on her gun. The man eyed her and finally got the rifles down and laid them on the counter with the holsters and revolver "Few boxes of ammunition as well."

"You're Blaney aren't you." The man said. It was not a question. She nodded and the man laid the boxes down.

She saw Josie on her right out of the corner of her eye. After she paid and they left Josie asked, "So your name was enough for him to do what you told him?"

"Fourteen years is a long time to build a reputation." she said.

"Wow"

She'd sent Pedro to buy them a couple of horses and saddles. He was leading the up to the boarding house as they walked up.

She thanked Bart again for teaching her Spanish. "Thank you, Pedro. Here you go," she said and handed him three dollars.

"Thank you miss, you come back anytime. " He ran off and Josie, still looking impressed said,

"You speak Spanish?"

"It comes in handy. Didn't you ever learn?" She shook her head. "Well I'll teach you. I also know French, Italian, and Latin. Though I haven't used Latin in a very long time."

Liz showed them how to properly store their gear while in the saddle. She showed them how to load their rifles and they mounted up. Alexis had it on good authority that the Burlaps had passed through a town a few days south and that there should still be a man there who could tell them where they had gone.

CHAPTER THIRTEEN

Liz actually knew the town where they were headed. She hadn't been there in five years, but she remembered it well. They dismounted and she looked at the other two. "Okay, I'll go in and meet with Dwight. Which one of you wants to wait and guard out here?"

"Why do we need to be out here?" Alexis asked.

"If someone gets out and tries to jump us coming out, or if more of their friends come in after us, one of you will be here to deal with it."

They both nodded their understanding. "I'll stay here." Alexis said.

Liz nodded and she and Josie headed inside. She leaned in and whispered, "Stay by the bar. I might need back up."

Josie nodded and they walked inside. The place was crowded. So crowded that she couldn't make out where he was. She went up to the bar and Joseph, the bald, withered old bartender who'd been here longer than god, said, "What can I get you Blaney?"

"I'm looking for Dwight Masterson." She noticed the fear in Joseph's eyes. It was a fair reaction. She and Dwight had met over the years and ever since Saint Louis someone always ended up dead or shot. He motioned with his head towards a table in the back of the room. Blaney got a beer and headed over. Dwight was older now, but he still looked mostly the same. His sunburnt face was caked with dirt and grime and his look told you that he had blood on his hands.

As she walked up she saw his back stiffen. He swallowed hard and she fought the urge to laugh seeing him hide his fear. "Rico get up." Dwight said.

A man Blaney's age looked at him. "The fuck would I do that for?"

"Cause if you don't I'll shove my gun so far up your ass you'll be licking lead. Now get the fuck up so my friend can sit down."

Rico looked up at Blaney. He briefly looked like he might cause trouble, but thought better of it. He stood and offered his chair to her. She picked a handful of cash out of the pot and handed it to him. "For your trouble." She looked at the other players."Dwight'll cover it."

They looked to Dwight and he nodded. Blaney sat down and said, "I'm looking for Burlap brothers." The other men scattered from the table, leaving Blaney and Dwight alone, and their chairs on the floor. She looked after them, "Is every man in this town a pussy? Shit, I've got one and I don't scare that easy."

Dwight smirked. "Why you lookin' for 'em?"

"They killed Bart. I've been hunting them for eight years. There are two left."

Dwight looked genuinely impressed. "Didn't know that was you. Nice work." Before he could say anything else Dwight looked down at the table. "Shit."

Blaney turned to see two men standing in the saloon. Josie was a few feet behind them, eyeing them with suspicion. She was so proud. The men wore large hats. They had shotguns on their backs, holsters, and belts of ammunition making an X across each of their chests. "They here for you?" she asked.

"Yep, killed their brother a few months back."

"What for?"

"Governor of Missouri wanted revenge for the death of his son."

The men walked over to the bar. One of them saw Dwight and smacked his brother on the arm. They began to walk over to the table. Blaney leaned in, "I kill 'em, you give me my information and collect any bounties they have on them. Deal?"

'Deal."

Blaney pushed her chair back and stood up. She drew on the men and shot them both in the heart before they had time to draw. They fell to the ground and she turned to Dwight, cocking her gun once again. "Well?"

"Left town three days ago. They were here for a long time getting men together. Offered me the job but you know how well I work with others."

"My left leg still tells me how well you work with others every time it rains."

"They went to a small town two hundred miles from the border. So small it don't have a name."

Blaney holstered her weapon and grabbed her hat off the table. She put it on and took a fistful of silver dollars from the table. "Until next time Dwight."

He tipped his hat. "Blaney."

She turned around and walked towards the bar. She laid the coins on the bar. "Sorry for the mess Joseph." She nodded towards the door and Josie followed after her. Her face was pale and she looked like she might faint. "Are you okay?" Blaney asked.

"I just uh...I....I knew you killed people but,-"

"If you don't want to go on, there is nothing wrong with that. Absolutely no shame whatsoever."

Josephine looked like she was briefly considering it before she shook her head. "No, I'm okay."

They headed out once again. As they rode, Josie was silent. Liz pulled up next to Alexis. "Is she okay?"

Alexis looked over at Josie. "She's thinking."

"It's just, she saw me shoot those men, -"

"It's fine. She's thinking. I believe she's realized that she's going to have to do what you did in there at some point and she's trying to figure out how she feels about that."

"Oh." Was all she could say. She pulled Roco to the side and they all rode in silence.

CHAPTER FOURTEEN

Three days in to their ride they crested a hill and found a house on fire. Liz want into a gallop and the others followed. As she got close to the house she saw two men coming out, they fired at her but missed.

She killed the first one and the second ran towards her, firing. She rode him down and shot him in the head to finish him. A girl's screams pierced the air. Liz hit the dirt and ran into the house. She found the girl with a man standing over her, starting to pick her up. She shot him dead and turned, seeing another man run. She brought the girl out of the house and saw another body on the ground.

Another man rode from behind the barn, that was what was on fire. She'd realized her mistake when she got closer. She went for her rifle but saw the man drop dead before it cleared her holster.

Looking over she saw Josie take her rifle down from her eye. She looked okay, and Liz didn't have time to worry right now. Alexis got down from her horse. "I don't understand, you missed that one?"

"No, I got another one inside. That one ran past me while I was retrieving the girl. Can you go get that body? Bring his horse back too if you can."

Alexis mounted up to go get the horse currently dragging a man's body away. She rode off and Liz turned to Josie, "Josie, see to them kids while I take care of these men."

"Yes ma'am." she said ,getting down.

Alexis got back nearly an hour later with the horse and body. "Great job," Liz said. "The last thing we needed was that horse headed home."

"Thanks, I stacked the body by the others. Figured he'll burn with them."

Liz turned to the kids. "I'm mighty sorry we couldn't save the barn."

"That's all right miss." said Amos, clearly the oldest. "We're just thankful you saved Janie."

Liz looked at Alexis, "We shouldn't lose too much time taking them to the nearest town."

"I ain't goin' nowhere."

Liz looked at Amos. "Is that so?"

Amos nodded "My Pa died protecting this place, and I intend to run it myself."

Liz sighed. "Well I don't reckon I have a right to tell you different. " She turned to the other two. "What do you want?" Amos started to speak, and she held up her hand. "You made your decision. Now they'll make theirs."

The little boy, Jonathan, stepped forward. "I'll stay with Amos. He's gonna need help running the farm."

Liz nodded and looked at the girl. She appeared to be about fourteen, but unlike Josie she looked fourteen. She was a pretty girl, but she still had the childish features and nearly flat chest that would typically mark someone her age. Her honey blonde hair was a rat's nest as she moved forward and said, "I'd like to go with you all."

Amos stepped forward angrily. "You're not going any-where." He grabbed Janie by the arm.

"Amos you're hurting me." Janie said.

He tried to pull her to the house. Liz brought her gun up and grabbed the barrel. She brought the butt down over his head. Amos slumped down and she looked at everyone else. "We'd better get going. You, um...Jonathan."

"Yes ma'am?"

"Do you and your brother know how to shoot?"

"Yes ma'am. Pa taught us."

Liz nodded. "Good, Josie get them the dead men's guns. I'll get one of their horses ready for Janie. Alexis can you find her some trousers?"

"Yes ma'am." She led Janie towards the house. "Come on sweetie."

An hour later they were outside the house, Josie was in the saddle and Liz standing in front of the kids as Alexis and Janie came out of the house. She went to her horse as Janie asked, "Why do I have to wear these?"

"I don't have time to listen to a bunch of belly aching bout how hard it is to ride side saddle or how much your quim whiskers hurt riding regular in a dress."

Janie looked at her brothers. Amos had a bit of blood in his hair. "I suppose this is goodbye." she said.

Jonathan ran off the steps and grabbed his sister in a hug. "I hope you can come back someday."

"I hope so too."

Amos returned his little sister's look with distain. He stepped off the porch. "Jonathan, we've got work to do." He walked off and she stared after him.

Jonathan followed and Liz handed Janie the reins of her horse. "We've got to get going." They mounted up and rode away.

Josie rode next to Janie the rest of the day and the next. Liz and Alexis both smiled at each other, they saw what was happening. The way that Josie stole glances at the new girl, tried to be her friend.

"Can we make camp soon? I'm sore." Alexis said.

Liz looked around and found a good spot. "We'll make camp here."

They made camp. It was kind of nice for it not to be just her. Everyone had a job, collecting firewood, making the food, tending the horses. She could tell that everyone else was sore.

They'd been in such a hurry the last four days that they'd barely stopped. It occurred to Liz that the others probably were sorer than they let on. "Everyone take your trousers off." she ordered.

"Why?" Alexis asked

Liz pulled a tin out of her saddle bag. "This is Indian medicine. It'll help with your soreness."

They seemed hesitant at first, but Alexis dropped her trousers and presented her rear to Liz. Alexis moaned in relief at the paste she was putting on her. Seeing Alexis so happy Josie did the same. Janie took some coaxing but eventually they were all laying around the fire happy and feeling much better. "Get some sleep," she said "I'll take first watch."

They didn't need to be told twice. In minutes they were all asleep. Liz wondered to herself how they were going to take the Burlaps, if maybe they should just leave it alone. She didn't want anyone else to die because of her. Late in the night she woke Josie up to relieve her. "It's your watch." she said. She stayed awake while Josie took a minute to get woke up, have some coffee, and be alert. "Are you doing okay?" Liz asked.

"What'd you mean?"

"It's a big thing to kill a man. You shouldn't take it lightly. There is no shame in being upset."

"No, I think what upsets me is that I liked it." Liz was a bit shocked but she let Josie continue. "I liked the feeling of knowing that he was a bad man, that he'd hurt people and that I killed him for it..."

Liz nodded, understanding. "Just know that if you aren't okay, you can talk to me. I've been where you are."

"Who was the first person you killed?"

"The soldier who came after me, trying to take me from the tribe. I flipped him over and killed him with a knife."

"Then it was the men who killed my Poppa right?"

Liz nodded. "After that I tied you to my chest, set you up to eat, and we rode together for two weeks until we got to town."

Josie looked shocked. "I don't think you've ever told me that one."

"I didn't think it wise to tell a young girl about riding for two weeks while her mother had a knife wound."

"You did?"

"Yeah. One of the men stabbed me. I cleaned it out the first night we made camp. I passed out from the pain and you were right there when I woke up."

"I can't believe you rode two weeks like that."

"I had no choice. I wasn't about to die without you being somewhere safe." Josie was silent for a long time. Liz finally spoke. "I'm gonna get some sleep. But you wake me if anything goes wrong. Alexis has the next watch in three hours."

CHAPTER FIFTEEN

The sun woke her up. It shouldn't have, they should have been gone by now. As she rose up and looked around she saw two men holding guns on her daughter and best friend. Janie was sitting against a log, looking between the men and Liz. "How long were you perverts gonna watch me sleep?" Liz asked.

"They've only been here a couple of hours they ate our food first." Josie said.

The man shoved his gun harder into her back. "I said shut up girl."

Liz situated herself so that she had her back to the log and her legs spread out in front of herself. Her hands were behind her back and she felt her knife and her derringer from where she'd put them under her bed roll. "Who are you boys?" she asked

"That don't need concern you." said the second man. He wasn't anything special. He had on a hat, a duster, and he had a big mustache. He could have been any one of a thousand men in the west.

"I see." She flipped her knife outward and hit the first man in the chest. She shot the second man in the heart. She was up before they hit the ground, walking over and laying a bullet in each of their heads. Janie screamed and Liz turned to look at her. "What?"

"You scared me."

"Oh christ's sakes. Quit belly aching and go fetch their wagon over yonder. Lead the team over here."

Alexis walked over to her. "Should we bury the men?"

"No, strip 'em and leave 'em. Buzzards gotta eat-too. And we've wasted enough time as it is."

She and Alexis stripped the men of their belongings while the girls brought the horses and wagon over.

Josie was riding one of them to get them moving She eyed the bodies and asked, "Why are the men naked?"

"We needed their stuff." They looked through the wagon and Liz recognized crates of dynamite and bullets. She smiled to herself and Josie asked, "What're you so happy about?"

"I know what our plan is now."

They put Josie to driving the team and they headed out. Over the next few days Liz filled everyone in on the plan. And when they got to the Burlaps' town, they were ready. They waited until the middle of the night, scouting around. Janie had proven very good at the rifle so Liz snuck her onto the rooftop of a building.

She knew the signal, and she knew her job. Liz just hoped hat she could pull the trigger. When the time came.

They set Janie up with enough food and water to last he day. They told her to stay low and hidden until the next night.

That night she unhooked the team from the wagon. She took one bundle of dynamite from the boxes and let the wagon loose. As it rolled she lit one stick and threw it into the wagon. The wagon rolled down the hill and into the center of town, and exploded. It took most of the two buildings on either side of the street with it, it sent bullets in every direction. Most of the saloon fell into the street and men came from the other buildings to see what was going on. "Give me five seconds and then come shooting." Liz said as she kicked Roco into a gallop.

She lit the first stick of dynamite and threw it at the crowd. It exploded, killing a few men.

The building where Janie was perched was behind the men, she popped up and started firing, sending all of them spinning as they were attacked from both sides. Dozens more men came out from the buildings and hit the dirt, dead, as Alexis and Janie rode down the hill shooting.

Liz threw dynamite through a few doors and windows as she rode past, buildings collapsed around her as she pulled up at the end of the street. Only a dozen men were left. Six more fell in between the other three women. Soon they were near Liz. She shouted, "Come out Burlaps! I know you're alive!"

Jona came from a partially standing building on the left, Mason from the right. "Who're you?" Mason asked.

"I'm the one been hunting your brothers."

Anger crossed their faces. In a flash of some of the quickest gun play she'd ever seen, Mason had his gun out. He fired at them but missed. Liz brought her gun up and shot, killing him. Jona turned and ran and she kicked her horse into a gallop. She rode him down, feeling the crunch of his bones underneath Roco's hooves. She loved it.

"Momma!" She heard Josie scream. She brought Roco around and she saw blood streaming out of Alexis' mouth. Liz cried out and she rode for her. Alexis fell to the ground and Liz leapt from her horse.

"Alexis, where are you hit?" She looked down at her and saw the hole in her gut. She ripped her shirt away and inspected the wound.

"I know...I'm gonna die." Alexis choked out. "It's okay." She erupted into a fit of coughing.

Liz could hear the panic in her own voice. "No, you'll be fine. It's okay. You're okay."

Josie looked at her. "What can we do Momma?"

Liz met her gaze and said nothing. She must have understood what she meant because she started to cry harder. "Alex," Josie said. "Don't leave me. Please don't leave me."

Alexis smiled at her. "You're gonna be fine. I raised you strong. You're beautiful...I. Am. So. Proud." She coughed for a while and then, having built up her strength, said, "Be good to your mamma. She'll need you."

Alexis looked to Liz. "I love you. You are the love of my life. Don't do anything stupid. You have a daughter to look after now."

Liz and Josie cried some more. Liz kissed Alexis and they both held her hands. Josie rested her head on her real mother's breast while she died.

CHAPTER SIXTEEN

They buried Alexis under a tree outside of town. Josie didn't even look at her the entire time they dug. She looked over Alexis' grave and said, "You were the bravest, kindest woman I will ever know. Thank you for being my Momma." She kissed her hand and placed it on the stones that they'd used to cover her grave. She walked past Liz saying, "I wish it had been you."

"Me too." Liz didn't know what to say over the grave. Finally, she said, "You saved my life, and I and failed you."

She walked away and got on her horse. Janie and Josie were mounted up and Josie said, "I'm not going with you."

"What?"

"Everyone who gets near you dies. Your parents, Poppa, Bartholomew, and now Alexis. I won't be next. I'm going west. You go wherever you want, but don't follow me."

Liz couldn't cry. She wanted to, but she didn't have anything left; and deep down, not so deep down she guessed, she knew what Josie was saying was true."Take this and be safe." She said taking off her gun belt. She also took the saddle bag that had all her money in it and put it over Josie's saddle. "Janie, you go with her. She'll keep you safe."

"What're you going to do?"

She spoke as she turned Roco around and started him walking. "Climb into a bottle and drown."

CHAPTER SEVENTEEN

...FIVE YEARS LATER...

Avasa loaded up her arms with whiskey bottles. She'd run out nearly a day ago and she was starting to sober up. Luckily, she had plenty now. She hated to be sober. Dreams and memories haunted her every moment, and it was best to spend them in a drunken stupor hiding her memories from her. She walked into her little shack, eyeing the two riders on horseback out of the corner of her eye" She didn't care. She went inside, popped a bottle open and started drinking, not bothering with a glass. Not that she owned any.

She sat in her squalid little shack with a fire going and she drank. She wondered how long she would have to wait for the riders to come in. She heard footsteps outside. Not long then.

"Come in! I've known you were there since I got home. I spotted you on the ride from town."

The door opened, and the riders walked in. They were wearing bandanas for the dust and the long dusters hid their sex from her. "Who're you?" Avasa asked. They pulled their bandanas down and took their hats off.

Josie hadn't changed much in the last five years. She still had that beauty that hid her age. She was nineteen now, taller, a bit fuller in certain parts, but apart from the battle-weary look in her eyes and a scar on her left cheek, she could have still been fourteen.

Janie was no longer flat chested. She had changed more so. She now had the eyes of someone who had seen a lot of fights, like she was watching in front of her and behind her at the same time. She had a scar on her right cheek, an inch under her right eye. It perfectly matched the one under Josie's left. "Nice to see you girls."

"You too Liz." Janie said.

"Not Liz, Avasa."

Josie looked quizzical. "You're going by your Indian name?"

Avasa hadn't spoken English in a long time. It hurt her mouth a bit. "Liz was Alexis' name for me. It died with her."

Josie got I more serious. "Why not Elizabeth, or Blaney?"

"They got everyone they cared about killed. My tribe changed names with significance and I'd say the death of most of your loved ones calls for a different name. One that didn't get anyone she cared about killed."

"Josephine's not dead."

"True," Avasa said. "But she had enough sense to leave, making her lost to me."

They were silent for what seemed like hours. Finally Avasa said. "I know you didn't come here to catch up."

Janie walked over, taking a seat in a chair on the wall by the foot of the bed. Avasa got into a sitting position. Josie remained standing. "We took a job to recover a child. He was kidnapped from a large ranch about a month ago. There is a meeting place a hundred miles south east of here. We heard tell you were here and we need help. We are a bit out matched and we don't know Mexico well."

Avasa looked from Janie to Josie. "You need my help Josephine?"

"Yes ma'am."

Avasa looked from one girl to the other. "Janie, you mind giving me a moment alone with my daughter?"

Janie looked at Josie for conformation. A look that Liz and Alexis had shared many times. Josie nodded and Janie got up, leaving the shack. "I'll tend to the horses."

When she had gone, and had time to get farther from the shack, Avasa spoke. "So tell me, what've you been doing?"

"When we left you, Janie and I went to California. I sent word to Rosie, she runs the house now. We found enough work to eat while we got better at hunting bounties. Since then we've been working as part bounty hunters part, gun fighters."

"Followed in my footsteps did you?"

"A bit." She bit her bottom lip and was silent for a few heart beats before she said, "I'm sorry for what I said to you. I was hurt when she died and I needed someone to blame. Add on to that the fact that I had only just seen you since I was five… I am sorry."

"You were right. I have gotten everyone killed. Death follows me, has since I was nine years old. And if you hadn't gone away I would have gotten you killed too."

Josephine looked hurt. She seemed to see what her mother had become and she seemed to blame herself. Avasa said, "So are you two just partners or is she your,-"

"Paramour? No." She shook her head. "I enjoy both sexes but Janie is strictly into men folk. Closest we've ever came is taking care of ourselves in camp at the same time."

"Probably could have done without that."

Josie blushed. "Sorry."

"I'll help you."

"Thank you, but will you forgive me for what I said?"

Avasa smiled. "Do you know what Alexis told me when I came back after eight years?"

"What?"

"She said I forgive you, mostly for me. I love you and I don't want to spend the rest of our lives angry. Not that I was ever angry with you Josephine."

"Thank you."

"And I'm sorry I got your mother killed."

"You're my mother."

"You know what I mean. I birthed you, but Alexis raised you." They were silent again. Avasa stood up. "I'd better saddle my horse. Do you have a gun I can use?"

"You know you'll have to sober up first."

Next thing she knew her daughter was dunking her head into the watering trough outside. She came up for air after several dunks. "I'm good."

Josie let go and she stood up. She flipped her wet mop of hair behind her head and found her hat. "Have you really had the same hat for twenty years?" Josie asked. "I remember trying that thing on when I was a kid."

"It was your Poppa's."

"Oh."

Janie got Roca saddled and Avasa walked over and patted him on the back. "Ready for another go at it old boy?" Roco nodded, huffing. She smiled and swung herself into the saddle Josie walked over and handed her a bundle she realized was Morgan's gun. "I didn't think you'd keep it."

"I'd never get rid of this. It's been saving me my entire life." Avasa took the gun out and saw that there was an A carved next to the LB on the side. She ran her thumb over the MB, J, and the B she had carved on the curve. She choked up a bit when she looked back at Josie. "I thought it fitting that one mother's name be next to the others." Josie said.

"I agree," She put the gun back in the belt and handed it to Josie. "I think you should keep it. Your Poppa would want you to have it."

Josie nodded, taking the gun back. "I'll get you something in town."

"Hold on." Avasa said. She went into Bart's old saddle bag and brought out his gun, still wrapped up and looking clean. She checked it just to be sure. She fired a round into the door of the shack. "Yep, still works." She wrapped the belt around her and they headed off.

CHAPTER EIGHTEEN

They talked a lot over the next several days. They slept mostly in saddle, stopping only when the horses needed. Avasa was regaled with tales of what the girls had been doing in the last few years. Including the bank robbers that they had trailed through seven states, eventually wearing them out.

She hadn't been on the road like this since coming to Mexico. But it didn't take her long to get used to it again. Her head hurt and every part of her body yearned for a drink. She wouldn't drink though. Not

only did she need to be ready at any moment, she wanted to relish in her pain for a little while longer.

They found the place where they were to meet the kidnappers. They camped a few miles away and Janie, who Josie said was excellent at moving silently, went to get a look. They made camp while they waited for her. It briefly reminded Avasa of hunting the Burlaps, with all of them making camp together. Her heart hurt that Alexis wasn't here.

Janie came back into camp looking grim. "We've got a problem."

"What is it?" Josie asked.

"They have a man on the boy. I watched them during a shift change, there is literally always a gun on him."

"Shit." Avasa said. They all sat around the fire that night, trying to think of a plan.

"I'm still not sure about this." Josie said the next morning as they broke camp and saddled up.

"It'll work." Avasa told her. "Or at the very least you'll get the boy out before I get shot." With another round of disapproving looks from both of the girls, they rode towards the other camp.

They broke off a mile away, each of them going one direction. Avasa rode into camp, the ransom box on the mule behind her. There were six men around the camp fire eating breakfast. She rode in and had a rifle on her immediately. An older man, about fifty, with a yellow poncho and a face so sun scorched he looked almost Mexican, stepped forward. "Can I help you?"

"I'm here for that boy right there." she said,pointing.

The man turned to look. "Well if you've got the ransom money I reckon you can take him."

"Look," she said, "I believe we are both civil and we can conduct our business as such."

"I suppose we can do that " The man said.

"Well then let's start with getting that rifle off me."

The yellow man turned to the one with the rifle on her. "Take it down Juan."

"No."

Avasa took out her gun and shot him dead. The yellow man whipped around to her. All eyes and guns were on her. "I apologize," she said, "I cannot abide men who don't follow given orders."

"I can agree with that. Bigger shares for all!" The men cheered. Behind them, Janie laid hands on the boy and started to lead him from camp. Two minutes. "Now can I see the money?" The yellow man asked.

"Box is awfully heavy, you'll need five of you to carry it." The boy forgotten, they all walked over and retrieved the box from the mule. Setting it down they popped it open and saw the rocks. Now.

Before they had time to react, the women were shooting them from three different directions. In moments they were all dead. Josie strode into camp and Janie went to retrieve the boy from the woods. "You okay?" Josie asked.

"Naw, I got hit." She said looking at her arm. She hadn't even realized that one of the men got a shot off. She got down and walked over to the fire taking out her knife. She slipped her duster off and tore her right sleeve away. She put her knife into the fire, getting the tip hot and sterile. Looking for a stick, she found one big enough to bite. Taking the knife out of the fire she bit down on the stick and started to dig the bullet out.

Pain seared through her and she felt the stick start to crack. The edge of the knife connected with the bullet and she bit down harder. She edged it out, tears streaming down her face.

She was vaguely aware of Janie and the boy walking out of the woods and soon the bullet and knife were free. She let go of the stick and sighed in relief. Josie was looking at her with wide eyes. "I've been shot three times and I have never been able to do that myself."

Gasping Avasa took a cartridge out of her belt and pried the projectile out. She laid sideways and poured the gun powder into the hole. She bit down on the stick again and picked one out of the fire, igniting the powder she cried out as her wound was cauterized.

She got up for some water from her canteen. She hadn't been shot in a long time. It hurt more than she remembered. She took a drink and poured some on her arm. They saddled up and she said, "Let's get him home."

CHAPTER NINETEEN

The boy's parents were very glad to have him back. The reward ended up being five thousand dollars. They went to the nearest town, where Josie and Janie had friends. Janie and Avasa were at the store while Josie had some errands to run. "I see you've been a good friend to my daughter." she said.

"She's been just as good to me. We take care of each other."

"Have you seen your brothers?" Avasa picked up another shirt checking to see if it would fit her.

"We stopped in there about a year and a half ago. Joseph had gotten so much bigger. I can only imagine how much he's grown since we were there."

"Did they get the farm up and running?"

"Built a bigger barn than before. Amos still hates me."

"I'm sorry to hear that. Some people don't know how to appreciate family while they're still here."

Janie looked gratefully at her. She started to speak but was interrupted by Josie coming into the store. "I got a reply." she said, practically bursting with enthusiasm.

"Really?" Janie said. "Where?"

"Oregon country."

"We've got to go. I'll pay, you tell her."

Janie walked away and Josie looked at her mother. "I have to tell you something."

"What is it?"

"I found Asha. "

All the air left her lungs. She just stared at Josie wide eyed. "'Wh...you..."

"I found Asha. She's on a reservation going by the name Elu." Josie must have seen the tears in her eyes and thought she was sad. "Are you okay?"

"I'm fine...I must go see her."

"That's our plan."

Avasa turned and walked out of the store. She got on Roco end they rode for Oregon country. It took weeks to get there. Every moment of every day she thought of Asha. Of the girls they were, laying in the tepee together. That seemed like centuries ago.

The reservation sat in a valley at the bottom of a hill. They sat on the top of the hill and Avasa opened her spy glass that Bart had given her. She'd used it to spy on kidnappers, Burlaps, bad men and women all over the country and into some others.

This was the first time she's ever really used it for something that might make her happy.

The Indians had been given a wooden cabin. They were set up in a long line. She could spot several different tribes all in the same place. This was not how they were supposed to be.

The third row of cabins, seven from the closest end. Asha, or Elu rather, was sitting outside on the little

porch, a baby in her lap. An older man, their age, came walking up with a man not much older than Josie. The younger man had a small girl with him. She assumed it was Asha's granddaughter.

She had a family. Three generations of family. A girl of about sixteen came out of the cabin, clearly pregnant. A big family. One by one they all walked away leaving Elu alone with the baby she held.

It wasn't like she expected her not to have moved on. They hadn't seen each other since they were fourteen. But seeing her first love with her family felt worse than any bullet she had ever taken.

Asha looked up the hill and her gaze, despite age, still pierced Avasa's soul. She knew that Asha knew it was her. With one hand Asha made the sign for, "I love you." Avasa repeated the sign. At the same time they both turned away. She turned her horse around and Josie called after her. "You're not going down?"

Beth heard Janie say, "No, she's not."

"Why not?"

"I'll explain later."

"Come on!" Beth called without looking back. "Let's go!

ABOUT THE AUTHOR

Ethan Thomas has lived in over twenty houses in his life and written stories in most of them. He lives in Wisconsin with his dogs and his beloved Hermes Ambassador that he uses to write his books.

ALSO BY

Freak House Novels

The Gathering Place
Reunited

Collections

Thought Bubble, Vol. I

www.ingramcontent.com/pod-product-compliance
Lightning Source LLC
Chambersburg PA
CBHW051945150726
47999CB00004B/1251